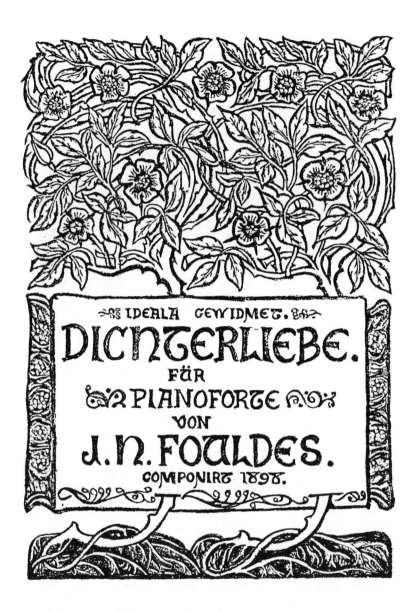

Foulds's own elaborate woodcut title-page from the manuscript of
Dichterliebe (see page 4). Note the dedication to "Ideala" and the
spelling of the composer's name which he used until about 1900.
(John Foulds Estate.)

Modern Music: Selected Essays
by Malcolm MacDonald
Volume 1

JOHN FOULDS
AND HIS MUSIC

An Introduction

*With a Catalog of the Composer's Works
and a Brief Miscellany of His Writings*

PRO/AM MUSIC RESOURCES, INC.
White Plains, New York

KAHN & AVERILL, LTD.
London

Pro/Am *P/A* General Music Series GMS-5

The present publication is a completely revised, rewritten and greatly expanded version of the author's *John Foulds: His Life in Music*, issued in 1975 by Triad Press.

Cover photo John Foulds c.1923: a studio portrait by the London photographers Vaughan & Freeman. (John Foulds Estate.)
Silhouette page *iv* dated 11 May 1923; on the reverse is the stamp of Hubert Leslie, silhouettist, of the West Pier, Brighton (courtesy John Foulds Estate).

MUSICAL EXAMPLES: ACKNOWLEDGEMENTS

Examples 1 and 11 © copyright by Hawkes & Son Ltd., by permission of Boosey & Hawkes Music Publishers Ltd. Example 18 by kind permission of Bosworth & Co. Ltd., London. Examples 3, 4, 5, 16, 17, 19, 20 by kind permission of Novello & Co. Ltd., London. Examples 7, 8, 27 and 29 by permission of United Music Publishers, London for Editions Salabert, Paris. All other examples courtesy of the Estate of John Foulds.

Published in the United States of America 1989 by
PRO/AM MUSIC RESOURCES, INC.
63 Prospect Street, White Plains, New York 10606
ISBN 0-912483-02-4

Published in Great Britain 1989 by
KAHN & AVERILL, LTD.
9 Harrington Road, London SW7 3ES
ISBN 1-871082-04-8

In Memoriam

MARYBRIDE WATT (née FOULDS)

1921–1988

Musarum filia fidelis

May 11.
1923.

Real music is not national — not even international — but *supranational*. I believe that the power of music to heal, to soothe, to stimulate and recreate, is just the same in Timbuctoo as in Kamchatka, and was the same in the time of Orpheus as it is today.

Anyone who believes that the phrase "the music of the spheres" is not simply an idle phrase but means something definite, will find no difficulty in accepting this idea, that real music is not an affair of Time and Space, but a series of vibrations coming we know not whence, going we know not whither, but some of which we humans are *permitted*, as it were, to overhear from time to time....

We incline to forget that music is a force in Nature as is Light, or Heat, or Electricity, and like these great natural forces, real music has nothing essentially national about it at all.

> — John Foulds (from "Is the Gulf Between Eastern and Western Music Unbridgeable?", a talk broadcast on All-India Radio, Delhi Station, 6 March 1937)

CONTENTS

Preface

This book is a completely revised, rewritten, and much expanded version of one published in 1975 as *John Foulds: His Life in Music*. That publication appeared as No. 3 in a special "Bibliographical Series" issued by Triad Press of Rickmansworth, England; and in conformity with its avowed "Bibliographical" purpose it was essentially an extended essay introducing a detailed catalog of John Foulds's musical compositions — published, unpublished, or missing — that included a listing of his remaining manuscripts, so far as I had been able to identify them.

The present book incorporates a catalog of Foulds's compositions in the shorter format favored by Pro/Am Music Resources (who have also made their catalog available separately in their series of *Composer DataCards*). Some of the information regarding Foulds's manuscripts — and their often complex relations — is now taken up into the main text. Apart from that, I at first envisaged this book as merely a new edition of the old, minimally updated where necessary and with certain passages I had formulated in the interim, in separate articles, lectures, or sleeve-notes, accreted to the main matter. However, in preparing this for the new publication I found myself, in the light of recently acquired information, inserting a great deal of new matter and rewriting some sections wholesale. While the text of the 1975 publication thus to a large extent remains embedded in this one, it now accounts for less than half of it; and in its latter stages it has been almost entirely suppressed and superseded by new writing. I have also introduced a large number of additional musical examples and illustrative materials, many of which have never been published before; and I have added a brief selection of some of Foulds's own writings, to act as an amplification for some of his ideas.

The result is therefore for practical purposes a "new" study of the career of the British composer John Foulds; but by no means a definitive one. The time for such a book has not yet arrived. In 1975 I had been interested in Foulds for less than two years. I had not yet heard a note of his music performed (apart from a few minor items on 78 rpm recordings). Since then a large number of his works have been played, and eleven of them (to date) made available in modern commercial recordings. These performances have greatly stimulated my thoughts on the music; my researches into it have continued; meanwhile I have in some cases come to a better interpretation and understanding of aspects of the manuscript remains. The results will be found throughout this book. But much of his music remains unheard; important works remain missing which may yet be found; and, so far, the biographical materials for a detailed (or even moderately coherent) account of Foulds's personal and professional life have remained elusive.

Thus I offer the present volume only as an "interim report" on the achievement of John Foulds, the composer of one of the most unusual, wide-ranging, and tantalizing creative legacies in the whole of British music.

A self-taught, Manchester-born composer who gained his practical experience first in seaside and theater bands and later in the ranks of the Hallé Orchestra, Foulds first came to public notice with the première of a tone poem, *Epithalamium*, at a Queen's Hall Prom in 1906 under Henry J. Wood. But for most of his career he was known to a wide public only as a composer of light music, reaching the apex of popularity with his once-famous *Keltic Lament*. Little interest was shown in his many more serious works, which displayed a different side (indeed, several quite different sides) of his creative gifts. Not many of them were performed, and even fewer were published, so that he was quickly forgotten after his sudden death, far from his native country, in Calcutta just before World War II.

Yet Foulds was one of the first European composers — and certainly the first British composer — to experiment with divisions of the octave smaller than a semitone (chiefly quarter-tones). His huge *World Requiem*, performed each Armistice Night from 1923 to 1926 by up to 1,200 singers and instrumentalists, was the origin of the annual Festival of Remembrance. Much in demand as a composer of theater music, and a close collaborator with Lewis Casson and Sybil Thorndike, he wrote the music for some of the most celebrated stage productions of the 1920s: probably the best-known was his score for the original run of George Bernard Shaw's *Saint Joan*. His interest in mysticism led him to produce works whose exploitation of harmonic stasis and repetition contain startling foreshadowings of today's "Minimalist" composers. His deep fascination with the music of the Orient, especially India, led him to experiment with Ancient Greek modes, non-diatonic scales, Hindu râgâs, and finally actually to write for ensembles of traditional Indian instruments, in a bid to unite the musical cultures of East and West.

These are only a few reasons why Foulds's *oeuvre* possesses a historical significance out of proportion to its current reputation. But more importantly its inherent quality gives his major compositions — many of them still unplayed — a living significance for the present day. I hope some of this has been demonstrated in the following pages.

* * *

A special debt of gratitude is owed to John Foulds's daughter the late Marybride Watt for her kindness, hospitality, and willing co-operation in all matters; and above all for preserving so many of her father's manuscripts. Without her contribution neither this book nor its 1975 forerunner would have been remotely possible. I have also received help and encouragement, greatly appreciated, from Foulds's sons — the late Ray Foulds and Major Patrick Foulds — and his step-daughter Joan Cragg.

Many other people have helped me over the years in innumerable ways — not least those who have participated in Foulds performances, contributing towards the current modest "renaissance" in his music's fortunes. Though not an exhaustive list, I gladly instance here Peter Broadbent, Brian Rayner Cook, Meriel Dickinson, the Endellion String Quartet, Leopold Hager, Vernon Handley, Raymond Head, Peter Hill, Peter Jacobs, Ann Measures, Timothy Reynish, Howard Shelley, Ronald Stevenson, Roger Vignoles, Rafael Wallfisch, and Moray Welsh.

Thanks are also due, for a whole variety of reasons, to Martin Anderson, the B.B.C. Music Library, Bernard Benoliel, Boosey & Hawkes Copyright Department, Susan Bradshaw, the British Music Information Centre, the Department of Manuscripts of the British Library, members of the British Music Society, David Brown, Theodore Buttrey, Cambridge University Library, John Casson, Paul and Liz Chipchase, Robert Cowan, Giles Easterbrook of Novello & Co., Lewis Foreman, the Hallé Orchestra, Graham Hatton, Peter Middleton, the Performing Right Society, Chris Rice, Bruce Roberts, Malcolm Smith, Ruth Smith, Celia Springate, Lance Tufnell, the Ralph Vaughan Williams Trust, and Roger Wright. This is also unlikely to be a complete list; Foulds's music has seemed to breed friendship and aid at every turn, and I have doubtless inadvertently omitted credit for some assistance or information that I have subsequently found invaluable. But any faults, obscurities, or inaccuracies I herewith acknowledge as my own.

Malcolm MacDonald
London, December 1988

CHRONOLOGY

DATES	LIFE	WORKS
1880	John Herbert Foulds born 2 November, Manchester.	
1894	Left home.	
1895	Works as cellist. Visits Vienna?	Sonata for 2 Cellos (lost).
1896		2 String Quartets, Piano Trio, Cello Suite (all lost), early piano pieces.
1897	First public performance.	*Rhapsodie nach Heine.*
1898	Performance of string quartet using quarter-tones.	*Dichterliebe* for piano
1899		2 more String Quartets (1 extant), *Undine Suite.*
1900	Joins Hallé Orchestra, under Hans Richter.	*Lyrics* (Op. 1) for piano.
1903		*Quartetto Romantico.*
1905	First publication — *Variazioni ed Improvvisati* for piano.	"The Waters of Babylon" for string quartet. Cello Sonata. Begins *The Vision of Dante.*
1906	Meets Mahler, Strauss, Delius and Humperdinck in Essen. Henry Wood gives *Epithalamium* Queen's Hall Prom première.	
1908	Completes *The Vision of Dante.* Begins writing "light" music.	*Holiday Sketches* for orchestra.
1909	Marries Maud Woodcock.	
1910	*Mirage* rehearsed but not performed by Hallé.	String Quartet No. 8, *Suite Française.*
1911	Cello Concerto premièred. Great success of *Keltic Suite.* Son Raymond born.	
1912	*Music-Pictures* series launched (*Group III* at Proms under Wood). Meets Lewis Casson. First theater work.	
1914	Moves to London.	
1915	Meets writer & musician Maud MacCarthy (whom he later marries). Study of Greek modes and Indian instruments.	*Recollections of Ancient Greek Music* and conception of *Gandharva-Music.*
1917	Works at Ciro's Club.	*Mood-Pictures.*
1918	Appointed music director of Central YMCA, London.	*The Song of Honour.*
1919	Leaves Ciro's. Public lectures.	Begins opera *Avatara* and *A World Requiem.*
1920		*Sacrifice.*
1921	Conductor of London University Musical Society.	*Deburau. A World Requiem* completed (April 14).
1922	Busy with theater music.	*Lyra Celtica* probably written now.

DATES	LIFE	WORKS
1923	First of four annual Albert Hall *World Requiem* performances (11 November).	
1924-25	Much theater work.	*Saint Joan, Masse-Mensch, Hippolytus, Henry VIII*, etc.
1926		*April-England.*
1927	To Sicily in summer, then settles in Paris.	*Isles of Greece, Essays in the Modes.*
1928		*Three Choruses in the Hippolytus of Euripides.*
1929		*Dynamic Triptych.*
1930	Returns to London in Autumn.	*Three Mantras* completed. Orchestrates Schubert's *Death and the Maiden.*
1931	*Dynamic Triptych* performed in Edinburgh (October).	*Quartetto Intimo.*
1932		*The Seven Ages, Hellas, April-England* (orchestral version).
1934	Publishes *Music To-day.*	*Puppet-Ballet Suite.*
1935	Passage to India (April-May).	*Indian Suite* for orchestra.
1935-36	Folk-music prospecting and journalism, especially in Punjab and Kashmir.	*Indian Scenes, Quartetto Geniale, Pasquinades Symphoniques, Deva-Music, Kashmiri Wedding Procession,* etc.
1937	Appointed director of European Music, All-India Radio, Delhi. Lectures on "Orpheus Abroad", starts auditioning Indian musicians.	Much light music, *Grand Durbar March.*
1938	Viceregal Concert, 28 March. Forms "Indo-European Orchestra".	Indian ensemble pieces, *Symphony of East and West, Symphonic Studies* for strings.
1939	*Symphonic Studies* performed Bombay, 10 March. Transfers to Calcutta and dies there, night of 24-25 April.	

1. Early Years

The composer of the music for Bernard Shaw's *St. Joan* could trace his ancestry back to Joan of Arc's France – to the Jewish banking family of Fouldes, which came to prominence in Paris at the beginning of the 15th century. Succeeding generations in France produced several important men of affairs, notably Napoleon III's powerful Minister of Finance, Achille Fould. Precisely when a branch of the family established itself in Britain is not known; but by the time of John Foulds's birth no trace of family wealth or Jewish religion remained with the English Fouldses, who had settled in the Manchester area. Financial security – like creative and professional security – was to elude the composer all his life.

John Herbert Foulds was born on 2 November 1880 in his family's home at 49 Dorset Street, Hulme, even then a rather undistinguished area of Victorian Manchester, in the southern part of the city, east of the docklands. The house – in common with almost the entirety of 19th-century Hulme – no longer exists: the destruction of the four-square-mile area, badly bombed during World War II, was afterwards completed when it was subjected to the largest city redevelopment in Europe, turing it into a concrete wilderness of "high-rise" housing.

John was one of the four children of Fred Foulds, a professional bassoonist who played in the Hallé Orchestra, and his wife Mary (*nee* Greenwood). Brought up in an atmosphere of continual music-making (not only by his father, but by an Italian godfather of whom he gives some anecdotes in his book *Music Today* – a man called Raspi, another bassoon-player, of "mephistophelean" appearance), the boy showed talent at a very early age. Piano studies commenced when he was four years old, and at seven he was also proficient as an oboist; when he reached the age of ten he took up the cello, which was to be his chief instrument. From the first, he was intended for the career of an orchestral musician. But by the age of seven he had also begun to compose – and chance has preserved for us the titles of all his juvenile works, from the year 1888.

Biographical details, however, are very scanty. Despite such artistic activity, Foulds's childhood does not seem to have been a very happy one. The family was not at all well-off; and with near-poverty was combined a narrowly religious atmosphere (they belonged to the Plymouth Brethren) which the boy found oppressive and constricting. Some reports of the composer in later life speak of him having a withered left arm – most probably the result of childhood disease, although it does not seem to have impaired either his cello or piano playing. His mother, to whom he was deeply attached, was an invalid; and at the age of twelve he was much affected by the death of his favourite brother, Ernest, who had been most akin to him in his artistic and literary interests, and whose books John now inherited. When he was 13 years old, he ran away from home.

The next years of his life are scantily known. Apparently he came under the wing of "a lady of ill-fame" (his daughter's description) who took a motherly interest in the boy and acted as his protector throughout his teens. He was always, in later life, profoundly grateful to this "guardian angel". She took care of his education, such as it was (he seems never to have had much formal schooling), and of his early career. For he entered professional life as an orchestral cellist at the age of 14, and until 1900 he made a living performing in pantomime and theatre bands and small local orchestras in and around Manchester and in the North of England. One town where he often played was Llandudno, where, in the closing years of the 19th century, several of the first public performances of his own works were given; and where he met his first wife, Maud Woodcock, the daughter of a local businessman. But he must have done some travelling on the Continent; in *Music Today* he mentions attending a rehearsal in Vienna at which Bruckner was present – which cannot have been later than January 1896.

By 1898, however, there seems to have been a rapprochement with his family. The *Manchester Directory* for 1898 until 1903 lists "Fouldes, Fred & John Herbert, professors of music" as living together in Dorset Street – though now at No. 80. The composer's father, who is first listed in the *Directory* for 1877, had not previously used the archaic form of his surname ("Fouldes"); John Herbert certainly uses it on his earliest surviving musical manuscripts of the mid-to-late 1890s, but seems to have dropped it about 1899.

In 1900, Foulds joined his father in the ranks of the Hallé Orchestra, with which he was to be associated until shortly before World War I. His years with the

Hallé were an extremely valuable experience, coming as they did during one of the most stimulating periods in the history of British music. They widened his already broad musical horizons, and brought him the friendship and professional esteem of many distinguished musicians—not only his conductor, the great Hans Richter, friend of Brahms, Wagner, and Bruckner, but also visiting artists and composers such as Busoni and the young Bartók, who came to Manchester for the première of his *Kossuth* in 1904.

Foulds's own compositions had continued unabated, and in 1905 the *Variazioni ed Improvvisati* for piano was the first of his works to find its way into print. A measure of performances continued, too—a large proportion of them due, apparently, to the efforts of three distinguished string-player friends, who regularly programmed his music: Arthur Catterall, a well-known Manchester violinist who was leader of the Queen's Hall Proms in 1909 and later leader of the Hallé; Arthur Payne, the first leader of the London Symphony Orchestra and later conductor of the Llandudno Pavilion Orchestra from 1900; and the Belgian violin virtuoso and conductor Henri Verbrugghen, another leader of the Queen's Hall Proms, founder of his own string quartet, who was active as a conductor in Glasgow (where some of Foulds's earliest performances took place) in the first decade of the century.

In 1906—perhaps through Richter's influence—the relatively unknown Foulds was invited as English composer-delegate to the Tonkünstlerfest des Allgemeines Deutschen Musikvereins in Essen, where he met, among others, Mahler, Strauss, Delius, and Humperdinck. About this time, too, he began to make his mark as a conductor. He acquired a lot of his experience conducting for touring companies in musical comedy. These took him as far afield as Holland, where once he had the experience of visiting the Ryks Museum in Amsterdam with the then-celebrated composer and conductor Sir Frederic Cowen. In later years he claimed to have studied with Sir Charles Hallé, Nikisch, Mahler, and Lamoureux, although nothing is known of the extent of these "studies". (Foulds would only have been 14 when Hallé died.) But Richter certainly appointed him conductor of stage-music for the Hallé concerts; he often rehearsed the orchestra, and until the outbreak of World War I he regularly visited the continent to gain experience (he was present at Munich in 1910, for instance, for the première of Mahler's Eighth Symphony). According to some reports, he also played under Richter at Bayreuth.

The same source which speaks of his conducting studies (see reproduction on page 79) locates these "in all the chief music-centres of Europe and America." There is no reason to doubt it, as long as we presume that the studies were in some cases *ad hoc* rather than formal—and yet I have not so far uncovered a single date or detail that would corroborate the statement that Foulds ever visited America. The fact is that adequate materials for a truly thorough biography of Foulds seem not to exist, or have so far not been discovered. Certain areas of his life and creative output are comparatively well-documented; others entirely unmapped. He appears only fleetingly in the published recollections of other musicians; we possess very little of his correspondence, and almost nothing in the way of a diary; often we are dependent on little more than hearsay. The story, therefore, is full of gaps and seemingly arbitrary shifts of focus—but its constant thread is the steady growth of Foulds as a composer. As a young man he may have lacked a formal education and formal training in composition. But by the first decade of the 20th century, when he began to produce music of some importance, he was already second to none of his generation as a practical all-round musician.

2. The Early Music

The first compositions of Foulds which are preserved are some small manuscript piano pieces, the earliest dating from his fifteenth year. During his late teens his interest was centered on piano and chamber music, including a number of works for his principal instrument, the cello; but these latter are unfortunately lost, along with several other items including his first three String Quartets. It's no surprise that the surviving representatives of his "juvenalia" are highly derivative: but the short piano pieces of 1895-96, though slight, are gracefully written and craftsmanlike. Moreover, the music of the immediately succeeding years, while still derivative in style, commands attention by virtue of its immense technical skill and confidence, and a boldly exploratory, un-academic outlook. The teen-age composer was learning fast, and producing work that was juvenile neither in technique nor imagination.

Some of these post-1896 works are quite substantial, beginning with a Piano Sonata in F sharp minor of 1897, to which Foulds gave the subtitle *A Study in Structure*. It was probably conceived as a one-movement form incorporating the various aspects of the conventional four-movement sonata, but after several promising and virtuosic pages it remained unfinished, for reasons now impossible to guess. (Foulds's *oeuvre*, we shall find, is littered with tantalizingly unfinished scores of equal and sometimes greater importance than many which he pursued to their conclusion.)

The year 1897 also saw him secure the first public performance of any of his music, when the violinist Rawdon Briggs (a member of the Brodsky Quartet and at one time leader of the Hallé Orchestra), with the pianist H.F. Webster, premièred Foulds's *Rhapsodie nach Heine* in Halifax in March of that year. This brilliantly violinistic display piece remained unpublished for nearly 20 years, when Foulds issued it during the Great War under the new title *Caprice Pompadour* — probably to avoid the effects of the then-prevalent anti-German sentiment — and with the misleadingly high opus-number of "Op. 42 No. 2". (Foulds did not begin to assign opus-numbers until 1900, and his numberings of his works are sometimes confusing; nor are they always a reliable guide to order of composition.) But *Rhapsodie nach Heine* seems to be how he continued to think of it, to judge by his remarks about it some 15 years later still in *Music Today*, which occur in the context of the interrelations between music, literature, and painting:[1]

> Heine declared that when he heard music performed his inner faculties at once translated it in terms of line, mass and colour, into a picture. Upon hearing Paganini play the violin he "saw" a veritable moving picture, the story of which he narrates inimitably in the *Florentine Nights*. Which, amusingly enough, the writer composed into a violin and piano piece many years ago: *Rhapsodie nach Heine*. Thus you have the full circle. A musical composition; a performance of it; this visualised by the poet as a moving picture; the picture described by him as a story; and lastly, the story retranslated into music. We do not know, by the way, which Paganini piece it was that wrought so potently upon Heine.

In his *Rhapsodie* Foulds made no attempt to quote from Paganini; instead, his music brilliantly "impersonates" the legendary violinist's manner by running the whole gamut of virtuoso pyrotechnics within a relatively small space. This ability to reproduce different "musical characters" at will is one of the distinctive qualities of Foulds's technical facility — and one of the most disconcerting elements to take into consideration when attempting to pin down the nature of his personal achievement in British music. The original 1897 manuscript of the *Rhapsodie* has disappeared, and it is difficult to believe that its 1916 version, *Caprice Pompadour*, was published without some revisions. But if the 1897 piece included passages such as this (Ex.1):

---

1   John Foulds, *Music To-day*, Opus 92 (London: Ivor Nicholson and Watson Ltd., 1934), p.97. A list made by Foulds (in about 1897) of the few books he possessed includes two volumes of Heine's poetry and prose, and one of his earliest songs (now lost) was a setting of Heine's *"Du bist wie eine Blume."*

Ex. 1

—including progressions built upon perfect fourths which were at that time practically unknown outside the last piano works of Liszt (whose *Third Mephisto Waltz* might indeed have furnished Foulds with ideas for the portrayal of the "Mephistophelean" fiddler) — then it was clearly the creation of a musical intelligence already well able to think for itself.

Another case in point is the extraordinary piano work entitled *Dichterliebe* (1897-98). This highly romantic suite is almost the most ambitious composition for piano he ever attempted, yet it remains unfinished. Nevertheless, six movements and part of a seventh were written down — in all perhaps half-an-hour's music. And such music: the pages grow black with notes through the ingenious contrapuntal elaborations, laid out in a piano style that calls for a virtuoso technique of the highest order, charged with a youthful ardor that is manifest not just in the notes but in the host of detailed and poetic instructions in both Italian and German that appear on every page. Not only the work's title, but various hints of a submerged program, recall Schumann: he is a chief influence in Foulds's early work, as is Wagner (and in fact one movement of *Dichterliebe* is a rhapsody on themes from *Das Rheingold*). The manuscript's woodcut title-page bears a dedication to "Ideala"; but we have no way of knowing whether this name conceals a real girl-friend or simply denotes the Feminine Ideal: similarly the *"Thema von Ideala"* which appears as a motto in several movements is as likely Foulds's own as the work of an aspiring woman composer. Such originality as Foulds had at this stage is glimpsed less in the musical language than in details of form and conception — for example in the remarkable prelude, whose terraced sonorities are clarified for the eye by being set out on no less than five staves.

At the very opening of the uncompleted seventh piece (*"Der Liebe Tod"*), however, a bold sequence of conjunct triads in contrary motion gives a faint foreshadowing of what was to be a consistent stylistic development: the exploration of triadic harmony in unusual combinations and fresh relationships. (See Ex.2, facing page, opening measures.)

As for his experimental leanings, Foulds was already tentatively exploring the use of intervals smaller than a semitone. Several times in later years (for instance in *Music To-day*, p. 59) he referred to his having used quarter-tones in a string quartet performed in 1898, adding that he still possessed the program of the concert to prove it. That program, however, can no longer be found, and the earliest surviving string quartet by Foulds (his Fourth, by my reckoning) dates from 1899 and contains no quarter-tones. Nevertheless, he had written his First and Second Quartets in 1896, and the performance in question might well have been of one of those. This latter date, 1896, would make the 15-year-old Foulds, without doubt, the first European composer to introduce such micro-intervals into his music — exactly contemporary with the Mexican, Júlian Carillo, and years ahead of better-known figures such as Charles Ives and Alois Hábá.

This first instance of quarter-tones, which he was to employ now and again throughout his career, was probably tentative indeed. The earliest (surviving) works that employ them are the Cello Sonata and a movement for string quartet which, under the title "The Waters of Babylon", was eventually assimilated into the suite *Aquarelles*, discussed in Chapter 3. Both works appear to date from 1905, and both show that Foulds tended to use these fine gradations as passing-notes, usually in slow-moving passages: in

Ex. 2. The first page of the unfinished finale of *Dichterliebe* gives some idea of the extreme care Foulds lavished on this manuscript, and of the fantastically detailed expression-marks found throughout. Copyright © Estate of John Foulds.

which surroundings, of course, they have most expressive point, and can most easily be distinguished by the ear. Certainly by 1905 he had developed his own symbols for them:

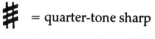

= quarter-tone sharp

quarter-tone flat =

—symbols which he later defended in print against those of Hába on the grounds, sensibly enough, that Hába's, unlike his own, confused the eye and could easily be taken for badly-printed ordinary sharps and flats.

Another kind of experimentation appears in Foulds's official Opus 1, the *Lyrics* for solo piano (1900). In extreme contrast to *Dichterliebe*, this work occupies only three exquisitely-calligraphed pages. Its subtitle is *Music-Poem No. 1*, and each page proves to contain a separate six-line "stanza". The music is unbarred: instead, it is punctuated, exactly as if it were an actual poem in words, by commas, exclamation marks, queries, dashes and full stops. The device, and something in the character of the music itself, seems to anticipate some of the later piano pieces of Satie.

Several other, more extensive "Music-Poems" followed in the next decade, though none quite approached *Lyrics* in the combination of verbal punctuation with musical text. Instead, we find Foulds adopting a kind of variation-form within a strophic framework, sometimes with prominent "refrain" passages (features which apply, too, to the impressively well-composed *Variazione ed Improvvisati*, Opus 4). Gradually, in fact, the "Music-Poems" became virtually symphonic poems for orchestra: for after 1900 Foulds began confidently to expand his efforts into larger forms.

It is worth looking at *Variazioni ed Improvvisati su una Thema Originale* (to give it its full title) in some detail; even though in some respects it is less original, less prophetic of its composer's later development, than either *Dichterliebe* or *Lyrics*: it harks back with enthusiasm and affection to great models—Chopin, Schumann, Liszt, Brahms—and stakes out a claim on their territory. Stylistically, therefore, the piece is undeniably derivative, though immensely assured: there are only fleeting hints of Foulds's personal voice. Yet beyond the surface influences and youthful excesses these more original features betoken a considerable creative personality in the making, and give the work some claim on the repertoire even

today: its full-blooded emotion, extraordinary inventiveness and natural feeling for large-scale architectonic design. These were presumably the qualities that brought it prompt publication. Indeed the composer Havergal Brian recalled many years later that in early 1905 he had asked Elgar's great publisher-friend August Jaeger, of Novello's, whether he had detected any new rising star among English composers who might rival Elgar's quality: Jaeger responded by sending Foulds's newly-printed *Variazioni ed Improvvisati*, which Brian then reviewed enthusiastically in *The Musical World*. It is difficult, indeed, to think of another set of piano variations from this period of the English Musical Renaissance that remotely approaches it in quality.

Formally, the work consists of a theme and nine variations, plus some rather freer development framed by two fairly "straight" restatements of the original theme. Foulds has, however, grouped the variations by a key-scheme and character to establish a large-scale three-part form: theme and variations 1-3, collectively subtitled *Il Pensieroso*; variations 4-9, subtitled *L'Allegro*; and the remaining music, which effectively constitutes a fast finale with slow introduction and coda.

The Theme itself (*Geniale, ma poetico*, B flat) has something of the lilting charm which Foulds seemed able to summon up effortlessly throughout his career (Ex. 3).

Its second half is repeated, and the first four variations follow suit. Variation 1 (*parlando*, B flat) elaborates the Theme in flowing semiquavers and begins to make something of the sighing progression in its second half. Low, tolling bass octaves underpin Variation 2 (*Calmo assai ma fervido*, B^b), a smoothly singing tune with a memorable cadential turn—soon to become a Foulds trademark in his many "Celtic"-inspired pieces, such as his once-famous *Keltic Lament* (1911) (Ex. 4).

This variation moves gorgeously to D flat in the middle, first of the work's many important structural linkages by thirds. In Variation 3 (*piu animando*, 3/8, B flat minor) the pace quickens somewhat but the mood remains rather darkly pensive.

The tonal centre moves—by a third—to G major for the beginning of the section Foulds calls *L'Allegro*. Variation 4 (*Non troppo vivace*, 6/8) is a skittish study in thirds, sixths, and off-beat accents. The fireworks really begin with Variation 5 (*Brillante*, 6/8, G major), a heroic piece of Chopinesque rhodomontade. Variation 6 (*alla marcia*, 4/4, G major) is a crisply strutting

Ex. 3

Ex. 4

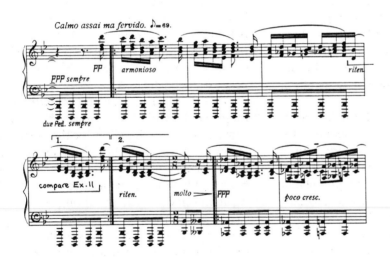

Ex. 5

march. Three variations in B flat have been balanced by three in G; the next three swiftly extend the chain of descending thirds. Number 7 (*Ardito, ma con umore*, 6/8, E minor) is a thunderous Brahmsian canon with chromatic thirds in contrary motion at its center, ending in a veritable fusillade of chords. Variation 8 (*Gaia, ma senza agitazione*) takes us to C major and a complete change of character, with a winsome tune spun above teasing rhythmic pulsation in alternating bars of 3/8 and 2/8 (Ex. 5).

Then Variation 9 (*Focoso*, 2/4, A minor) switches the mood back to ardent keyboard virtuosity. That variation contrives to end in F, at which point the Theme returns complete, richly harmonized in D flat, *Lento molto e con intimo sentimento*.

A massive sequence of triads in contrary motion (*Grave*, 12/8)—the most prophetic indication of the later Foulds in the whole work—swings the tonality firmly back to B flat, minor at first and then brightening with "Forest Murmurs" figuration towards the major. This introduces the finale-section (*Allegro*, 12/8) which strenuously and athletically continues the variation-process to a heaven-storming climax. But the bravura heroics subside suddenly into pensive meditation, and the work ends *Tempo Primo* with the lilting tune in its original innocence, and B flat confirmed in rolling arpeggios the whole length of the keyboard.

This impressive confidence in the handling of large-scale structure, and of the chosen medium, also manifests itself in the chamber and orchestral music of the period. By the time he turned twenty in 1900 Foulds had already composed five string quartets, although only the fourth of these is known to have survived, in the form of a set of parts. These very early quartets occupy a similar position in Foulds's *oeuvre* to the early and mostly missing quartets of Schoenberg: as prentice works which must on the one hand have reflected an intense love of the Classical and

Romantic masters in the medium, and on the other the first stirrings of a personal mastery gained in practical experience of chamber music—these were works written in the first instance to play with friends. So much we can gather from Foulds's Quartet in F minor of 1899, analogous in its way to the Schoenberg D major of 1897, and just as dominated by the shades of Brahms and Dvořák. Foulds never assigned numbers to his many quartet compositions—which eventually totalled at least ten, in addition to the suite *Aquarelles (Music-Pictures Group II)* and quartet versions of some of his lighter pieces. But from the early worklist previously referred to we know that the F minor work is chronologically his Fourth String Quartet, and it already displays an easy familiarity with the ensemble. The 18-year-old composer writes effectively for strings and can construct a textbook approximation of a sonata-movement. The overall form shows some slight originality: there are three movements, the finale being a set of free variations or "Impromptus" on the dramatic introduction to the first; and the most individual music seems to be the second movement, a delicate intermezzo-like piece marked *All' Arabesco* which introduces, perhaps for the first time in Foulds's output, a whiff of Orientalism which he was eventually to follow to some very exotic conclusions.

His Sixth Quartet, *Quartetto Romantico*, of 1903 was long listed as his Op. 5 until the composer appropriated the designation for the much later *Three Marching Songs* when those were published in 1929. This quartet, too, is at present only extant as a set of parts; but it shows a great advance on the F minor. Again in three movements, though on a bigger scale than the F minor quartet, it is an extremely assured piece of work which demands considerable prowess from its performers—perhaps significantly, it is dedicated to Foulds's friend the Belgian violin virtuoso and conductor Henri Verbrugghen. As the title sug-

Ex. 6

gests, the idiom is warmly and expansively romantic with that "sheer vitality and natural musicality" (Hugh Wood's phrase) which distinguish Foulds's music throughout his career. Again, the most personal writing occurs in the slow movement, which has a striking opening (Ex. 6).

This is something of a seminal passage in Foulds's work. He was an inveterate re-user and adapter of his own good ideas. The guitar-like chords, slightly modified, went straight into the slow movement of the Cello Sonata; while the beautiful and wholly characteristic violin tune—which eloquently demonstrates why he could have become such a "natural" writer of light music—provided the basis for the Adagio of the Cello Concerto, Op. 17 (1908-09).

Quartetto Romantico seems to contain the seeds of a creative epiphany; and the mid-1900s were in fact a period of creative breakthrough for Foulds. They saw his emergence as an orchestral composer with *Epithalamium* and other symphonic poems; saw him carry through a very ambitious project indeed in the huge "Concert Opera" *The Vision of Dante*; and saw him take a decisive stride towards mastery in the remarkably powerful and original Cello Sonata, Op. 6, of 1905[2]—a large-scale piece, a real duo-sonata in

which both players are taxed to the limit by writing of magnificent bravura. Like most of his best works, throughout his career, it combines several different areas of interest, several contrasting stylistic tendencies, into a powerful unity. Foulds was in some respects a musical pioneer, but his wide-ranging mind made him also a highly intelligent eclectic, and his real originality seems to me to lie precisely in this receptivity to all kinds of contemporary musical developments, to take whatever he felt was useful for his expressive purposes, and to create a quite individual synthesis which could be the work of no other composer.

Some of the Sonata's main motives are, according to Foulds's published program-note, "traces of two old English Puritan tunes which had been in the composer's mind since early boyhood". One of these is the first movement's opening theme (Ex. 7)—simple in itself, but accompanied with great harmonic sophistication: the conjunct-triad motion we noted in Ex. 1 is already bearing distinctive fruit. Moreover, the whole work exhibits a kind of "progressive tonality" from B minor to G major. The first movement is a powerful, highly-chromatic, foreshortened sonata-form in which the first subject (our Ex. 7) is omitted entirely from the recapitulation but forms

Ex. 7

---

2   It was certainly revised for publication in 1927, but I think little of the basic conception was altered. Even if (as is just possible) the present finale was composed then, its basic material had already appeared in the first movement of the sturdy Cello Concerto, Op. 17.

Ex. 8

the basis of a brusque coda. The following *Lento* contains music of great beauty written with the most intimate knowledge of the cello's capabilities, featuring arpeggiated pizzicato chords, pizzicato harmonics, and — in two transition-passages — double-stopping in quarter-tones. The finale, which ranges from a forthright diatonicism to some extraordinary whole-tone writing, is basically a sonata-design with a fine striding main theme (Ex. 8).

The form is telescoped, however, to accomodate three cadenza-like displays of virtuosity: the first for the cello, after the exposition; the second for the piano, after a combined development and recapitula-

tion. The third, for both instruments in octave unison, occurs as the culmination of a huge coda which combines most of the materials of the whole work over a passacaglia-like ground bass. It is a notable work, one of the finest, if not *the* finest, Cello Sonata by an English composer, brilliantly and gratefully written for both instruments, and well worth the attention of any players who love the Brahms, Fauré and Debussy sonatas and may be looking for a new addition to their repertoire.

The Seventh String Quartet, presumably composed in about 1906, has disappeared (it was performed in 1907, and used quarter-tones, as well as

Ex. 9

having a *"finale in modo popolare"*); but No. 8 (Op. 23, in D minor) is still extant, with a complete set of parts and a score of the first movement. It seems to show Foulds irresolute at a turning-point in his musical career; and it was the last full-blown quartet he was to write for over 20 years. Certainly it must have given trouble: it has only two movements, but while the first was completed in 1907 it took him until 1910 to produce the other;[3] and they look Janus-like in opposite directions. In the Cello Sonata, he had reached out from the secure basis of a post-Brahmsian style to embrace a large number of other devices (quarter-tones, whole-tone harmony, open fifths, pentatonicism, a personal brand of diatonic dissonance he had been experimenting with in small pieces since the 1890s, and a melodic style which incorporated specifically "English" elements without actual quotation of folk tunes) and pulled them together into a highly successful, but by its nature precarious, eclectic mixture. In the light of the Sonata, the Andante first movement of the Eighth Quartet is a regression to Brahmsian models, though composed now with a melodic generosity and richness of sonority that leaves most of Foulds's contemporary English post-Brahmsians looking even more palely academic than usual (Ex. 9).

The second movement appears an uneasy amalgam of disparate elements — a whispering chromatic perpetuum mobile in contrary motion; a gruffly rhythmic passage in triple and quadruple stopping; a cocky little "English" tune, spun over an ostinato bass; a mysterious chorale with wide chordal spacings; and a floridly emotional cadenza-like solo for the first violin — all these are developed to a grandiose, almost orchestrally resonant coda which ends with a major-key apotheosis of the first movement's principal theme. Only a good performance will enable one to tell whether Foulds brings off his formal balancing-act: one can only note that this kind of structural risk often brought out the best in him.

During the same general period (1905-10) Foulds composed no less than three concertos for his own instrument, the cello. He seems to have abandoned the bulk of the earliest, his Op. 12, within a year or so of

writing it, but he retained from it a *Lento e Scherzetto* (the original second movement), which he himself performed in Manchester at a Hallé Promenade Concert in January 1907. Soon afterwards Foulds produced a new three-movement Concerto in G major, Op. 17 — his official *Cello Concerto No. 1* — dedicated to Carl Fuchs, the leader of the Hallé Orchestra's cello section. He followed it with a *Cello Concerto No. 2*: although this latter work (his Op. 19) was in fact an arrangement for cello and chamber orchestra of a Concerto Grosso by Corelli. Op. 19 has disappeared without trace — and, as far as we know, without ever attaining a performance. But Foulds himself conducted the Op. 17 Concerto during Hans Richter's last subscription concert with the Hallé on 16 March 1911, the soloist being Carl Fuchs, the work's dedicatee.

From contemporary press reports it was not a particularly auspicious occasion. The large audience had come to bid farewell to their great conductor, who seems in any case to have monopolized the preliminary rehearsals, so that the orchestra was almost certainly sight-reading Foulds's Concerto — which is quite a tricky score! Not surprisingly, the critics afterwards spoke of "orchestration more interesting than effective"; but they were not wholly unfavourable. The slow movement came in for especial praise, and the *Manchester Guardian* critic found the orchestral interludes in the finale provided evidence of a substantial orchestral composer in the making, whose "imitative passages stride boldly along and witness to his mastery of the contrapuntal style." But the Concerto was never heard again in Foulds's lifetime; it had to wait until a recent (1987) recording of it, for the BBC, to demonstrate that Foulds's orchestration, when properly rehearsed, is an admirable foil to the solo part.

As already noted the Cello Concerto shares some material both with the Cello Sonata and the *Quartetto Romantico*. The spacious first movement is in fact largely built upon Ex. 8, which is treated in a quite different way to its appearance in the finale of the Sonata. The orchestral colors and harmonies frequently suggest the influence of Richard Strauss (as

---

3   It seems certain that compositional progress was more complex than this summary suggests. Although the set of parts is in fine condition and perfectly represents the work's final form, at the end of the now fragile and stained manuscript score of the first movement, and beneath a boldly-inked date "Fine / about July 1907" (which is itself clearly a later addition), is a very faint and not altogether decipherable pencil note which appears to read: "[?sl]ow movement (III) made out in [?smaller?] score (now 2)". No "smaller" score, if that is how the word should be read, has come to light — and neither of the movements that comprise the quartet's final form is slow. It looks as if in 1907 Foulds conceived the work in three (or more) movements, shuffled them, and arrived at the present form only after a radical re-thinking of the whole structure.

some critics noted), but combined with a "Nordic" coloring more reminiscent of Sibelius. The soloist propounds material of his own, notably a rhetorical "motto-theme" in wide-spread pizzicato chords, similar in style to those in Ex. 6. (This recurs in all three movements.) The solo writing is, if anything, even more virtuosic than in the Sonata, and includes a breath-taking cadenza.

The slow movement, founded upon the tune already shown in Ex. 6, is in a comparatively short ternary form, its soulfully melodious outer sections contrasting with an elegiac middle episode in the style of a slow march. The finale is a vivacious Rondo, whose main theme is notable for its ferocious double-stopping. There is something of a "gypsy" quality to this music, as in some of Brahms's concerto finales—and this is certainly the movement which relates most closely to the well-loved recent musical past of Brahms, Dvořák, and Tchaikovsky. There are plenty of soloistic pyrotechnics, with space for an improvised cadenza, and the coda—where the music moves into compound time—is rather clearly modelled on that of Brahms's Violin Concerto. But it is no less enjoyable for that.

The Concerto was, in any case, by no means Foulds's first orchestral effort. He had already been active in this field since the late 1890s, and his earliest surviving orchestral score—a suite entitled *Undine* with a memorably dark barcarolle for its middle movement—had been performed in Llandudno around the turn of the century. As I remarked above, Foulds soon turned to the orchestra in order to extend his "Music-Poems" upon a larger and more colorful canvas.

Foulds's first orchestral "Music-Poem", *Epithalamium*, Op. 10, was also the first work to bring him before a wide public. Early in 1905, Foulds approached Granville Bantock, who was then conductor of the Liverpool Symphony Orchestra, to show him the first part of the work which occupied so much of his energies at that time, the huge "concert opera" *The Vision of Dante*. Bantock, though impressed, thought it beyond his capabilities, but mentioned that he would be interested to perform a smaller work. That Autumn, therefore, Foulds sent him the newly-completed *Epithalamium*, a vivacious and optimistic orchestral poem in six "stanzas", played without a break. Bantock was again unable to per-

form it himself, but his sympathetic reply, from the office of the Liverpool Orchestral Society, is interesting and typical of the man:

> I am returning the score of your Epithalamium today by registered post. I have been much interested in reading the score, & congratulate you on so good a work. It ought to be very effective.
>
> I have got into such trouble lately with our members for introducing so many novelties by "freaks", this is the term they use for British composers—myself among the number—that for the present, I shall hesitate about including or recommending new works in subsequent programs. Meanwhile, take your score to Richter, & send it to Dr. Sinclair, & Dr. Brewer, of the Hereford & Gloucester Festivals, also let Mr. Wood see it; & if you should not be successful in these quarters, let me know & I will do what I can for you with our committee.[4]

Foulds followed Bantock's advice to "let Mr. Wood see it": and Henry Wood performed *Epithalamium* with great success in the 1906 Queen's Hall Proms. The young composer received an ovation, the critics found "much to praise", and the work was performed again in Manchester towards the end of the year, and in Edinburgh in 1907.

Epithalamium would still, I think, make an enjoyable short work in the concert hall, and it displays already Foulds's remarkable gifts for deft and telling orchestration. But two later, more substantial orchestral poems seem to me of more lasting interest. One is *Apotheosis*, Op. 18, an elegy in five "stanzas" in memory of Joseph Joachim. This is a noble and deeply-felt work, cast basically as an extended funeral march for orchestra with a meditative, rhapsodic violin obbligato and an interesting key-scheme that passes gradually from the gloom of F sharp minor to the final radiance of the relative (A) major. *Apotheosis* had only one performance, in Liverpool in 1909; but the last and most ambitious of the "Music-Poems", *Mirage*, Op. 20, of 1910, has never been heard in public at all—though it recently had the good fortune to become one of the first of Foulds's orchestral works to appear on LP. Scored for a large orchestra with a fine sense of colour and large-scale effect, this is an extended symphonic poem in six sections, whose titles

4   Bantock to Foulds, 14 November 1905 (Letter in B.M.Add.Ms. 56482). Punctuation as in original.

The first page of *Mirage,* Op. 20, in Foulds's autograph. (Courtesy Trustees of the British Library. Copyright © 1980 by Musica Viva and the Estate of John Foulds.)

reveal a program more spiritual and philosophical than narrative: "Immutable Nature", "Man's ever-ambition", "Man's ever-unattainment", "Mirage", "Man humbled", "Man's self-triumph". The musical language owes something to Richard Strauss — most of all (and not unnaturally with such subject-matter) to *Also sprach Zarathustra*; but the work as a whole is highly original. The very opening, with a grand mysterious chorale-theme looming majestically on woodwind and horns through a shimmering haze of string oscillations, is a remarkable inspiration, as is the muted, icy scherzo that depicts the spiritual "Mirage" itself. In the third section, Foulds introduces quarter-tones in the strings; the fifth includes some fine Elgarian *nobilmente* writing; and the finale provides the chorale with a serene apotheosis of mystic, Brucknerian grandeur.

Mirage really brings Foulds's earliest period of musical development to a close, but one other work of the 1900s deserves especial mention. *The Vision of Dante*, Op. 7, a "concert opera" or operatic cantata, on which he worked from at least 1904 to 1908, is one of the largest works in Foulds's entire output. The forces called for, though large, are not unreasonably gigantic, and the text is the composer's own skilful précis of the *Divina commedia*, well-tailored to make the maximum number of dramatic and musical points. The work is in three parts, each corresponding to the three divisions of Dante's poem; each of them is through-composed, with recurring development of leit-motives. The first part, "Hell", is naturally the most sheerly dramatic, though it opens with a dark, meditative orchestral prelude, "Dante Alone", which could well be performed on its own as a concert item. There are some suitably violent demonic choruses, and a remarkable orchestral depiction of the region of eternal ice in which Dante's Satan is finally discovered. In Part II, "Purgatory", the music moves into a region of spiritual contemplation which we often encounter in Foulds's more serious works: the chorus sings in broad chorales, and a strikingly beautiful passage, dominated by string harmonics, recurs at the end of each section, marking Dante's ascent one stage higher towards the "Paradise" which is the subject of Part III. Here the character of Beatrice becomes increasingly prominent, and the work culminates in a truly grandiose hymnic apotheosis.

The term "concert opera" denotes a dramatic work for purely concert performance, its spiritual subject-matter being treated in an operatic rather than ecclesiastical manner. Clearly, Foulds was aiming at

performance in one of the great English choral festivals, which were then experiencing the break-up of the Victorian oratorio traditions under the impact of such works as Elgar's *Dream of Gerontius*, Delius's *Mass of Life*, Bantock's *Omar Khayyam* and the "Sinfoniae Sacrae" of Parry. In common with most of his earliest music, *The Vision of Dante* is steeped in the late 19th-century Romantic masters, particularly Liszt, Wagner, and Bruckner. But it is very much a work of its time (the influence of *Gerontius* is also detectable), and contains some prophetic foreshadowings of the composer's later development. The motif of "God the Lord" — three long, quiet, slowly-descending triads — recurs in many of the scores he wrote during the next 30 years.

Ex. 10

The score was read by Elgar, whose opinion (recorded in a letter now in the British Museum) was that it was one of the finest modern works to have come to his notice, and deserved an immediate and prestigious performance. Foulds's mentor Hans Richter declared his intention of performing it; but for reasons which are not clear he had not managed to do so by the time he retired in 1911. Foulds appears to have made few attempts after that date to have the work mounted, and in fact — apart from a few extracts which he later arranged for chamber orchestra — the work has still never been heard. Havergal Brian, who saw the score in Foulds's house soon after it was written, felt that this was a particular disappointment to the composer, and one of the reasons that he turned his hand to light music.

3. Light Music, Theater Music, "Music-Pictures"

In 1909, Foulds married Maud Woodcock. They established themselves in a house at 80, Acomb Street, in the Fallowfield district of Manchester. Havergal Brian, who visited him there on occasion, found him well able to continue composing in the midst of domestic hubbub. They had one son, Raymond (b.1911), who was to grow up to be a versatile instrumentalist like his father, and eventually became Manager and Director of Charles Foote & Sons, the well-known London firm of instrument-makers. The few known photographs of John Foulds at this period show a young man giving every appearance of zest for life; his pince-nez, high forehead, and dark swept-back hair occasionally reveal a striking resemblance to Gustav Mahler. In addition to his musical activities, he was a keen amateur painter[5] and woodcarver. One photograph of him in the living-room at Fallowfield (taken no earlier than 1910) shows Foulds playing the piano to one side of an impressive and ornately-carved wooden fireplace, the result of his own labors.

This fireplace is intricately inlaid with strange designs and mystical symbols—among them the Swastika (at that time still an untainted alchemical symbol) and the Egyptian Ankh. It also bears Foulds's personal monogram (J,H,F superimposed into a single character), which is found in many of his manuscripts, as well as a motto that reads *HO EX-ORIENTES FOS* (a macaronic and oddly-spelt mixture of Greek and Latin, meaning "The Light from the East"). This magnificent piece of carving[6] testifies to Foulds's early-awakened occult interests—which at this period seem to have tended in the direction of the Theosophy of Madame Blavatsky, with its specifically Oriental roots. Having escaped from a family atmosphere dominated by one of the narrowest aberrant forms of Christianity, it is perhaps not unnatural that Foulds was drawn towards its opposite pole in a much more esoteric form of spirituality—one, moreover, which was exciting many artistic people at the time, such as W.B. Yeats and the composer Cyril Scott.

Meanwhile, however, Foulds's music was beginning to reach a wider public—but chiefly in a sphere that was anything but esoteric.

It is always difficult to draw the line between "light" and "serious" music; but Foulds undoubtedly crossed that line in 1909 with the first performance of the Suite *Holiday Sketches*, Op. 16—the first of a whole series of light-orchestral and salon pieces whose appeal for the listener lay, not in contrapuntal or structural elaboration, not in exploratory harmonies or microtones, not indeed in any depth of emotional content, but simply in sheer tunefulness, simple forms, a dash of conventional mood-painting, and highly professional orchestration. Those are not qualities to be sneered at: they came easily to Foulds's fluent and inventive pen, and much of his light music is very good of its kind—the best pieces still retain a sparkle and insouciant melodic charm which would make them effective in performance even today.

At first, we may surmise, Foulds threw off such pieces as a kind of relaxation from his serious composition. But they soon became necessary to a composer with a wife and child to support—for unlike his more ambitious works, they were saleable. *Holiday Sketches* and its two successors, the *Suite Française* and the *Keltic Suite*, soon found publishers and plenty of performances, as did other little pieces in the same vein that he produced up to the First World War; and this trickle of "pot-boilers" had to continue, for it remained one of his main sources of income throughout his life. Even so the financial reward was usually moderate, and his efforts in light music, however much he must sometimes have enjoyed the task, were finally counter-productive. Light music of various kinds came to bulk very large in Foulds's output—so large that he came to be known simply as a light-music composer and found it almost impossible to interest conductors or publishers in the works which *he* set store by. Light music (and arranging) was what was wanted from him, and so he had to write it—leaving little time for what he conceived as his real task.

---

5   As a boy he became friendly with John Yeend King (1855-1924), a then-fashionable landscape and genre painter who exhibited in both London and Paris; he took the young Foulds on outdoor sketching expeditions.

6   Its ultimate fate is unknown. The house no longer exists.

John Foulds (seated at the piano) and his first wife at home at 80 Acomb Street, Manchester, with the elaborately carved fireplace discussed in the text (page 15). (Courtesy of the late Raymond Foulds.)

All Foulds's light music maintains his customary high standards of craftsmanship; but the musical interest is highly variable. The best and worst of his early efforts in the *genre* are to be found in the *Suite Française*, Op. 22, with its exciting toccata-like first movement ("*Les Zouaves*") and the delicate "*La Fée Tarapatapoum*", which is succeeded by a dreadfully empty, bombastic "*Hymne Heroique à la France*". However it was with the *Keltic Suite*, Op. 29 (1911) — itself derived from a slightly earlier set of *Keltic Melodies* for strings and harp — that Foulds had by far his biggest popular and commercial success. This was his first work to employ a generalized "Scottish" style — with the conventional attributes of Scotch snaps, pentatonic melody, drone basses and a mild modality — which Foulds was to exploit with greater degrees of effectiveness and sophistication in such later works as the *Keltic Overture*, the 5 *Scottish-Keltic Songs* for chorus, the Suite *Gaelic Melodies*, and the vocal concerto *Lyra Celtica*.

The worst that can be said against the *Keltic Suite* is that it is not a very interesting piece of music. It is not *bad* music — just a potboiler, a musical picture-postcard, no less and no more. The tunes are pleasant rather than memorable, the scoring is clean-cut, the outer movements are lively and contain two or three ingenious modulations. There is some life in them yet. That said, the objective critic of a later generation has exhausted its virtues. But it was not written for such a critic, but for an ordinary low- to middle-brow concert audience in 1911 — and something in the second movement struck home to that audience with great force.

This movement, titled "A Lament", consists of a simple, shapely melody (Ex. 11) presented by solo cello against a sparse chordal accompaniment; repeated in fuller scoring; and then recalled briefly a third time by solo violin to form a coda. In Foulds's own original scoring, this modest little piece was at least restrained and unsentimental — the string-writing in the coda even distantly recalls Sibelius. But it was not long allowed to remain so. Only a few years after the *Keltic Suite*'s first performance, the *Keltic Lament* was being issued and performed separately as a favourite popular number — for full orchestra, for brass band, for cello and piano, as a song, as a chorus,

Ex. 11

John Foulds playing the cello at home in Fallowfield, Manchester. (Courtesy of the late Raymond Foulds.)

in arrangements sometimes by Foulds, but more often not. It became his one real popular "hit", and during the inter-war period it was performed and broadcast innumerable times, often more than once a week. Even as late as the 1950s it was occasionally to be heard; and in present times it still crops up, once every three or four years, in the odd light-orchestral program (and usually attributed to "the Scottish composer John Foulds"). Until the mid-1970s, it thus retained the dubious distinction of being the *only* work of Foulds that was still, if very infrequently, heard in his own country—a mere trifle, which gives no hint of his real achievement, and of whose popularity he had grown sick long before his audiences had.[7] Moreover, its occasional revivals were usually in one of the versions for brass band—a medium to which the piece is fundamentally unsuited.

However, at first this success must have been very welcome. And his talent for tuneful, evocative, atmospheric music could be turned in another useful and remunerative direction—that of the theatre. About the same time as he began to produce his lighter pieces Foulds became friends with Lena Ashwell, Lewis Casson, and Sybil and Russell Thorndike, and wrote his first incidental music for plays for Lewis Casson productions in Manchester and London. His very first theater score, for a children's fairy play entitled *Wonderful Grandmama* which Casson staged in Manchester at Christmas 1912, was a substantial one: it required nearly 40 musical numbers, and Foulds was given only a few days in which to compose them. Yet the music was a great success, and he afterwards thought well enough of it to recompose some of the numbers into a *Miniature Suite* for orchestra. Long believed lost—even by the composer—this *Suite* was rediscovered in the library of the Hallé Orchestra in 1982 and proved to be a work of considerable sparkle and delicate instrumentation, several of whose musical ideas Foulds developed in subsequent works.

Thus began a long association. During his career Foulds was to write at least 32 theater scores, almost a third of these being for Casson and Thorndike. Though their quality was variable, the finest of them

are certainly of greater artistic stature than the general run of his light music. Unfortunately only a few pieces were published from them, and many of the manuscripts were apparently destroyed during World War II: but even so, enough remains to show how well his talents were exercised in the field.

One by-product of Foulds's theater associations at this time was *The Tell-tale Heart*, Op. 36—a "dramatic monologue" in which Edgar Allan Poe's grisly story is turned into a melodrama for reciter and orchestra (or piano). This was written for Russell Thorndike, who performed it several times with great success. The orchestral material seems to be missing, but the published piano score shows it to be a musically distinguished and dramatically viable piece, one of the very few thoroughly effective contributions to a notoriously difficult medium. Though it has not been heard in this country for many years, it is, in the piano version, one of a handful of Foulds works which still find an occasional performance abroad.

Foulds's output of more "serious" music, though slowed down, did not cease in those years just prior to the Great War. It was at this time that he began his series of suites of so-called "Music-Pictures": pieces designed to reflect, in sound, the composer's reactions to various aspects of the visual world, and especially to specific paintings. Of course such a general scheme provided an excuse for very diverse musical styles, light as well as serious; the first few, however, Foulds definitely ranked among his major works. The first set, for piano trio (Op. 30), is lost; and the second—the *Aquarelles* for string quartet (Op. 32)—had to wait many years for performance; but the third (Op. 33), for full orchestra, was taken up by Henry Wood and was quite a sensation at the 1912 Proms.[8] Other performances followed in 1913 (after which the work has never been heard again complete, although the first movement was revived in Manchester in 1980). The press was very favourable. The *Morning Post* critic wrote of the première thus:

> The affinity between sound and colour has long been recognised, but the new orchestral compositions by Mr. J.H. Foulds, performed for the first time at the Queen's Hall

---

7   In the early 1920s Foulds seems to have made a deliberate attempt to supplant his own work (and repeat its success) with a new piece in similar vein, *Gaelic Dream-Song*. Though equally unpretentious, this is musically more distinguished than the *Lament*: but it failed to dislodge it from popular affection.

8   This apparently straightforward sequence is belied by Rosa Newmarch's analytical notes for the Queen's Hall première of *Music-Pictures Group III*, on 5 September 1912. Clearly based upon contemporary communication with Foulds (who is quoted verbatim at several points), these notes tell a rather different story. As of that date, she informs the audience: [continued next page]

Promenade Concert last night, are not mere reproductions of colour schemes. Their aim is to show how the musician can be inspired by the painter. Mr. Foulds does not attempt to transfer colour to sound.... he has sought to reproduce in music the mental impression created by the picture.... Thanks to a clear-sighted vision, a command of melody, and an excellent constructive technique, he creates a picture that conveys a definite impression. The pictures show Mr. Foulds as a musical colourist of great versatility. Much of his work is masterly.... His introduction of quarter-tones hitherto absent from the Western scale, but present in the Eastern, is justified by its effect.... It is not too much to say that these "Music Pictures" are the most satisfactory native effort in orchestral program music that has been heard for a long time. They mark a definite departure and a definite achievement.

Reviewing a later performance, early in 1913, the *Musical Standard* complained that the recent Musical League Festival in Birmingham could with profit have dropped "more than one work in Mr. Foulds's favour, for to my mind there was then no equal to the solemn breadth and power which is so ingeniously wrought amid the strangely moving tonal colouring in... the first of these Pictures". The *Yorkshire Post* concurred: "Undoubtedly these endeavours are as-

tonishing essays on the part of the young Englishman.... The prevailing characteristics are an utter disregard of the limitations of the diatonic, or even the chromatic scale... a contempt for merely related keys... and a most up-to-date acquaintance with all the shades of instrumental scoring.... a work which as a whole gives the listener more to think about than to gush over."

Music-Pictures Group III is, indeed, a fine, characterful work, wide-ranging in its stylistic references as is all Foulds's best music. The first movement, "The Ancient of Days" (after Blake's famous watercolor which Foulds had seen in a Manchester exhibition), uses only woodwind, brass and percussion to convey an impression of archaic austerity, founded on the solemn opening theme reproduced as Ex. 12, below.

The delicate and ingenious second movement, after a picture by Brunet of a dancing Columbine which had impressed Foulds at the Paris Salon of 1906, is subtitled "A study in full tones, half-tones and quarter-tones". It is cast in A-B-C-B-A form, the "A" sections using only whole-tone intervals, the "B" sections being mostly chromatic, and the central "C" section for strings alone moving in streams of quarter-tones. The overall scheme of a gradual refinement and then relaxation of the gradations of harmony looks, in score, as if it should sound most natural and effective in performance. The third movement, "Old Greek Legend", was inspired by a sketch of a sage by John Martin, and is one of the earliest examples of

Ex. 12

Footnote 8 *(continued)*

He has written in all four groups of Music-Pictures: the first is for pianoforte solo; the second, from pictures in water-colour, is for string quartet; and the fourth, for orchestra, is based upon Watts's "Love and Death" and "Love and Life".

Mrs. Newmarch's reference to the second group accords well with the *Aquarelles* described on page 20 — although the manuscript as we have it seems to be of significantly later date than 1912. All of Foulds's surviving worklists indicate that the first group of *Music-Pictures*, now missing, was for a trio of violin, cello, and piano; but we may perhaps concluded that it originally existed in a version for solo piano. However, the "fourth group", for orchestra, after pictures of G.F. Watts, has not only completely disappeared — so has all mention of it in any work-list yet found. Since little more than a month had elapsed between Foulds's completion of Group III and the concert for which the notes were written, this "fourth group" may still have been at the sketch-stage at that time. However, it remains curious that all trace of the work seems to have vanished. The suite for string orchestra, after paintings by Degas, Farguharson, and Morland, which Foulds published in 1922 as *Music-Pictures Group IV*, is clearly no relation.

Ex. 13

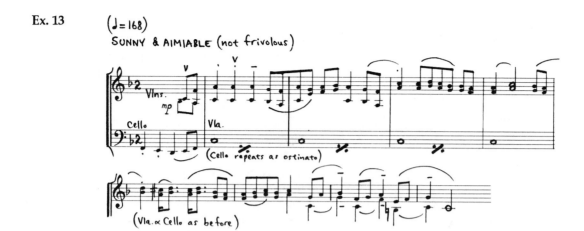

Foulds's interest in strict modal composition, being written entirely in the Phrygian. (It was this same interest which produced, in the virtually contemporary incidental music for Lewis Casson's production of *Julius Caesar*, an unaccompanied modal setting of a Pindaric Ode—now lost—and was to lead Foulds to several diverse artistic conclusions in later years.) The suite's finale, "The Tocsin", with its brilliant scoring, off-stage bells, and poignant cor anglais solo, provides a rousing conclusion. Its point of departure was a painting by Boutigny.

Music-Pictures Group II, for string quartet, may well have been assembled from various sources at a later date than *Group III*. The Eighth String Quartet's "English" tune had already been parodied to provide a march in the music for *Wonderful Grandmama* for a character identified in the cast-list as —Captain Scarabang of the Horse Marines"—when, according to the critic of the *Manchester Guardian*, it seemed "in danger of becoming a popular tune before the season has run through." Here, somewhat re-cast (see Ex. 13), the same tune forms the basis for the first of these three *Aquarelles*, entitled "In Provence" after a painting by Henry Herbert La Thangue (1859-1929), a well-known landscape artist of the day. Here the heavier aspects of the Brahmsian inheritance are entirely absent: the final movement, ")Arden Glade", after John Crome, is indeed a romp of almost Graingeresque gusto. But the central movement, entitled "The Waters of Babylon" after another William Blake

watercolor, is not without expressive weight. It begins with a mysterious progression of which more will be said before the end of this book:

Ex. 14

Foulds uses these wandering harmonies to turn the music onto distant and unexpected keys, and later reinforces their plangency by having them move against one another in quarter-tones. Their characteristic contrary motion is echoed in passages where all melodies are inevitably accompanied by their own inversions—deliberately suggesting reflections in water, and so making the movement as a whole (which according to a manuscript note by Foulds was originally conceived as early as 1905) a fascinating study in mirror-forms. *Aquarelles* was only performed once in Foulds's lifetime, in 1926; but in the past decade, due to the advocacy of the Endellion Quartet, it has become perhaps his most-played work of recent years.

4. Maud MacCarthy — The War

Foulds seems to have moved to London in late 1913, although there is evidence that he continued to play with the Hallé occasionally until 1915. In London—like so many composers before him—he worked as a musical odd-job man: cellist, pianist, theater musician, conductor, arranger, music-copyist—only incidentally, as far as the rest of the world was concerned, a writer of music. When the First World War broke out in August 1914 he volunteered for army service, but it was considered that he would be more usefully employed in a civilian capacity as a musician.

Not long afterwards, John Foulds met the woman who was to have a decisive influence on his life. Maud MacCarthy (1882-1967) was a most remarkable person: musician, mystic, writer, lecturer, actress, ethnomusicologist, poet, champion of women's rights—these were some of her talents and activities. Born in Ireland, the daughter of a surgeon, she spent her early childhood in Australia. She was a child prodigy violinist, who made her concert debut at Crystal Palace at the age of 9 and later studied with Arbós. Before she was 20 she had appeared as a soloist in all the major Classical and Romantic concertos in Britain, Europe, and America, and was hailed in some sections of the press as no less than "the legitimate successor to Joachim". But the onset of neuritis, crippling her hands, forced her to abandon the career of a concert soloist when she was only 23. Yet she found many other musical activities to occupy her mind. Her interest in Eastern mysticism and metaphysics drew her to India, and to the study of Indian music: she began collecting authentic Indian folk-melodies as early as 1909 when travelling throughout the country with Madame Blavatsky's pupil, the social reformer Mrs. Annie Besant. She devoted two years to a study of Indian music—especially that of Southern India—in considerable depth, and became proficient on Indian instruments and in singing the microtonal intervals of oriental music. Among her voluminous writings are nine volumes of unpublished notes on the music of the Indian subcontinent. On her return, from 1911 to the mid-1920s, she toured Britain giving lecture-recitals on the subject at universities and colleges, singing her own musical examples and accompanying herself on the appropriate instruments. For example in January 1912,

speaking under her first married name of Maud Mann, she read a paper on "Some Indian Conceptions of Music" to the Musical Association in London, attended by several prominent composers and musicians. She is known to have given advice and examples of Indian râgâs to Gustav Holst, who was deeply interested in Indian literature as a source of musical inspiration throughout the 1900s.

It was probably not only their common musical concerns, but their shared attitude to occult forms of spirituality, that drew Foulds to this remarkable woman. How he first acquired his occult interests is one of the points on which biographical details seem to be non-existent, and it would certainly be rash for the present writer, as a non-occultist, to attempt to delineate the confusing, shadowy landscape of turn-of-the-century British occult groups: a territory inhabited by many people well-known in the public life of the time, but for which no really reliable maps exist. I will simply reiterate that Maud had been closely associated with Annie Besant, one of the leaders of the Theosophical movement; we should note also that Foulds knew the architect Edwin Lutyens and his wife Emily, both of whom were practising Theosophists; and that Annie Horniman, for whose Manchester Gaiety Theatre Foulds conducted, and wrote his first theater scores, is known to have been a leading member of The Golden Dawn—the celebrated magical school founded by S.L. McGregor Mathers in 1888, whose most famous adept was the poet W.B. Yeats.

Maud MacCarthy and Foulds met in London in 1915. From all accounts it was love at first sight. Both were in the toils of unhappy marriages at the time; but rather than enter into a clandestine affair, they immediately laid the matter before their respective spouses. The two couples met together, discussed the situation amicably and agreed on divorces so that John and Maud could get married. (However, Foulds's wife was then dissuaded by others from this agreement, so it was actually some years before the marriage could take place.) Foulds and MacCarthy set up house together, and eventually had two children—a son (Patrick) and daughter (Marybride) in addition to those of their respective first marriages (Foulds's son Ray, and Maud's daughter Joan). It proved a stormy conjunction—the fiery, assertive, outgoing Maud MacCarthy and the more inward, reserved Foulds were very contrasted in temperament and valued their own independence; nevertheless they were devoted to each other, had a high regard for each other's artistic capabilities and firmly believed in each other's work whatever their personal differences.

What Maud MacCarthy gave Foulds, in musical terms, cannot easily be assessed. She was a constant inspiration to him, that is certain (sketches of her face appear time and again in the margins of manuscript scores). She had a particular influence on certain works, particularly the *World Requiem*. As a singer and violinist she was a faithful interpreter, collaborator and assistant (often leading the theater orchestras he conducted). She aroused his interest in Indian music and especially in modal and râgâ-based composition; and her mysticism, with its strong Oriental influence, provided him with a metaphysical basis for his work. Indeed, if we are to believe a short appreciation of her he wrote in the last year of his life, he came to regard her as an "incarnate devi". Moreover, she cultivated in him the faculty he called "clairaudience": the ability to hear, and take down as if from dictation, music apparently emanating directly from the world of nature or of the spirit. The first "clairaudient" pieces Foulds produced, in 1915, included the *Recollections of Ancient Greek Music* — a five-movement piano suite in the Greek modes which, at least in their piano guise, have something of the flavor of the Greek-inspired pieces of Satie and Debussy. (For this flavor, see his citations from the work in his nearly contemporary article "A Chat on Ancient Greek Music", reproduced in the Appendix.) However, Foulds was not satisfied that the piano was their proper medium; and throughout the next decade he tinkered with them, scoring individual movements for a wide variety of ensembles (the most impressive is probably the richly resonant version of the Dorian-mode *Temple Chant* as arranged for 20 wind instruments). Finally in the early 1930s he added a quick sixth movement and scored them all for double string orchestra, harp and percussion with the new title *Hellas: A Suite of Ancient Greece*, thus contributing to the English string repertoire a work of singular beauty.

Another "clairaudient" inspiration of this period — though not finally written down for over ten years — is the strange *Gandharva-Music*, Op. 49. Published as a piano piece, this extraordinary little composition brings to mind the music of today's "Minimalist" composers. Unbarred, without accent of any kind, it presents over an undeviating ground-bass pattern a swirling, interweaving network of D major figuration, which builds up and ripples along in a continuous stream of melody for four or five minutes, finally evanescing into thin air rather than coming to any formal end. There is no harmonic movement, and no themes appear apart from the melodic content of the ever-repeated figurations themselves. Foulds himself conceded that it was "of a *naïveté* almost incredible from a purely intellectual point of view"; yet properly played it does have a certain hypnotic fascination, attaining a kind of suspension of the sense of time for which many more recent composers have striven (Ex. 15).

Maud MacCarthy was herself a composer in a modest way — she produced, for example, several patriotic songs for circulation to the forces, which Foulds helped her arrange for performance. He also produced harmonizations for melodies she had collected or herself created. In early 1917 they collaborated on the theater music for W.B. Yeats's play *At the Hawk's Well* — a Nôh-inspired drama in which music plays a considerable part. History (and Yeats himself in the collected edition of his plays) has only recorded that the music was provided by Edmund Dulac, who also devised the scenery: but Dulac, though musical, had no known compositional gifts and it is likely that he simply gave indications for gong-strokes and the like which were used at the first night. In subsequent performances Foulds and Mac-Carthy, who were among the stage musicians in the production, supplied a score that was probably partly improvised — certainly none of it seems to survive today.

During a single week in 1917 while staying with Frederick and Emmeline Pethwick-Lawrence (the prominent socialists and associates of the suffragette movement) at their house in Holmwood, Surrey, Foulds composed perhaps his finest set of songs, the

---

Footnote 9 *(from preceding page)*

Foulds described this process more fully in *Music To-day*. I offer no comment on the phenomenon itself. One is reminded, however, of the somewhat parallel case of W.B. Yeats's marriage, and the experiences thereafter — including automatic writing — which he summarized in *A Vision* and which aided the composition of much of his late poetry. That such experiences do not admit of "rational" explanation does not necessarily deny them a reality; equally, when the result is independently assessable as a work of art, the nature of the experience need not necessarily detain us.

Ex. 15

A page from *Gandharva-Music*, Op. 49

Mood-Pictures, Op. 51. Foulds's songs in general have much to offer the recitalist: they range from a would-be sentimental Irish ballad handled with taste and restraint ("Eileen Aroon"), through infectious exuberance and *joie-de-vivre* ("Spring Joy", from Op. 69), rapt beauty ("To One in Paradise" from Op. 11) and atmospheric drama ("Phantom Horseman"), to the Straussian harmonic richness of "Life and Love" from the cycle *Garland of Youth*, Op. 86, and such oddities as "The Fairies", from the same cycle, where the lowest octave of the piano keyboard is kept permanently depressed, allowing the voice to emerge among a haze of harmonics. In sheer sustained melodiousness his setting of Byron's "There be none of Beauty's Daughters" (also from Op. 11) is as gorgeous a creation as any British song-composer has wrought. But the *Mood-Pictures* are probably his most sustained achievement in the field.

Foulds chose his texts from one of the quintessential poets of the "Celtic Twilight" movement: William Sharp (1855-1905), who wrote under the pen-name of "Fiona McLeod". Possibly the recent success of Rutland Boughton's opera *The Immortal Hour*, based upon a play by Sharp and produced at Glastonbury in 1914, might have attracted Foulds to "Fiona McLeod"'s poetry—if he didn't already know of it through his own strong Celtic interests. But his approach is distinctive. He selected his enigmatic stanzas from some 25 so-called "prose rhythms" that appear in Sharp's 1895 volume *From the Hills of Dream*. For Foulds's purpose—the exploration of moods beyond merely verbal sense—they were ideal; and they allowed him a great diversity of approach. Though conceived as a cycle (a fact that was long concealed since they were eventually split between two publishers), the songs seem to be five separate creations, as if five pictures by different artists of the same school have been hung side-by-side in a gallery.

"Lances of Gold" is a virtuoso study in flashing, shimmering arpeggios, whirling ever higher as the voice soars from low to high register. In "The Reed Player" the voice has only two sung phrases, during a dramatic central section—the rest is rhythmicized speech, while the piano reiterates a delicate, unconcerned, piping tune interspersed with knowing, gently mocking cadences. "Orchil" emerges impressively from cavernous depths of piano and voice, until it reveals itself as one of the most beautiful of

Foulds's triadic studies. This aspect of his style sometimes brought him close to Vaughan Williams: but it is a surprise indeed, at the words "and the sound of the weaving is Eternity, and the name of it in the green world is Time", to find "Time" poised above exactly that famous minor-major oscillation (only a semitone higher, E sharp minor/E major) which Vaughan Williams was to use 30 years later to conclude his Sixth Symphony!

"The Shadowy Woodlands", by contrast, is like no other composer and is even practically unique in Foulds's output. It is tenuous and highly chromatic in a quite individual way, the voice low and *parlando* among mysterious motions and distant bird-cries in the piano—sole example of a kind of dark Impressionism the composer never seems to have explored again. Finally, "Evoë!", with its titanic piano part, impulsive galloping rhythms, shifting, Busoni-like modulations and final rocketing cadence which ends on an impetuous G sharp major instead of the expected F sharp—this is quite simply one of the most exhilarating songs ever written by a British composer.

About the time he wrote *Mood-Pictures*, Foulds had begun to perform his chief "war service" by providing music and conducting at Ciro's Club in Orange Street, off Leicester Square. Ciro's was at this time under the management of the Y.M.C.A. and was run specially for the benefit of "Members of His Majesty's Forces and their lady friends"—regardless of rank—almost as a charitable institution. Duchesses and debutantes waited at table upon other ranks, and distinguished musicians and artistes provided the entertainment. Foulds, with a resident chamber ensemble, gave concerts to large audiences every evening. For these occasions, presumably, he wrote the 24 *Dedicated Works* and the 12 *Pièces d'occasion*, now missing. Early in 1918 he was taken onto the staff of the London Central Y.M.C.A., and was appointed Musical Director for the Y.M.C.A. National Council on 28 September 1918—a post he held until January 1923. He was popular with all those who worked with him, unassuming but a good mixer and an excellent organizer. He himself provided a resumé of his activities during this period,[9] which I quote in slightly abbreviated form to give some idea of the sheer amount of work and energy his duties entailed:

---

9   Typescript, now in British Library Add. Ms. 56482.

Above: The first page of "Evoë!" (*Mood-Pictures* Op. 51 No. 2, in the original Paxton printing — now copyright © Musica Viva). **Next page:** The ending of "The Shadowy Woodlands" (*Mood-Pictures* Op. 51 No. 1. For the original publication by Curwen this song was transposed upwards to D minor, but the Musica Viva printing, shown here, restores Foulds's original key of B minor. Copyright © 1980 by Musica Viva).

Daily attendance at Ciro's Club from inception of Y.M.C.A. work there, early 1917 to its close end of 1918. *106 Special Sunday Concerts* of dedicated and sacred music at Ciro's from 9 June 1917 till closing concert 15 June 1919....

Commencing 3 February 1918.... to January 14 1923, weekly Sunday afternoon concerts at London Central Y.M.C.A..... in all 106 concerts, averaging 10 works per programme—nearly all of these I have had to *specially arrange* for the combination of instruments at my disposal.

Commencing February 13 1919, weekly Thursday meetings at the Mansion House, arranging hymns, etc. for the city men's meetings; continuous up to and including November 20 1919.

Commencing 26 November 1919, half-hour midday concerts up to and including May 5, 1920.... also several organ recitals of 1/2 an hour to precede Thursday talks.

Commencing March 1919, 20 public lectures.... last two seasons in King George's Hall (capacity about 1,500).

Commencing September 15, 1919 formed & conducted the Centymca Orchestral and Choral Societies....

Commencing October 4, 1919, 25 Popular Orchestral Concerts have been given in King George's Hall.... Professional orchestra & artists, conductor—myself....

Full as the above list is of my musical ativities for Central Y.M.C.A., it did not represent my whole working capacity because the salary paid me by the Y.M.C.A was not sufficient for my whole time, and therefore I did not give whole-time work to the Association. If I had been able to do so I believe I could have shown a correspondingly increased musical result....

It seems almost incredible that he had time left to engage in other activities at all. But, in fact, he was active in many other ways—as conductor of the University of London Musical Society from 1921; providing incidental music for plays and often conducting the orchestras for the duration of the production as well; and, of course, continuing with his more serious composition. Supreme among his serious works, in the years immediately following the War, was the *World Requiem*.

He also taught some budding musicians; for instance, the young Elisabeth Lutyens—later to be one of Britain's leading women composers—came to Foulds for study at the urging of her parents, who shared his Theosophical leanings. In her autobiography, *A Goldfish Bowl* (London: Cassell, 1972), she allows (pp.26-27) that Foulds was "an able musician, but also a Theosophist"—as if the two terms ought to exclude one another. It is not certain whether Foulds would still have called himself a Theosophist by this time (see p. 101, note 53), and her brief account of Foulds seems confused by her own deeply sceptical reaction against her parents' Theosophy. She is the only source I have encountered who seems to have felt there was anything "sinister" about Foulds's interest in meditation and devic contacts; and she is also the only person to claim that the *World Requiem*—which was being given its annual performances during her time of study, and which she did not like—was "not eligible for criticism" as it was "directly dictated to him by St. Michael"; this seems an embroidery of the story recounted below, on page 28. It seems unlikely that such remarks have any real bearing on the nature and quality of the *World Requiem*; in any event, it is to a consideration of this supremely important work in Foulds's public career we must now turn.

5. The *World Requiem* and Its Vicissitudes

The idea of a large-scale piece commemorating those who fell in the Great War, which could be "A tribute to the memory of the Dead — a message of consolation to the bereaved of all countries" and give meaning to the trauma through which the world had passed, had taken hold of Foulds's imagination gradually. The result was *A World Requiem*, Op. 60, which was to bring his name before a wide public as an "ultra-serious" composer — but only for a few years.

According to one account:[11]

> The idea of writing a work of this nature occured to the composer toward the end of 1914, but although gradually maturing in his mind as time passed, and taking a greater and greater hold on his imagination, it was not until October, 1918, that he found himself able to begin the actual composing. The giving of hundreds of daily concerts for His Majesty's Forces, and all the difficulties and disturbances of those times had held back and, as it were, dammed up the work, but when the floodgates were opened pent-up ideas poured through so copiously and with such rapidity that the whole of Part I was completed by the beginning of December 1918, that is, in three months. Again circumstances intervened and prevented further composition for a time, but only with the same result, that when the next clear interval was reached the composer, resuming toward the end of 1919, completed his work in one long sweep and brought all to a conclusion by the beginning of 1920.

These dates must apply to the sketching of the composition only; it is pretty clear from the manuscript full score that the orchestration occupied Foulds at intervals between mid-1919 and April 1921.

Considering the number of other commitments to which he devoted himself at the time, this was a very short period in which to compose such an ambitious piece, the largest (with the possible exceptions of *The Vision of Dante* and the unfinished *Avatara*) he was ever to write. It seems that Foulds did indeed feel himself in the grip of a powerful inspiration, and worked directly into the enormous full score from mere rough sketches. Apparently some sections were heard "clairaudiently": Maud MacCarthy used to tell how she had "heard" some beautiful music in her head and, going in search of Foulds, found him writing down *the same music*. She was, in fact, his close collaborator, providing some of the text and helping to select the rest from a wide range of sources. The completed *Requiem* was dedicated to her.

The result was not a liturgical composition but an extended sacred cantata of elegiac and benedictory tone, implicitly Christian, but supra-denominational in spiritual focus, intended for performance in a cathedral or other large building on a national occasion. The texts — which include passages from John Bunyan and the 16th-century Hindu religious poet Kabir — express a desire for a new era of peace which will prepare for the coming of the Kingdom of God. It was a grand, noble, idealistic theme, undertaken in a profoundly pacific spirit. In two parts of 10 movements each, the work was written for soli, large choral forces and large orchestra; but, as Foulds later wrote:

> Although the words "colossal", "enormous", etc. have been used.... large numbers of performers are not necessary. It may be performed by a small choir of 20 voices upwards & organ; or by larger choirs with string orchestra & organ....; or by the average Choral Society of about 200 voices with orchestra of 60; or by large choruses of 350 voices with orchestra of 80.... orchestral parts are copiously cued.

His desire that the work should become part of the general choral repertoire did not cause him to "write down" to his potential audience. In some ways the *World Requiem* is a very austere score, though rich in others. There are few clearly-defined themes: the piece is a seamless, slow-wheeling interplay of orchestra, soloists and chorus, an ebb and flow of ac-

---

11 Presumably by Foulds himself, but unsigned; this appeared as part of a "historical note" in the program of the first performance in 1923; the programs for the three subsequent performances all contained different preliminary matter, and the paragraph quoted above did not appear again.

John Foulds and Maud MacCarthy at Eastbourne, Sussex,
around Christmastime 1923. (Author's collection.)

cumulating and receding textures, articulated by certain motifs which as often as not are basically harmonic in their appeal — such as the solemn sequence of unrelated common chords with which the opening *"Requiem Aeternam"* movement begins (and which is in fact adapted from the opening chorale of *Mirage*, Op. 20): see Ex. 16, on next page.

The *Requiem* is remarkable among Foulds's larger works for its general avoidance of counterpoint or the extreme registers of the voices. Though this helps to make it stylistically one of Foulds's most highly unified compositions, it shows his characteristic skill in incorporating many disparate elements into a convincing whole. Quarter-tones are used at certain points, as is what he called "counterpoint of timbres" — a technique using gradually-changing chord-colorings similar to that found in *"Farben"* from Schoenberg's *Five Orchestral Pieces*. Among the most original sections is the movement entitled "Elysium" (Section XII), a duet for soprano and tenor soloists with a small female chorus accompanied by a small orchestra. Its proto-Minimalism relates to the world of *Gandharva-Music*, though in a much more sophisticated way. Here a chromatic ostinato figure

Ex. 16

Ex. 17

of six rising semitones, ceaselessly repeated in voices and instruments but surrounded by ideas of a more direct, diatonic lyricism, creates an effect both other-worldly and hypnotic. Other noteworthy features include antiphonal brass fanfares from the corners of the auditorium during the invocation of the peoples of North, South, East and West in Section V; a gigantic, continually unfolding "synthetic melody" (without phrase-repitition) stated in a massive octave unison at the beginning of Part 2, uniting in a single vast melodic line many of the *Requiem's* principal motifs, some of them at that point previously un-heard; such unusual cadences as Ex. 17, precipitated

by a great stacking up of superimposed fifths; and the use of *glossolalia* (open vowel sounds conveying mystical ecstasy), more than 40 years before Michael Tippett was to use them in *The Vision of Saint Augustine*.

The *Requiem's* basic language, however (as Ex. 16 shows) is "pan-diatonic" in that its harmony most frequently consists of the movement of chordal blocks, usually triadic, against one another. The only modern writer to have glanced at *A World Requiem* (Alec Robertson, in his book *Requiem*) duly notes this fact and opines that Foulds was a skilful imitator of Vaughan Williams. But as we have seen, this kind of harmonic movement had been original with Foulds from the 1890s: and the most characteristic Vaughan Williams works which the music does occasionally bring to mind—namely *Sancta Civitas*, the *Pastoral Symphony* and *Job*—were all written *after* the *World Requiem*. (It is of interest that Foulds sets in Section XVIII some of the same words from the Book of Revelation—notably "Behold I come quickly. I am the bright and the morning star"—which Vaughan Williams later set in *Sancta Civitas*. There are other parallels, too, such as Foulds's distant chorus of boys' voices coldly proclaiming the glory of God in Section IV: a device Vaughan Williams uses for the proclamation of the destruction of Babylon.)

Another much later work which the *Requiem* prefigures is Herbert Howells's *Hymnus Paradisi*— both in general outline and in the special quality of the vocal writing, where the close interweaving of parts gives the choral sound a great luminosity (indeed, like Howells, Foulds makes the idea of *"Lux Perpetua"* central to his *Requiem*). In the end, however, the work cannot be judged simply on the strength of the published vocal score, where the orchestral portion is often drastically simplified. One needs to study the manuscript full score to realize that Foulds, always a master orchestrator, strove to achieve a radiant, shimmering sound-fabric of extraordinary incandescence. Whatever its ultimate effect might be in a modern performance, one can say confidently that it contains some dazzlingly beautiful music, and the nobility of its aims compels admiration.

As soon as the *Requiem* was completed, Foulds sent it to the British Music Society (which had been founded in 1918 by Eaglefield Hull "to champion the cause of British composers and performers at home and abroad") to enlist their support for a performance. On 29 April 1921 Hull wrote to Foulds to inform him that

> Our Committee of Management, which is the National Executive of the British Music Society, have adopted unanimously the recommendation of the Selection of Music Committee to allow your "World Requiem" to be given definitely under the auspices of the British Music Society. They lay great stress on the advisability of giving the work in a Cathedral, in preference to a performance in a concert room. Should it be possible to arrange such a performance in St. Paul's Cathedral or

Westminster Abbey, they will do all they can to make the event a national one.... We were very much impressed with the work and feel sure that it will not be unworthy of the great occasion.

The Committee whose unanimous opinion was thus recorded consisted of Arnold Bax, Arthur Bliss, Edward J. Dent, Eugene Goossens, Hamilton Harty, Adrian Boult and Hull himself. Sir Hugh Allen, Chairman of the Society, took a great interest in the score, and sent it to Charles Kennedy Scott (conductor of the London Philharmonic Choir) who was fired with enthusiasm. After permission for a performance in Westminster Abbey had been refused (on the grounds that the text of the work was not liturgical) plans were set in train for a performance in Scotland. In mid-1922 some of the music was heard for the first time when Donald Tovey (an old friend, and once the suitor for the hand of Maud MacCarthy in her concert-artist days) ran through some sections privately with the Reid Orchestra. The Scottish performance did not materialize; but in 1923 the work was accepted by the British Legion for performance in the Albert Hall on Armistice Night. When he heard of this, Tovey wrote to Foulds a characteristic letter which is worth quoting almost in full:[12]

> I am very glad to hear that there is a prospect of hearing your *World Requiem* in London. My recollection of the enjoyment of running through it with a holiday remainder of my orchestra in Edinburgh last year will remain vivid until I get an opportunity of knowing the work as permanent monuments of that calibre ought to be known.
>
> It must and shall make its mark. I shall not be surprised if it makes an immediate impression of a more popular kind than is usual with work of such calibre: and if so, its popularity will be one of the best signs of the times. It will be the popularity of something that is true, definite and masterly.... I question whether any work of this calibre has been more practically devised; and I see no reason why any of its problems should hinder an impressive execution if proper arrangements are made.... On the other hand it is not, in our muddle-through state of musical fashion, wholly to the advantage of your work, at the

---

ROYAL ALBERT HALL
Manager   :   :   :   :   HILTON CARTER, M.V.O.

UNDER THE MOST GRACIOUS PATRONAGE OF

THEIR MAJESTIES THE KING AND QUEEN

AND IN THE PRESENCE OF

H.R.H. THE PRINCE OF WALES
(Patron : BRITISH LEGION)

FESTIVAL COMEMMORATION

FOR ALL WHO FELL IN THE GREAT WAR
ARMISTICE EVENING
———1923, AT 8———

A WORLD REQUIEM

By JOHN FOULDS.
(FIRST PERFORMANCE)

IN AID OF

BRITISH LEGION
(Registered Under the War Charities' Act, 1916)

FIELD - MARSHAL EARL HAIG'S APPEAL
FOR EX-SERVICE MEN OF ALL RANKS
SOLOISTS:
IDA COOPER   WILLIAM HESELTINE
OLGA HALEY   HERBERT HEYNER

Chorus   and   Orchestra   of   Twelve   Hundred

Conductor: JOHN FOULDS
Leader of Orchestra: MAUD MacCARTHY.   At the Organ: C. H. KEMPLING
Programme: PRICE ONE SHILLING

moment, that your style is so masterly and practical. We are apt to be so proud of reading at sight that the only things we will practise till we get our best tone and style into the rendering are the passages we *can't* read at first sight. I confess to being sometimes rather tired of hearing an experienced orchestra's hundredth performance when it is merely the hundredth sight-reading *minus* the freshness of the first! I hope, then, that the first performance of the *World Requiem* will, like the work itself, be so masterly as to raise our popular demands as to the standard of such occasions.

The effect of the work will be invigorating in all its aspects: as representing its title and occasion it faces facts and uses symbols which are "not dark and dumb": as a piece of choral music it centres its invention on the voices, and uses the richest colours of the orchestra without deviating from its true centre. I forbear to go into details.... but the generalities I mention here mean, to me at all events, things of decisive importance in a work of art.

The practicality of the *Requiem*, on which Tovey comments, was one reason for its appeal to the British Legion. It was hoped to replace the "Armistice Jazz" which had celebrated the first few anniversaries of the war's end in rather frenetic fashion, with a more exalted kind of festivity—in which the Albert Hall performance of the *World Requiem* would be only the central one of a nationwide series of performances, wherever sufficient choral and instrumental forces could be assembled. However, the Albert Hall performances seem to have remained the only ones, and it was in connection with them that the name "Festival of Remembrance" was first coined—apparently by Maud MacCarthy.

There is some evidence that, while performance of the *Requiem* hung in the balance, Foulds was considering seeking a position abroad. The composer W.H. Bell, who had become Professor of Composition at the University of Johannesburg, almost tempted him onto his staff in 1921; and in 1923 he supported Foulds in an application for a post in Australia. But the British Legion's initiative seems to have put paid to that.

Foulds and Maud threw themselves whole-heartedly into the task of preparing the performance. In the event, the British Music Society was little help to them. They sank what little money they had into the preparation of the printed parts; Maud became Fes-

tival Organiser and was to lead the orchestra; Charles Kennedy Scott was an active helper; Paxton took on the work and issued the vocal score; Kennedy Scott and Arthur Fagge rehearsed the choirs. Foulds renounced all royalties and profits on his composition for the first five years of performance—those were to be donated to the British Legion. The demand for tickets broke all previous records at the Albert Hall. On Armistice Night, 11 November 1923, *A World Requiem* was premièred to a packed auditorium by a chorus and orchestra of over 1,250, under the composer's baton.

It was a tremendous success—with the general public. The audience was ecstatic, many of them in tears: the ovation at the end for Foulds lasted ten minutes, and literally hundreds of congratulatory letters arrived in the following days (so many that more than 30 years later Maud MacCarthy was able to publish a large booklet of extracts from them). Roger Quilter, Eugene Goossens and Josef Holbrooke were among composers who hailed Foulds's achievement; Sybil Thorndike wrote that it was "such an exquisite wondrous thing"; the

The composer at around the time of the last performance of *A World Requiem*. (John Foulds Estate.)

baritone Norman Allin declared it "one of the finest things produced in English music for a long time"; Bernard Shaw called Foulds "a great composer"; conductors, choristers, orchestral musicians and many, many ordinary music-lovers added to the chorus of praise and superlatives. F.W. Pethwick-Lawrence's comment—"It went deeper down and higher up, it was bigger, broader, nobler, and reached out more into the eternal than music as it is ordinarily understood and interpreted, or as any music other than that

Two pages from the vocal score of *A World Requiem*, from movement 12, "Angeli".

Paxton

15180

heard by the great masters — has ever done. It is indeed a world heritage...” — was merely typical of the response.

On the other hand, its failure with the critics was almost total. One reason for this may be adumbrated in Tovey's letter, and was indeed amplified in the program-note for the performance written by W.H. Kerridge (conductor of the South London Philharmonic Society) when he noted that—

(By kind permission of Novello & Co., Ltd.)

Paxton

...it is not exclusively a religious work.... it is not a distinctively national work.... nor is it primarily an emotional work, calculated to work upon the feelings of people who are already overwrought. It is an appeal to the spirit, and upon a man's spiritual reaction to the ultimate problems of life its acceptance and appreciation will depend. Thus although it must be judged upon its musical merits, it is not to be regarded solely, or even primarily, as a contribution to musical literature and aestheticism. Its universal appeal demands that its broad basis and central themes be of the utmost simplicity, even at the risk of seeming, to more musically tutored minds, too obvious in statement and progression.[13]

In a sceptical world (and the musical climate of the 1920s was turning increasingly sceptical) this was a dangerous ground on which to take a stand. With the exception of the *Musical Standard*, and of Edward Dent, who contributed a highly appreciative review to *The Nation and Athenaeum*, the "musically tutored minds" confessed to various degrees of boredom and distaste. Ernest Newman found the piece "unpleasantly pretentious" but admitted "there is considerable skill in the handling of the large masses of tone, and some personality in the harmonic writing.... Altogether the work shows a talent that may come to something when the composer clips the wings of his ambition a little." The *Musical Times* dismissed it in a snappish paragraph, and never bothered to send a reviewer to any of the subsequent performances. A longer review in *Musical Opinion*, a notable exercise in damning with faint praise, took umbrage at what was obviously considered a "conspiracy" to upset the accepted ranking of English composers and establish Foulds at their head. The *Daily Express* was particularly abusive, and was to remain an implacable foe of the *World Requiem*.

The wide disparity of response between audience and critics was not, perhaps, very surprising. The *World Requiem* was in effect the victim of its own occasion. *Pace* Newman, it is not a pretentious piece, but a reflective, meditative one. It does not seek to exploit anyone's emotions—but, with an Armistice Night audience who had mostly lost family or friends in the War, an enormous amount of emotion must have been projected onto it. As long as it was competently written and reasonably exalted in tone, it could hardly fail to move the hearts of thousands. The critics, well aware of this fact, were on guard not to be so easily moved, and suspicious of the feelings that were aroused all about them. Faced with a piece that turned out to be more quiescent than grandiose, it was easy enough for them to be bored.

Foulds's *Requiem*, in fact, was the first notable casualty of that depressing tendency in British Music, after the Great War, to distrust anything which seemed too large-scale, too serious, or too visionary in conception—a tendency which aided the eclipse of several fine composers (Havergal Brian is only the most striking instance). Precisely because the *World Requiem* offered itself as a "monument", and because the British Legion hoped to make it a permanent one, it was most exposed to the contrary currents of opinion. Between the audience's rapture and the critics' distaste, the musical reality of this large, genuinely aspiring creation was somehow mislaid. That reality can only be rediscovered through a modern performance, now that the Great War—and the 1920s—have faded into the distant past.[14] In the meantime, Tovey's opinion, as expressed above, remains a powerful tribute to Foulds's achievement.

There were three more annual performances—all given to equally large and equally enthusiastic audiences. But they were mounted against a groundswell of critical disapproval. The full story of the campaign against the *Requiem* is certainly not known to the present writer: many reasons for its abandonment remain mysterious. But there was evidently intrigue against Foulds. It is known that one distinguished member of the British Musical Society Committee which had recommended the work in 1921 approached Earl Haig after the 1924 performance to tell him that, in his opinion, Foulds was a fraud and his Requiem a "hoax", and that the Legion ought to withdraw its support. It did not do so immediately, but the 1925 performance was moved to the smaller venue of Queen's Hall (though there was the compensation that year of a B.B.C. broadcast of

---

13   Kerridge later wrote an interesting essay, "Some Comments on the Music of *A World Requiem*"—printed in the program of the 1925 performance *only*—which rather changes tack by stressing, instead, the symbolic and technical aspects of the composition, its links with Eastern music, Busoni's modal theories, and Schoenberg's orchestral and vertical/horizontal methods.

14   The revival of a few sections of the *World Requiem* in the context of a concert, by limited forces, at St. John's Smith Square, London in 1983, continued to leave a somewhat enigmatic impression: the piece clearly needs to be heard entire for a proper assessment to be made.

certain extracts, recorded in Glasgow). The 1926 performance returned to the Albert Hall, but it was the last. After this the London Cenotaph Choir (specially formed for these concerts) was disbanded — despite the vigorous protests of the choristers, who loved the work — and the *World Requiem* was dropped.

Foulds and his wife — who had expended enormous energy, time and effort on the performances, and had never made a penny out of the proceedings — did not blame the Legion, whose first function was of course to raise money for ex-servicemen by any means it could. They had hoped, in these first Festivals of Remembrance, to add a spiritual dimension to that function, but it was not to be. The *World Requiem* has never been performed complete — anywhere — since 1926. Nor was it re-printed. The published vocal score, which can still occasionally be picked up in music shops with a second-hand department, actually represents the form of the *Requiem* as it existed before its first performance. In practice

Foulds introduced many changes to its structure and detail, deleting a substantial "meditation" for orchestra alone (which he nevertheless retained as an independent concert item as the short tone-poem *Peace and War)*; substituting for this a new soprano aria; replacing an *a capella* chorus with an extended contralto song; and revising aspects of many of the other movements. His personal conducting copy, which is fortunately still extant, collates all such changes and was intended as the basis for a "Second Edition" of the score; but this was never issued.

The failure of the *World Requiem* to establish itself in the repertoire was, in a sense, the crucial setback in Foulds's career as a serious composer. In following years it seems to have become an albatross around his neck, an apocryphal "white elephant" of British choral music, that helped to confirm his reputation as "basically a light music composer". The tragedy is that this failure had apparently so little relation to the *World Requiem*'s actual value as music.

Cover of the program-book for the last complete performance of *A World Requiem*. (John Foulds Estate.)

6. Other Works of the Early and Mid 1920s

The period of the *World Requiem* was also the time when Foulds—established with Maud and their children in a house at 59, Abbey Road in the St. John's Wood area of London—was most in demand as a composer of incidental music for plays. Several of his most important scores in this genre were composed during these years. The music for a 1921 production of Sacha Guitry's Pierrot-play *Deburau* well illustrates the variability of Foulds's inspiration, for it yielded two pieces of "light music". The *Suite Fantastique*, published by Hawkes, is lively but thin and merely workmanlike in invention; whereas the Overture, published by Paxton under the title *Le Cabaret*, is a sparkling, zestful, irresistible little work whose splendid tunes and scoring, deft sense of structure and infectious high spirits makes it an excellent curtain-raiser to any light-music program even today.

Deburau was produced by Foulds's friend Robert Lorraine; but it was with Lewis Casson and Sybil Thorndike that he was most closely associated at this time. Unfortunately, the majority of the scores he wrote for them seem to have perished in the Blitz; but enough indications remain to give us an idea of them. An incomplete set of parts for *Hippolytus*, for instance, suffices to give the flavor of this modally-based music, whose substantial and beautiful orchestral prelude re-works ideas from the *Recollections of Ancient Greek Music*. Some of these scores were highly elaborate, like that for the spectacular 1925 production of Shakespeare's *Henry VIII*. Here Foulds used deliberate archaism to suggest the music of the period: the effect being as approximate, and as personal, as (for instance) William Walton's film score for *Richard III*—in comparison with which Foulds's music stands up well.

His biggest success in the theatre was of course with the music for the first production of Bernard Shaw's *Saint Joan*. Foulds and Shaw first met when the playwright came to hear the première of *The Tell-Tale Heart* in 1923; he immediately approached the composer (who had been conducting) and asked if he would consent to write the music for the "Chronicle Play" he had just finished. First heard at the play's British première at the New Theatre, St. Martin's Lane, on 26 March 1924 (in a glittering production by Lewis Casson with sets and costumes by Charles

Ricketts, and Sybil Thorndike in her most famous role as the Saint), Foulds's music had literally hundreds of performances all over England and on the continent during the 1920s. Shaw was delighted with it, and the critical response was favourable, too. Horace Shipp, for instance, devoted a lengthy review to the music in *The Sackbut*, saying that *Saint Joan* was

> a profound work of art. And John Foulds's music enhances it. One is not oblivious, one does not treat it as an irrelevance or desire to chatter or eat chocolates during its progress. It is part of *Saint Joan*, bearing through the oral-emotional medium of music the message which Shaw's words are urging through the oral-intellectual one of literature. It exactly achieves its end—taking its place, keeping its place, not failing to bring in its quota of support to the aesthetic of the play, not obtruding between the author's written word and his audience.... John Foulds's experience of theatre work and his appreciation of the work of the dramatist have dictated the limits of his contribution, and by defining those limits he has become Shaw's collaborator. Thus it is that we carry away from the theatre the helpful, joyous memory of his music.... if I saw *Saint Joan* without his music I should feel something lacking.

Foulds drew orchestral suites for concert performance from both *Henry VIII* and *Saint Joan*. The former is essentially a series of formal dances in Elizabethan style; the emotional intensity which Foulds was able to bring to this idiom, however, is well illustrated by the grave melancholy of the music for "Queen Katharine's Vision" (see Ex. 18, following page).

Unused in the Suite, and still nestling among the loose pages of Foulds's cued manuscript conducting score for the production of the play, is a simple yet beautiful setting of "Orpheus with his Lute", scored for voice, lute, and strings, that should be ranked among his most affecting songs.

The *Saint Joan Suite*, which Foulds conducted at the 1925 Queen's Hall Proms, is an even more substantial addition to the repertoire. It is dominated by a motto-theme representing Joan herself, heard in its simplest form in the third movement, "The Maid": a charming character-study that originally functioned as the prelude to Shaw's play (Ex. 19, "in mediæval style").

This haunting yet unassuming tune proves capable of many developments in personality — martial in the exciting battle-music of the "Orleans" movement, noble yet anguished in the movement representing Joan's martyrdom. Most substantial of all is the first movement, "Donrémy", which Foulds seems to have amalgamated from several pieces of the theater-music into a virtuosic and wide-ranging structure, varying in moods from the pastoral to the heroic, and in his most glittering full-orchestral style. A recent recording of this Suite, issued in 1982, has shown that it has plenty of life in it yet.

One of Foulds's most intriguing theater scores — his next after *Saint Joan* — was the music he wrote for the first English production of Ernst Toller's revolutionary socialist drama *Masse-Mensch* (billed in London as *Man and the Masses*). Intriguing because of the subject, because nearly all the music is missing, and because it caused considerable stir and was widely reviewed as one of his most powerful contributions in the field of incidental music. "The music.... seemed to me to have more in it of the spirit of revolution than the whole of the play," commented the *Evening Standard* critic; and the *Times* opined that the music — which apparently ran almost continuously — should be performed on its own, or as a ballet. All that now survives is the haunting character-study *Sonia*, in an arrangement for violin and piano, which suggests

Ex. 18

"Cause the musicians play me that
sad note I named my knell."

Ex. 19

that *Masse-Mensch* was harmonically one of his most advanced scores.

Foulds's theatrical work for the Union of East and West, a multi-racial organization promoting cultural exchange between Britain and India, is evidence of his continuing interest in Oriental music. His scores for Kalidasa's *Sakuntala* and Nirjan Pal's *The Goddess* are lost without trace, but the two brief, haunting songs he contributed to a production of Rabindranath Tagore's *Sacrifice* show an attempt at extreme simplicity, the vocal lines being carried over humming drone basses. One version of the songs calls for the accompaniment of a tambura, the first instance of Foulds actually using an Indian instrument in one of his scores, although—doubtless under Maud MacCarthy's influence—he had been learning to play the tabla as early as 1915.

An *unfinished* theater score of some importance was actually for one of Maud's own plays: *Veils*, a mystery-drama or "Ritual for the Autumn Equinox" conceived for performance either in a church or within a puppet-theater. Although Foulds never completed work on it (and no production of the play is known), his extensive drafts and sketches constitute some of his most notable theater music of the early 1920s, and it would be welcome if some pieces at least could be put into performable shape.

The composer's flow of "serious" compositions continued alongside this copious theatrical activity, although not suprisingly at a rather reduced rate of production. Only those of fairly small dimensions—such as the set of five *Scottish-Keltic Songs* for chorus, and the brilliantly extrovert tone-picture for piano, *April-England*, appear to have reached completion. *April-England*, composed on the morning of the Vernal Equinox, 21 March 1926, was indeed intended as only the first in a projected series of works to be collectively entitled *Impressions of Time and Place*. (A second, *Isles of Greece*, for small orchestra, was written about a year later, while a third, *Sea-Moods*, remained a fragment despite a highly promising opening.)

In a short program-note attached to the manuscript of *April-England* Foulds explains the title thus: "Such moments as those of the Solstices and Equinoxes always seem to be particularly potent to the creative artist, and no less significant the place in which he happens to be at such time." He further points out that the two main motifs on which the piece is based—a bright, fanfare-like and highly characteristic figure of chiming, alternating triads (see Ex. 21, below) and a sturdy tune with something

of the character of a folksong—are connected respectively with the ideas of "April" and of "England"; while a striking passage of quiet, solemn chords towards the end brings with it "the thought of the beneficent Power under which all operates." Perhaps the most remarkable portion of the composition is the vertiginous, cadenza-like central section, in which glowing polyphony of a Bach-like poise gradually accelerates into a riot of exuberantly exfoliating figuration, rapid keyboard runs, and roulades—all over an absolutely undeviating, deliberate, unchanging ground bass. According to Foulds, the passage symbolizes "the boundless fecundity, opulent burgeoning of Springtime." The whole work is a scintillating show-stopper. It's no surprise that in 1932 Foulds extended and elaborated *April-England* into a sumptuous tone-poem for full orchestra.

Two of the larger compositions in which Foulds invested a great deal of creative effort during this period, but which he never managed to complete, call for especial mention. The first is *Lyra Celtica*, a Concerto for the unusual combination of wordless contralto voice and orchestra. Even more unusual, the voice is required to sing several passages in microtones—indeed, the work opens with a microtonal cadenza! The idea is bizarre, to say the least—till one remembers that Foulds was married to a woman who could sing the Hindu scale of 23 tones to the octave with flawless accuracy.

Two complete movements and the bulk of a finale (lacking only, it would appear, a final cadenza and coda) exist in full score. Unfinished though it remains, *Lyra Celtica* looks like a very individual— and extremely attractive—creation, a characteristic celebration of the *sunlit* aspects of the Western Isles, not of the more familiar and conventionalized "Celtic Twilight". Its title is that of a once-popular anthology (published 1896) of Celtic poetry from ancient times to the 1890s, edited by William Sharp—whose "Fiona McLeod" poems Foulds had set in *Mood-Pictures*—and his wife Elizabeth. Foulds obviously possessed a copy of this anthology, for he drew some of the texts for subsequent songs and part-songs from it. Yet his vocal concerto is entirely wordless—although an early sketch for the slow movement suggests that he first thought of it as a setting of lines from a translation of Ossian by Thomas Pattison. We might be surprised that Foulds did not use Sharp's own edition of Ossian; but a reference on the same sketch-page to a song, "Sleeps the noon in the deep

The last complete page of *Lyra Celtica*, from the autograph full score. (By courtesy of the Trustees of the British Library. Copyright © 1980 by Musica Viva and the Estate of John Foulds.)

blue sky" by "K.F.", is sufficient to indicate that he was deriving his text from Volume 3 of *Songs of the Hebrides* by Marjorie Kennedy-Fraser, the indefatigable collector, arranger (and some might say bowdlerizer) of Gaelic folksong. Foulds's movement makes no attempt to reproduce her melody for "Sleeps the noon..." (set to an air from the Patrick MacDonald collection of 1781)—indeed, it is difficult to see how the long-spanned, tranquil theme he eventually fashioned might be fitted to the poem. Clearly, therefore, this was an idea early abandoned; but the fact that the Kennedy-Fraser setting was not published until 1921 is one of the few indicators we have to the dating of this frustratingly abandoned and enticing score.

Indeed, *Lyra Celtica* even in its unfinished state is to all appearances the finest of all Foulds's "Scottish" works, blending the customary pentatonically and modally-inflected melodic lines with sophisticated whole-tone and "pan-diatonic" harmonies in an evocative, iridescent sound-fabric (in which the trumpet, celesta and harp are prominent). Like many of his works of this period, it gives further evidence of his inventive and individual use of basically triadic harmony. In *Saint Joan*, for instance, the motive of Joan's "voices" is a floating chain of root-position triads (Ex. 20). While a simple triadic oscillation is the seed of *April-England*—Ex. 21. The unfinished piano piece *Sea-Moods* has the bold but still basically triadic opening idea of Ex. 22; while the beautiful second subject of *Lyra Celtica*'s first movement obtains its languorous effect by not dissimilar means (Ex. 23).

In music of this kind Foulds was breathing a fresh and quite distinctive life into the familiar harmonic world of diatonic tonality. But as some earlier works had hinted, he was capable of taking an altogether more radical and abrasive approach; and of no score is this more true than the one I must now examine in some detail.

Ex. 20

Ex. 21

Ex. 22

Ex. 23

Epilogue Saint Joan 105

business, not mine. There was no use in both of us being burned, was there?

CAUCHON. Ay! put the blame on the priests. But I, who am beyond praise and blame, tell you that the world is saved neither by its priests nor its soldiers, but by God and His Saints. The Church Militant sent this woman to the fire; but even as she burned, the flames whitened into the radiance of the Church Triumphant.

The clock strikes the third quarter. A rough male voice is heard trolling an improvised tune.

Rum tum trumpledum,
Bacon fat and rumpledum,
Old Saint mumpledum,
Pull his tail and stumpledum
O my Ma—ry Ann!

A ruffianly English soldier comes through the curtains and marches between Dunois and Joan.

DUNOIS. What villainous troubadour taught you that doggrel?

THE SOLDIER. No troubadour. We made it up ourselves as we marched. We were not gentlefolks and troubadours. Music straight out of the heart of the people, as you might say. Rum tum trumpledum, Bacon fat and rumpledum, Old Saint mumpledum, Pull his tail and stumpledum : that dont mean anything, you know; but it keeps you marching. Your servant, ladies and gentlemen. Who asked for a saint?

JOAN. Be you a saint?

THE SOLDIER. Yes, lady, straight from hell.

DUNOIS. A saint, and from hell!

THE SOLDIER. Yes, noble captain: I have a day off. Every year, you know. Thats my allowance for my one good action.

A page from the pre-publication copy of Shaw's *Saint Joan* which Foulds annotated in preparing his theater score—with his comments and corrections to Shaw's notation of the Soldier's Song in the Epilogue. (John Foulds Estate.)

7. *Avatara* and the *Mantras*

One further "unachieved" work of this period remains to be considered: and considered it must be, for the three orchestral extracts which are all that survive from it are in themselves among Foulds's most brilliant achievements. These are the *Three Mantras* which originated in his mysterious opera *Avatara*, a work to which he assigned the opus number 61. Of all Foulds's operatic projects (*Solomon*, *Cleopatra* and *Undine* had been earlier ones, and little survives of any of them), this was by far the biggest, and evidently it was stylistically one of his most advanced creations. It was conceived in 1919, not long after he had begun composing the *World Requiem*, and he worked on it at intervals until at least 1930. It seems likely that he did not start the orchestration until 1926, but by 1930 he had certainly completed more than two acts, amounting to some 420 pages of full score.

Yet equally certainly, he never finished it, and seems in the end to have discarded, and perhaps even destroyed, four-fifths of all the music he had written. This obviously major creative effort is thus extremely difficult to discuss. We know very little indeed about the opera itself; nothing has been preserved of its libretto; its subject or story remains obscure; and even the title is illuminated only by a note on the title-page of the orchestral preludes: "From the Sanskrit. AVA, down: TRI, pass over. A descent into—incarnation in—or manifestation upon earth, of deity". (A brief note dating from September 1926, at which point the title was in the form *Avatar*, gives a similar explication, with a reference to "Sanatana Dharma, Benares 1902".[15]) The term "Avatara", from which our English word "avatar" is derived, however plays a very specific role in Indian mythology—for it denotes especially the various human or supernatural incarnations of the god Vishnu, by means of which he intervenes in the successive cycles of history. Some of those incarnations (for example Krishna, and Rama) are great mythical heroes in their own right, and in some versions even Buddha himself is reckoned another "avatar" of Vishnu. It seems likely that Foulds's *Avatara* may have dealt with one or more of these figures.[16]

The only other thing known about the opera is that orchestral music seems to have played a major part in the conception of it: each of its three acts, as well as opening with a large-scale prelude, was to be framed by an introductory ballet and a concluding "tableau". The ballets, tableaux, and the acts themselves are lost; the only portions that Foulds preserved from *Avatara* were the preludes, which he extracted from the opera's full score and had bound together to form a self-sufficient suite of symphonic dimensions, about 25 minutes in duration: the *Three Mantras*, Op. 61b. These three movements, on their own, constitute one of the most astonishing things Foulds ever wrote—certainly his most extreme, and

---

15 I am indebted to Raymond Head for the information that "Sanatana Dharma" is a Hindu philosophical concept: the Primordial Tradition (including and transcending all branches of human activity) which, though hidden, alone survives without change throughout all the Manvantara (the successive cycles of manifestation of terrestial humanity). It is therefore the descent of the Avatar that rekindles this primordial tradition in the lives of the people. The Great War was seen by many people, and certainly by Theosophists, as the ending of one cycle and the beginning of a fresh one, which perhaps adds significance to Foulds's beginning *Avatara* in 1919. His note appears to be a bibliographical citation, possibly to a publication from the Hindu University at Benares.

16 A further piece of evidence has recently come to light in a letter written by the distinguished orientalist E.B. Havell, founder of the Calcutta School of Art, to the Secretary of the Maharaja of Baroda. The purpose of the letter, dated 20 September 1928 from Headington, Oxford, seems to be to introduce both Foulds and Maud MacCarthy to the Maharaja, and Havell speaks of Foulds as "...an eminent musical composer and conductor who is at work on a grand opera on the subject of Sri Krishna, [who] would very much appreciate any assistance and advice H.H. the Maharaja could give him in making the music a true expression of Indian musical thought and in showing the way for a musical renaissance in India." The language here anticipates the views Foulds would put into practice a decade later in India itself; and the existence of the letter suggests that he and Maud were already looking for ways to travel to the subcontinent. The reference to an opera "on the subject of Sri Krishna" can only be to *Avatara*. Raymond Head has pointed out to me that to write an opera about this or any other avatar of Vishnu might strike a Hindu rather as an opera about Jesus might strike a Christian, i.e. bordering on the blasphemous.

probably his most profound and powerful orchestral work.

A "mantra" is, in its ultimate derivation, a verbal formula, a Word (or Words) of Power, whose repetition (spoken, sung, or chanted) acts as an aid to meditation or magical work. In the practice of Mantra Yoga, different mantras are used to focus the inner being upon different planes of reality, each plane being conceived as having its own particular rate of vibration. Foulds defined the term "mantra" in *Music To-day* (p.117) as "a short rhythmic arrangement either of words or musical sounds of an evocative nature, which, when constantly repeated — in conformity with laws not generally known but as definite as a mathematical formula — set going causes which produce predicable results." Like Stockhausen half a century later in his *Mantra* for two pianos, Foulds in his *Three Mantras*[17] builds up very large-scale and complex processes of variation upon tiny basic cells (e.g. a chain of ascending fourths, or a one-bar rhythmic ostinato), resulting in vast spans of continuous development. The suite's organic unity is particularly impressive in view of the fact that the score gives clear evidence of having been worked upon at widely-separated periods of time (*Mantra III*, indeed, properly belongs to Foulds's Paris period at the end of the 1920s, although the basic ideas of all three movements are found together on a pencil sketch inscribed "Begun Aug. 18. 1919, at Penn, Bucks."). All three movements share transformations of the same basic materials (doubtless *Leitmotifs* from the opera proper), and *Mantras II* and *III* both recapitulate themes specific to *Mantra I* in new forms.

Taken together (and Foulds clearly intended them to be performed as a single entity), the *Mantras* are the greatest orchestral showpiece of a master orchestrator. The orchestra itself, though quite large, is not of unreasonable dimensions, and even the few unusual "extras" required (the sistrum for a few bars in *Mantra II*, a small wordless female chorus in the same movement, and the Latin-American gourd

drum or "tamburo di guero", practically throughout *Mantras I* and *III*) constitute no serious problem.[18] But the utmost virtuosity is required from every player, and both in its most statically ethereal and its most unremittingly rhythmicized passages, the work calls for a considerable investment of sheer stamina. The enormous bravura and textural complexity of the writing, the wide-stepping nature of the themes, and the brilliant exploitation of the extreme registers of the orchestra, are far removed from the homophonically simplified style of the *World Requiem* — in fact, they may be a deliberate reaction against it, an expression of "the other side of the coin" — yet knowledge of the *Mantras* is vitally necessary for a properly balanced understanding of the *Requiem*'s composer.

If one were to seek stylistic parallels, one would have to mention Scriabin (whose late works, particularly *Prometheus*, Foulds greatly admired); perhaps also some of his younger contemporaries in France such as André Jolivet, or Honegger, whose dramatic works much interested Foulds and whose characteristic machine-like rhythms are paralleled by certain passages in *Mantra I*. At other moments one may think of Gustav Holst — especially the Holst of *The Planets*. That work seems to have a little of the moods and spirit of the *Mantras*, and there is a certain technical affinity in Holst's melodic use of fourths, though Foulds tends to be more consistently dissonant. The first *Mantra* has something of the pace and gusto both of Holst's "Uranus" and his "Neptune"; the second combines the lyric warmth of his "Venus" with the austere remoteness of his "Neptune"; the third is a worthy adversary in controlled violence to his "Mars". But much of the work is more extreme than any of these composers attempted; and, in truth, this music really sounds unlike anything else. The more Foulds puts his enormous musical facility at the service of really challenging ideas, the more utterly individual he becomes.

It is important, however, to recognize that for Foulds the *Mantras* were no mere display pieces, but

---

17 Maud MacCarthy objected to the full form of Foulds's title (*Mantras from Avatara*) on the ground that this literally means "Words of Power from a Divine Being" — which she felt was far too exalted a name to give to one of Foulds's most "modernistic" and cacophonous scores! However, despite her dislike of the work, she carefully collected the few surviving sketches — which she discovered inside the full score after her husband's death. The present writer found them in an envelope on which she had written "to be preserved under cover with great care. They may be needed before the 'Mantras from Avatara' are performed or published. J.F left no instructions regarding them...." The note is dated "Lahore 1940". In the event, the sketches were not needed for the performance, but they provide almost our only, tantalizingly cryptic insights into Foulds's developing musical conception.

18 In the first performance (for Lyrita records in March 1988) the part of Foulds's invented vibrating wire "sistrum", which no longer exists, was supplied by a Greek-pattern hand sistrum combined with small high sleighbells. No "tamburo di guero" large enough to produce a sufficiently penetrating tone could be located in the short preparation time available, but it was most satisfactorily imitated by a deep tom-tom.

were devoted to a high expressive purpose—to producing "predicable results". (As, indeed, Holst's work is both an orchestral *tour-de-force* and an evocation—or invocation—of the astrological powers attributed to the seven planets.) For there is no doubt that Foulds viewed himself as composing music that would actually have "mantric" effects, similar (but presumably enormously magnified) to the Words of Power employed by a Buddhic sage in ritual or meditation.

One of the central elements of the book, *Music Today*, which Foulds published in 1934, is an attempt to classify the various levels of aesthetic achievement reached by different composers and their works, according to what he calls "a five-planal conception"— the five planes corresponding to the lower five of the seven interpenetrating spheres of nature, "subdivisions of the universal consciousness", according to ancient Sanskrit philosophical teaching. He supplies a diagram to make this clearer:

SANSKRIT	ENGLISH
UNMANIFESTED { 7. ĀDI	DIVINE
6. ANUPĀDAKA	MONADIC
MANIFESTED { 5. ATMA	*IMMORTAL INDIVIDUALITY* { SPIRITUAL
4. BUDDHI	INTUITIONAL
3. MANAS	HIGHER / LOWER MENTAL
2. KAMA	*MORTAL PERSONALITY* { EMOTIONAL
1. STHULA	ETHERIC / DENSE PHYSICAL

Each of these "planes" is understood to be characterized by its own proper "vibration-type".

Foulds's thought here is deeply colored by the tenets and vocabulary of Theosophy, which is no reason to dismiss its active significance within and contribution to his own creative work. He pursues his discussion in *Music To-day* by averring that, until the 20th century, music had largely—though with signal exceptions—been confined to the evocation of (or "contact of vibration upon") the first two "planes", especially the emotional; and that one of the most valuable qualities of "modern" music is precisely its attempt to break free of these restrictions into new areas of expression. What follows reads like a personal credo, and a splendidly robust advocacy of the genuinely New in music:

> The vast majority of us are so obsessed by the emotions that a recent pronouncement that no new possibilities in music remain to be exploited has gone almost unchallenged. No new possibilities! Think of that. Consider... that the upper levels of the Mental plane (the Causal world), the glories of the whole of the Intuitional world (the Buddhic) and the wonders of the Spiritual (Atmic) realm remain practically unexplored by composers, or, more precisely, not conveyed to us in their music. Having realized this, what will be our reaction to such statements as these; that we have reached a terminal point; that to progress further is a manifest impossibility?
>
> It will surely be abundantly clear... that no additions to our technical equipment—no quarter-tonal, no modal systems, no additions of new *timbres* to our orchestral resources, in short, no technical means whatever—will in themselves aid us in our efforts to widen the field of musical appeal. What is needed is the spirit of the intrepid explorer; his contacting instrument the human consciousness; his driving power the Will, and his recording instrument the brain. Once able consciously to contact and freely roam the hitherto neglected higher-mental, intuitional and spiritual realms, once able to realize these extremely rarified vibrations in his brain, assuredly all the technical devices we have so far evolved *and many new ones* will be needed by the composer adequately to transcribe for us the records of his pilgrimage.

Some pages later, Foulds concludes his discussion with reference to a work that was fated to remain unheard for another 54 years:

> I permit myself to mention what is perhaps the first conscious essay along these lines: an opera, *Avatara*, each of the three "Acts" of which is preceded by a *mantra* apposite to it, which aims to set in motion the basic vibration-type of the whole act. The first—Mantra of Activity—appertains to the "higher" third plane (Manas); the second—Mantra of Bliss—

to the fourth plane (Buddhi); the third—Mantra of Will—to the fifth plane (Atma).[19]

These are indeed the titles which the three movements bear. But in the 1919 sketch referred to earlier, we glimpse a different (though perhaps complementary) conception. There, the titles are rapidly pencilled as follows:

1 Apsara Mantra
2 Gandharva Mantra
3 Rakshasa Mantra

Apsaras, Gandharvas, and Rakshasas are all different forms of devic entities encountered in Hindu mythology. The first two categories are male and female spirit-musicians: we have already met the Gandharvas in *Gandharva-Music*, and Foulds was to return years later to an attempted evocation of the two types in a projected symphonic work, his *Deva-Music* of about 1936. The Rakshasas, however, were demonic (though not necessarily malefic) beings, most celebrated as the soldiers of the demon-king Ravana. This early title of "Rakshasa Mantra" helps to explain the sinister and violent character of the music of the eventual "Atmic" Mantra of Will. (And the scheme as a whole may supply a clue to the possible basis for the *Avatara* opera in the realms of Indian myth: Ravana was eventually killed in battle by Rama, the "avatar" of Vishnu, as is told in the *Ramayana* of Valmiki—a story which was the basis of Holst's early opera *Sita*.)

Let us turn, at last, to the music of the *Three Mantras*. *Mantra I* (of Activity) begins *Impetuoso* with a veritable hurricane of swirling string figuration (on the lines of Ex. 24a), against which a bold, aspiring, but irregularly accented theme (Ex. 24b) spring to life on horns and cellos.

This material is developed in an exhilarating onward-rushing movement of teeming orchestral inventiveness, the harmony full of the zestful diatonic dissonance of superimposed triads. The mood is one of passionate, surging *élan vital*. The idiom in some respects anticipates that of William Walton's First Symphony by over a decade. The form of this initial portion is indeed rather like a symphonic exposition: the opening music centers around A, and then a vaunting new transition-theme, *con slancio*, leads to a grandly aspiring "second subject" in a modal E major (Ex. 25a). This builds to a tremendous climax reintroducing Ex. 24a, before trombones begin to sound a minatory fanfare based on perfect fourths and tritones (Ex. 25b)—a "call" that "goes right through the work" (as Foulds noted in the sketches).

A wildly pulsating machine-rhythm is built out of Ex. 25b, treated as a multiple ostinato in the whole orchestra; and then, at the movement's center, the music withdraws into relative calm and stillness. The motion is slower, but there is still "Activity", for the texture is built out of interweaving canons on an augmentation of Ex. 25a. Then the fanfaring fourths

Ex. 24

---

19   Quotations from *Music To-day* (London: Ivor Nicholson and Watson, 1934), pp.166-67 and 177.

Ex. 25

return, and Foulds builds up a pounding orchestral toccata in C major, continuously accelerating in pace while the bars themselves get progressively shorter. This is founded on Ex. 25*b*, against which the other themes are recapitulated, before the energy is whipped up to a thunderous climax (at the incredible metronome-market of dotted minim=200, equivalent to crotchet=600!) and then suddenly cut off short. (The movement's tonal structure, moving from A to C, anticipates the tonality of the others: *Mantra II* is in A major, *Mantra III* in an exotic mode upon C.)

Exx. 25*a* and *b*, in various guises, are heard in all the three *Mantras*. Also, at a more basic level, all three movements share the concerns with the salient intervals of fourths, fifths and tritones out of which Ex. 25*b* is formed. We find these features treated quite differently in *Mantra II* (of Bliss), though this movement is also one of the most elaborate and sophisticated examples of Foulds's pan-diatonic style, much concerned with serene streams of superimposed triads (and therefore also varying the harmony of the opening portion of the preceding movement).

In the 1919 sketch already twice referred to, *Mantras I* and *III* are represented by rapid jottings of early forms of distinguishing themes. But the "sketch" of *Mantra II* is purely verbal:

A Mantra.

Beginning with long sustained note in middle register (as I always hear music) then the trills and exchanges, these spreading to higher & lower octaves, then the overtones, & the "exquisite inter-tracery" of the Consilium Angelicum.[20]

This succinctly describes the actual technique of the opening portion of *Mantra II*, marked *Beatamente*, which fans outward very slowly to the heights and depths of the orchestra from a single central long-held A on a horn, resonated by flageolet notes on two double-basses. (As such details may suggest, Foulds's scoring throughout is of exquisite refinement.) In this music, all is calm, but elaborated in some of the most shimmering textures that he ever devised, with distant horn-calls of ascending fourths, an evocative triadic trumpet motive closely akin to Ex. 21 (the opening of *April-England*), and a wordless female chorus—spirits even more distant and other-worldly than Debussy's *Sirènes*.

Eventually the music accumulates motion and filigree textures ("exquisite inter-tracery" indeed) over an ostinato bass in 5/8 meter, with the tolling of deep bells. Although there is no exact quotation, the

---

20   *Consilium Angelicum*, which Foulds listed as his "Op. 62", appears to have been a book rather than a musical composition, but is wholly missing, so the point of the reference is unclear.

passage seems to be an expansion of the character and techniques of *Gandharva-Music*, which is especially interesting as Foulds seems originally to have planned this movement as a "Gandharva Mantra". The motion ceases; the wordless voices rise and fall in ecstatic fourths. Then Ex. 25a sounds out very quietly in extreme high and low registers, doubled on piccolo and double-bass; and this inaugurates a capricious, ethereal, much-transformed and compressed recapitulation of most of the themes of *Mantra I*; after which the music dies away on its peaceful, rocking fourths, arriving at no proper cadence but fading away gently in a series of still echoes.

The final *Mantra* (of Will), marked *inesorabile*, is a strict modal study (like the *Essays in the Modes* and the first movement of *Dynamic Triptych*, both to be discussed in our consideration of Foulds's Paris years, in Chapter 9) — in fact, the most elaborate, violent, and harmonically acrid example in Foulds's entire output. Cast in 7/4 time, and driving the orchestra to an extreme pitch of virtuosity and polyphonic density, it is basically a fantastic, storm-riding chaconne on this fierce one-bar theme:

Ex. 26

MODE:

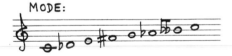

For all that this is the movement intended to contact the "Atmic" sphere, its character is heavy, barbaric, fateful, probably as a result of Foulds's original conception of a "Rakshasa-Mantra". It is also the only one of the three movements that seems to possess a strongly Indian character, partly as a result of the mode itself, which corresponds to a Southern Indian râga.[21] The important thing about Ex. 26 is not its shape, which is varied in countless ways as the music proceeds, but its *rhythm*, which is "inexorably" present in almost every bar of the music, and creates a gigantic cumulative kinetic energy. This is the basis on which Foulds constructs some hair-raising polyrhythmic complexities. Multiple time-signatures are often employed, and the brass, with their apocalyptic tritonal fanfares, are virtually an independent entity throughout. The culmination — an orgiastic superimposition of themes from *Mantra I* simultaneously upon the brass fanfares and the Ex. 26 rhythm — is one of the most shattering explosions of sheer orchestral power in 20th-century music.

Foulds completed this amazing movement in Paris in April 1930, but he never heard the *Mantras* performed. Almost 58 years later they finally came to life when the London Philharmonic Orchestra, conducted by Barry Wordsworth, performed them for a future commercial recording in a studio session. The present writer was privileged to be present on that occasion; and he feels confident in forecasting that this suite is one of the cardinal achievements by which Foulds will be known to posterity. The *Mantras* show him at his most individual, his most uncompromising — and at the very height of his powers as a composer.

---

21 The mode will be found as Mode "IIIG" in Foulds's "Table of 90 Modes" reproduced in Chapter 9 (see page 58).

Above & opposite: Two pages from the manuscript full score of *Mantra III*.
(Copyright © 1980 by Musica Viva and the Estate of John Foulds.)

8. Interlude: Eclecticism, Impersonation, and Self-Quotation

By the time Foulds embarked on the *Avatara* full score he was in his mid-forties and, although several of his most important works remained to be written, his musical attitudes and vocabulary had fully matured. It is worth pausing at this point to consider them — and to consider the musicological issues which they raise.

It should be emphasized that those issues are "problems" only for critics and analysts: problems of aesthetic criteria and the standards by which 20th-century artistic theory has come to judge "orig-inality". For the ordinary listener or performer such considerations should be irrelevant. Foulds seldom wrote a piece that was not an active pleasure to listen to, or was not sympathetically conceived for his chosen instruments. His profound "musicianliness" (by which term I try to combine the not entirely identical concepts of "musicianship" and "musicality"), and his utter professionalism in the actual writing of his scores — however large, idealistic, or even nebulous his governing conceptions may sometimes have been — are in fact distinguishing features of his output. Although he was capable of creating musical structures of great complexity and extreme dissonance (as in the *Third Mantra* just described), he also possessed in abundance the contrary talent, rarely found in the same composer, of a natural, spontaneous melodist. He had the gift for writing tunes that are wholly characteristic and immediately (even infuriatingly!) memorable. His music — through, and sometimes seemingly in spite of, its technical facility — conveys a rich and coherent personality, with the charm, humor, passion, and zest for life which seem to have been typical of the man.

It is very necessary to stress that Foulds *has* a strong musical personality, easily recognizable to anyone who has heard a reasonable cross-section of his music; because that personality does *not* seem to be determined (or at least, is only partly determined) by the presence of specific technical features. "Eclecticism" — selecting and blending elements from different styles and systems — is usually a pejorative term in 20th-century music criticism, which likes its major figures to be self-parturiating "great originals", or at least a "logical development" from their predecessors. Reading the descriptions which I have offered of various Foulds compositions, and the

names of other composers I have adduced as stylistic parallels, it would be easy to imagine that he was, by contrast, a wholesale eclectic, a magpie collector of styles with no defined personality of his own. And an enthusiastic, unashamed eclectic he undoubtedly was — but one who, by a fine paradox, turned eclecticism itself into a form of originality: the means by which that "rich and coherent personality" could express itself to the appropriate extent in any given musical situation.

Briefly stated, the original foundation of Foulds's self-fashioned musical vocabulary was the Romantic period of the Austro-German tradition: not only the Schumann-Brahms line (as he would have been taught at, say, the Royal College of Music), or the Liszt-Wagner line (as he would have imbibed at the Royal Academy of Music), but an intelligent blend of them both. This blending is already a kind of eclecticism, and it was being attempted in Vienna at exactly the same period (the late 1890s) by Arnold Schoenberg and Alexander von Zemlinsky (indeed Zemlinsky, whose music exhibits several interesting parallels to Foulds's, has in recent years, after long neglect, been forgiven *his* arch-eclecticism and hailed internationally as a rediscovered master). In Foulds (as in Schoenberg and Zemlinsky) the first great underlying stylistic model was probably Brahms.

But to this Brahmsian basis was wedded from the first a specifically "English" melodic sense whose origins seem to lie in Puritan hymns (which influence the Cello Sonata) and folksong (a very early work indeed, now lost, was an 1890 set of violin variations on "The Ash Grove"). Although Foulds was never a "folksong composer" in the manner of Vaughan Williams, Holst, or Grainger, this folksong background underlies many of his "maddingly memorable" tunes, and shapes their cadences and contours.

To this already rich mixture he was adding some personal refinements as early as the 1890s: quarter-tone passages, post-Wagnerian chromaticism, and a fondness for streams of triads in root position (a phenomenon more often associated with Debussy). As we have seen, as time went on he continued to enlarge his stylistic resources with new harmonic and coloristic elements, partly stemming from contemporary French practice but also from increasingly exotic concerns of his own — "Celtic" pentatonicisms,

Ancient Greek modes, and a growing receptivity to Oriental music and the sense of timelessness and stasis that such music often seems to evoke.

Foulds's creative direction, therefore, presents no simple picture of development along a straight line. His basic harmonic language evolved from a typically late-19th-century chromatically-decorated diatonicism to a much suppler medium making highly individual use of diatonic dissonance. But in other respects he developed "outwards", encompassing a larger and larger range of stylistic resources, pushing several separate but related interests abreast, upon an ever broader front.

This very wide stylistic range is paralleled by (and helped to make possible) the range of musical *genres* to which Foulds contributed. At one end of the scale are the huge, deeply serious choral works and orchestral compositions; at the other, distinctly "lowbrow" pieces produced for sheer entertainment value. Yet there are sometimes specific links from one to the other: the little piano rag *Mississippi Savannahs* of the mid-1920s actually parodies the solemn "God" motif (shown as Ex. 10) that appears in both *The Vision of Dante* and *A World Requiem*! And between these two extremes are many different levels and styles, represented by various forms of light music, sentimental ballads, music for the comic and the serious theater, experiments in music of a basically non-European type, music relating to the visual arts, and so on. Elgar, and Sibelius, and Frank Bridge wrote light music as well as their more weighty works, but none of them covered a range to equal Foulds's activities. Percy Grainger's output shows something of Foulds's grand miscellaneousness, but he never achieved anything comparable to Foulds's compositions in sonata-style, nor did he attempt anything on the sheer scale of his larger pieces.

Foulds was himself keenly aware of these divisions, as his writings (and his categorizations of his own works) show. In part he viewed them as artificial — seeing light music such as the *Keltic Suite*, for instance, as a possible stepping-stone which would help untutored listeners to cultivate in time a taste for the more developed forms of classical music. But at the same time his personal grasp of so many different styles meant that he was able to turn his hand to each and every one of these categories with equal facility. It was only in a relatively few large works that he was

able to draw upon the full range of resources at his command, allowing them fruitfully to cross-fertilize in the service of a single all-embracing musical idea.

"Jack of all trades, master of none": the old saw lies behind much of the conventional distrust of fluently eclectic composers. But Foulds was self-evidently a master at each of his "trades"; and to grasp the protean nature of his achievement we should perhaps abandon the metaphor of the tradesman for that of the gifted actor. It comes easily, in any case, to a composer so concerned with the theater — and in his baritone scena *The Seven Ages* (discussed in Chapter 10) Foulds himself seems to accept it as a fitting characterization of his varied skills. The true actor enters into the personality of the character he may be playing, appearing to vanish behind a mask; but there, behind the mask, he has to remain himself, using his own intelligence to manipulate his given material, so that the "impersonation" may succeed.

I commented in Chapter 2 that in the early *Rhapsodie nach Heine* Foulds "impersonates" Paganini — in musical manner, not by quotation; and this often seems to be the basis on which his lighter works are conceived. In *Holiday Sketches* he is a tourist, a sightseer, in Germany — and then in France for the *Suite Française* (which was first performed as *French Holiday Sketches*); in the *Keltic Suite* he dresses up as a Highlander, complete with dirk and kilt. In the *Music-Pictures* series he impersonates a number of different painters. In some of his Greek modal works he has "dreamed himself into the mood"[22] of an Ancient Greek musician; the *Sacrifice* songs show a similar attempt at entering into the spirit of Indian style; while in the *Henry VIII* music he gives a passable impersonation (for the 1920s, at any rate) of an Elizabethan composer. But each of these "impersonations" seems to involve only part of Foulds's musical personality. He gives us his "all" in works which merge all the various aspects into a real creative totality. In some of the earlier works of this type the stylistic mixture is not always wholly successful: *Mirage*, for instance, does not really achieve consistency of utterance, though it remains an impressive score, full of memorable ideas and real sincerity of musical thought. In later pieces Foulds has blended every element into a superb and stimulating unity — nowhere more so than in the *Quartetto Intimo*, whose "intimate" baring of his inmost soul paradoxically

---

22 To use his own phrase: see his 1915 essay "A Chat on Ancient Greek Music", reproduced in the Appendix to this book.

reveals a full-blooded modern romantic of enviably integrated personality (see Chapter 10).

An unusual feature of Foulds's music as a whole — and it is one of the things that proclaims a unity underlying all its diversity — is what we might term its "self-reflectiveness". Specific, clearly identifiable musical ideas, motifs or themes crop up in many different works, at different stage of the composer's career, and are put to many different uses. The student examining Foulds's scores in bulk soon finds himself wandering in a maze of self-quotation.

Of course, to the extent that *any* composer who develops a distinct personality will show a preference for certain types of idea — often with strong rhythmic or melodic similarities — all composers engage in a generalized form of self-quotation. Some will quote specifically from one work in another with a particular expressive or extra-musical purpose in mind (a classic instance is the "Hero's Works of Peace" section of Richard Strauss's *Ein Heldenleben*, where he summons up a host of quotations from his previous masterpieces as an answer to his critics). Some, such as Shostakovich in his late works, have developed the art of meaningful self-quotation as an integral (usually ironic or pathetic) aspect of their style. But Foulds's use of the device is more widespread, seems to arise from a larger number of causes, and has a quite different effect.[23]

His recycling of ideas certainly *doesn't* denote lack of inspiration, for he was enormously prolific and many important works seem to take no part in the self-quotation process. In some cases it may simply indicate a lack of available time — for instance when the finale of *Music-Pictures Group IV* for strings turns up practically verbatim as a country-dance interlude in the *Henry VIII* music: presumably in this instance Foulds's deadline simply did not allow him to compose a new movement at such length, or perhaps the requirement for the interlude arose at a late stage of preparation for the production. It is also quite likely that, since many of the works Foulds most valued remained unperformed, he saw no crime in resurrecting some of their most characteristic passages in later scores that seemed to have a better chance of being played.

But more often one has the impression that certain themes and ideas came to dominate Foulds's auditory imagination — either they became a store of personal *Leitmotifs* which he inevitably associated with particular emotional states or philosophical concepts; or they simply proved so fruitful that he continued to see possibilities for their exploration and development (and possible combination) beyond the confines of a single work.

Several examples of this process have already been noted. Ex. 6, from the slow movement of the *Quartetto Romantico*, was subsequently split into two segments, one going into the respective movement of the Cello Sonata, the other into that of the Op. 17 Cello Concerto. But Ex. 8, from the Cello Sonata's finale, was also take over into the Concerto — for its first movement. So not only can one composition give ideas to two others, but one can absorb material from two (or more). Likewise in the *Saint Joan Suite* the fifth movement, "The Martyr", revives Ex. 12, from *Music-Pictures Group III* (though in new scoring), and combines it with a theme from *Mirage*. The *World Requiem*, though of course generating much material of its own, is in some movements a veritable palimpsest: taking over its opening wind chorale from *Mirage*, the ground bass of one of its movements from *Gandharva-Music*,[24] the substance of another movement from the Fiona MacLeod setting *Orchil*, the "God" motif from *The Vision of Dante*, the chromatic mirror-progression given as Ex.14 (which probably has the same ultimate source — see below), and so on.

For certain ideas Foulds showed an especial fondness, and in consequence they developed a particularly complex internal history in his *oeuvre*. Consider, for instance, the chromatic progression I have just mentioned. It is shown as Ex. 14, the form in which it appears at the opening of "The Waters of Babylon" from *Aquarelles*. That movement dates from 1905 — but at about the same time, while working on the "Hell" section of *The Vision of Dante*, Foulds had used the self-same idea for the setting of the inscription that appears over the gates of the Underworld: "Abandon Hope all Ye who Enter Here". Subsequently, forms of the same foreboding progression are found in the section of *Mirage* subtitled "Man's

---

23 A closer parallel might be with Busoni, who conceived some of his smaller works as "studies" for larger ones, and frequently interchanged elements between them.

24 Or perhaps vice versa, as *Gandharva-Music*, though conceived in 1915, may not have been finally written down until 1926 (although an undated sketch for it is clearly much earlier than 1926).

Ever-Unattainment", and in the "Ancient of Days" movement from *Music-Pictures Group III*. As already mentioned, it then makes an appearance in the *World Requiem*, and is prominently featured in the powerful orchestral meditation *Peace and War* (which itself originated in the *Requiem*). In every instance Foulds seems to associate it with ideas of threat, tension, impending tragedy. But its career was not over. In the early 1930s it makes an unexpected appearance—in almost the exact Ex. 14 form—as the basis of a short movement in the fundamentally positive and outgoing *Quartetto Intimo*; and it returns in sketch-form as foundation for a prelude to a skittish (but never-completed) *Pasquinade* for four woodwind instruments. In these later pieces it maybe seems to represent something of "the past", an emotional heaviness which his music was now trying to escape.

Less complex but still quite involved is the history of the tune I have quoted as Ex. 13, which is its appearance as what Foulds called a "Refrain Roccoco" in the first of the *Aquarelles*.[25] This had appeared first, in a slightly different form, in about 1910 in an episode in the finale of Foulds's Eighth String Quartet. Between that work and the *Aquarelles* there was almost certainly an intermediate form in the second movement of the lost *Music-Pictures Group I* for piano trio, which like the relevant *Aquarelle* was entitled "In Provence (after La Thangue)". Around the same time (it is difficult to be more accurate about successive developments, as the chronology of the early sets of *Music-Pictures* is still obscure), Foulds used the tune in a spikier, parodied form in his music for *Wonderful Grandmama*, whence it found its way into the finale of the *Miniature Suite*, an *Andante Burlesco* entitled "Scarabang and his Minions". Finally, many years later, he made an orchestral version of the *Aquarelles* movement—but much-revised, with different key-relationships and a new middle section—as the finale of his *Sinfonietta*.[26]

I could cite many other examples of this phenomenon; but I conclude with a case where one of these "recycled" ideas undergoes a substantive musical development at each appearance. The large-scale coda of the Cello Sonata presents a synoptic review of the work's main themes, in skilful contrapuntal combination, over a sonorous, bell-like ground bass motif (Ex.27).

Ex. 27

This idea crops up again in the 1917 Fiona Mac-Leod song "The Reed Player", whose central section is founded upon it (Ex. 28, next page).

The section is relatively short, and the ostinato-figure is only repeated a few times before it concludes. But the next year (1918) Foulds made use of it in the central portion of *The Song of Honour*, a dramatic work for speaker, female chorus and chamber orchestra on a text by the poet Ralph Hodgson. Here the bass, on pizzicato strings, becomes the foundation for an ever more elaborate accumulation of instrumental textures, in eventually riotous profusion, to accompany the poet's vision of a paradisal natural harmony—"The everlasting pipe and flute of wind and sea and bird and brute and lips deaf men imagine mute in wood and stone and clay". (One of the counterpoints, a bird-like flute figure, eventually landed up in the *Saint Joan* music by way of *Peace and War*; and the opening section of the *Song of Honour* also contains music that is further developed in the first movement of the *Saint Joan Suite*.) And when, in 1926, Foulds came to write his virtuoso piano piece

---

25   There is no connection between this tune and the violin and piano piece *Ballade and Refrain Roccoco* of about 1909.

26   A word of explanation about this title. Foulds never wrote a composition called *Sinfonietta*. However, he did write, in rapid succession in 1934-35, two works called *Three Pasquinades*—one for two pianos, Op. 93, and one for orchestra, misleadingly labelled Op.37—plus a third 3-movement score entitled *Pasquinades Symphoniques*, his Op. 98. Simply to avoid confusion I suggest re-naming the Op. 37 set as *Sinfonietta*, not least because that points up its relationship to the "symphonic" Op. 98 set as a "littler and lighter" companion piece. Typically and confusingly none of these scores survives in an absolutely finished state (Op. 93 is largely missing, and the two orchestral sets both break off in the middle of their finales; though there is a sketch-basis for an easy completion of Op. 37), and the three are interrelated by the "self-quotational" phenomenon being examined here. The *Sinfonietta*'s first movement has been developed from a sketch for a "Pasquinade" movement in Foulds's *Puppet Ballet Suite* described on a later page. Its finale, as already noted, derived from *Aquarelles*; and its central slow movement, which features a pair of solo violins, is founded on the main melody of a piano-piece of the mid-1920s called *Moonlight: Sorrento*. But the slow movement of the 2-piano *Pasquinades* is founded on exactly the same melody—though sufficient material is extant to show the harmonic and textural treatment was entirely different; and the same sketches also show that the *first* movement of the *Pasquinades Symphoniques* is itself a vast elaboration and expansion of the first movement of the 2-piano set! The reader may by now have grasped what I meant to indicate by the phrase "wandering in a maze of self-quotation".

April-England, he returned to the conception worked out in *The Song of Honour* for *its* central vision of "boundless fecundity" and "opulent burgeoning". The ground bass is the same; the figures and textures which ride upon it are entirely different, and tailored to the very different medium of the keyboard (Ex. 29) — but the proportions of the passage, and its harmonic content, are identical to those of the comparable section of the earlier work.

Examples of this kind cannot be written off as mere "self-borrowing"; they show a progressive development of one idea (sometimes in combination with others) that is pursued through several different compositions. But they make the listener's experience of Foulds's music rather different from that of many composers' — shocks of recognition occur more frequently, and it may be that one's appreciation of an individual score may come to be colored by the recollections of others, sharing its material, that lie behind it.

Ex. 28

Ex. 29

9. Working Abroad (1927-30)

In 1927, after it became obvious that there would be no performance that year of *A World Requiem*, the Fouldses quit the London musical scene and ventured abroad. Maud travelled to Taormina in Sicily, where she was involved in an attempt—ultimately successful—to reopen the ancient Greek theater there for dramatic performances. (The project was fraught with difficulty, as the Fascist authorities imagined she was a political spy!) Foulds joined her in Taormina for a time, and to this sojourn we owe some of his most elegant light music in pieces like *Isles of Greece, Strophes from an Antique Song*, and *Sicilian Aubade*.

With the end of the summer Foulds moved to France, where he lived—principally in Paris, at a flat in the Rue des Acacia—for the next three years. Here he worked, as he had done in London, as a composer of incidental music, an arranger, a conductor, and according to some reports as an accompanist for silent films. Maud, pursuing her own interests, joined him for part of this period, and continued to lecture on Indian music: on one occasion she appeared in Paris with the Indian classical dancer Uday Shankar in a program of "*Danses et Chants de L'Orient*" sponsored by the Association Française. (It seems very likely that the young Olivier Messiaen may have attended this event.) But for much of the time Foulds remained in France on his own.

In many ways he must have found the artistic climate freer than in London. He had always kept abreast of developments in contemporary music, and now continued to do so, making the personal acquaintance not only of "*Les Six*" but also of Korngold, Stravinsky and Varèse; and he formed a closer friendship with George Migot, a fellow enthusiast for Oriental music. The years in France saw the completion of some of his most important compositions: the third *Mantra*, the first and only volume of his *Essays in the Modes* for piano (which he was able to publish, along with the revised Cello Sonata, in handsome editions issued by the house of Senart—practically the only two of his serious works which Foulds was to see issued in a form that satisfied him); and he composed one of his finest creations, the *Dynamic Triptych* for piano and orchestra.

As already noted, Foulds had shown considerable interest in using Ancient Greek modes as a basis for composition. But in addition to those, he was much intrigued by the possibilities of the many *other* modes that exist apart from the diatonic major and minor scales on which so much of Western music has been founded since the 17th century; and from his knowledge of Oriental music he knew that many were in use as the râgâs of classical Indian music. By about 1920 he had tabulated a collection of 90 modes—90 seven-note scales in which the octave was differently divided—which he thought fruitful for exploration in music. Seventy-two of these (including diatonic major and minor) correspond to the 72 classical râgâs of Southern India: that is, they accomodate the interval-structure of the Indian scales to their nearest mean-tempered equivalent on the piano. Foulds's idea was that pieces written in strict conformity with the non-diatonic modes would (in addition to whatever purely musical value they possessed) help to acclimatize ordinary listeners to tonal systems other than those of familiar diatonicism, and therefore form a bridge to greater understanding and appreciation of the wide varieties of music that were being composed in the enormously expanded harmonic vocabularies available to the 20th-century composer. His "Table of 90 Modes" was eventually published in a preface to *Essays in the Modes*, his major composition for solo piano (see next page).

Speculation along these lines naturally brought Foulds close to the thinking of Busoni, who had already adumbrated the possibilities of modal composition in his epoch-making book *Sketch for a New Aesthetic of Music* (1907). But Foulds's Table of 90 Modes contains a smaller number than Busoni's proposed total of 113, because he preferred to exclude those modes which flattened or sharpened their fifth note, thus losing the effect of a perfect cadence. He also took issue with Busoni for wishing to introduce, into modal compositions, harmonies foreign to the prevailing mode itself; Foulds felt that "the power of mode resides in its utter purity" (*Music To-day*, p.49). Certainly each piece in *Essays in the Modes* uses only the seven pitches of its respective mode, plus octave transpositions. Thus Foulds denies himself the resource of modulation; but to compensate for that he deploys quite extraordinary inventive powers and a lavishly imaginative range of textures, utilizing the entire gamut of the keyboard (and every conceivable

A TABLE OF NINETY MODES

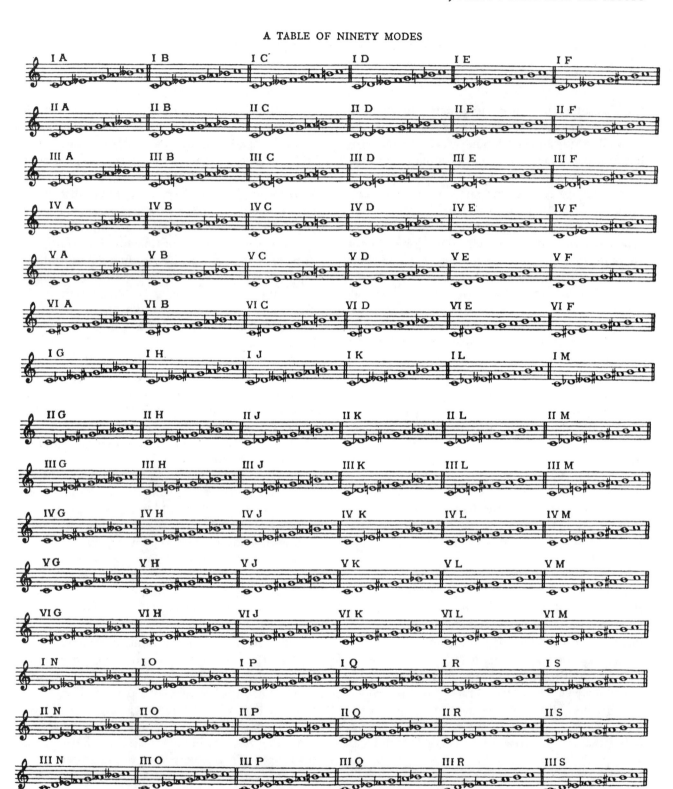

Foulds's "Table of 90 Modes". (Author's Collection.)

skill of the pianist). As a result, there is no sense of limitation or constraint. These are no mere exercises in harmonic novelty but highly evocative compositions of genuine musical worth and not a little charm. When I showed them to the composer, pianist, and Busoni-scholar Ronald Stevenson in 1975, his first verdict after playing them through was: "This is the music of Busoni's *New Aesthetic* made audible!"

Foulds had initially planned a vast cycle of no less than 72 piano pieces, apparently on all the modes corresponding to râgâs; later he reduced this to a cycle of 36, to be issued in six books. But in the event only one volume, containing six pieces, was issued; one other complete piece remains in manuscript, and there are sketches and drafts for several more. The seven complete pieces, however, comprise an impressive and substantial collection; and though little-played during Foulds's lifetime, they have been taken up by several pianists in the past decade, and have been broadcast and recorded. Many of Foulds's earlier works had displayed "French" attributes of wit and elegant polish; but in the *Essays* he seems consciously to be matching himself against the great French masters of the piano, especially Ravel.[28] Despite their unusual modal basis, they are the most essentially pianistic, and virtuosic, of his solo piano works.

The first piece in the published set, "Exotic", is founded on a mode spelt $C- D^b- E^b- F- G- A^b- B^{bb}$, and is a slow preludial savoring of the extended sound-world. It begins with innocent, intriguing chord-sequences (Ex. 30), moves on to a darkly sonorous tune in the tenor register that would sound equally at home on a cello, and rises to an impassioned climax in which the Oriental coloring is most pronounced.

"Ingenuous" (on the mode $F^#- G^#- A^#- B^#- C^#- D^#- E$) is a nonchalant fugal invention that casually generates a glittering, bell-like excitement. "Introversive" (mode $D- E^b- F- G- A- B^b- C^#$) is a tense, almost anguished oriental nocturne, growing from subtle rhythmic heterophony (Ex. 31—page 61), assuming touches of Debussyan impressionism, and revealing glimpses of a slow, funereal march.

The fourth piece in the published volume, "Military", is actually founded on the diatonic major scale (which Foulds included in his Table of Modes, as it corresponds to the Hindu râg Shankrabhara), but an unusual harmonic dimension is retained in this movement too: by composition in two simultaneous transpositions a semitone apart—so that the

Ex. 30

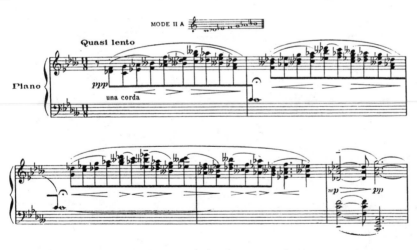

---

28 As an interesting instance of parallel development, we should note here the work of the French musicologist-composer Maurice Emmanuel (1862-1938), who at this period held the chair of History of Music at the Paris Conservatoire, and whose pupils included Messiaen. Deeply committed to the revival of both Ancient Greek and Gregorian modes, Emmanuel had published books on Greek music as early as 1895. In 1920 he composed his splendid *Sonatine IV* for piano, *"sur des modes Hindous"*, which was published in 1923 with a dedication to Busoni. This is a remarkable work in its own right, although Emmanuel's methods are very different from Foulds's; he uses two Hindu modes and freely modulates among several transpositions of them. Since Foulds also began the *Essays* in 1920, Emmanuel's Sonatina can hardly have been an influence on him: but he can hardly have remained wholly ignorant of Emmanuel's works, especially during his years in Paris. Nevertheless, there is no mention of him in the pages of *Music To-day*.

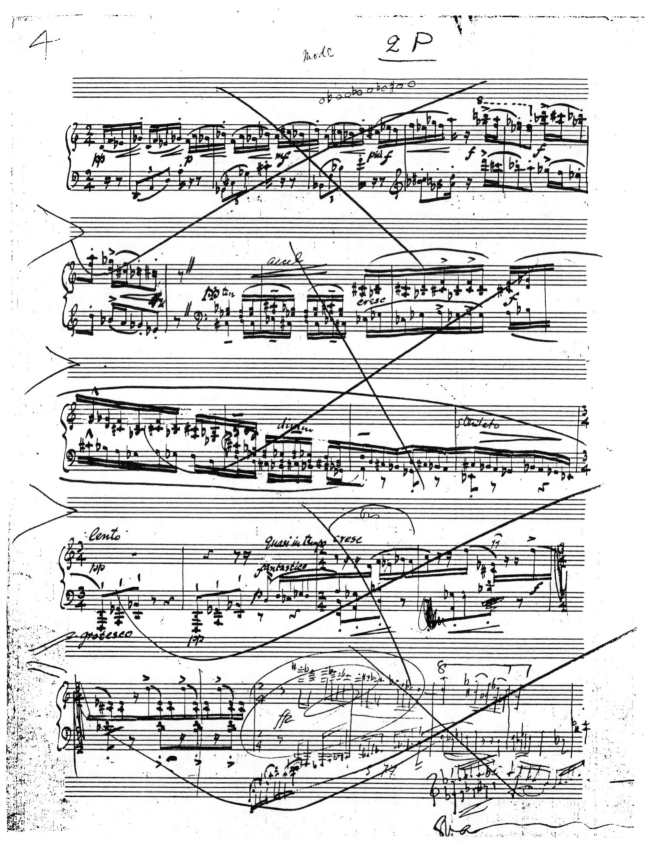

A cancelled sketch for the modal *Essay*, "Prismic". On the reverse of this sheet
the evolving piece is titled "Mineral Elemental". (John Foulds Estate.)

right hand is always in D major, the left in D flat. This is a brilliant bitonal study in the form of a swaggering patrol whose cheeky main theme and pounding accompaniment, Alkan-like at opposite ends of the keyboard, suggest the sonorities of fife and drum. "Strophic" (on mode E– F$^\#$– G$^\#$– A$^\#$– B– C$^\#$– D$^\#$) then presents four increasingly elaborated forms of a nobly elegiac tune, like four stanzas of a poem (a throwback, perhaps, to Foulds's early conception of "Music-Poems"). A great resonant tolling, as of gong and bells, enshrouds the final bars in melancholy.

The mode used in "Strophic" represents the Hindu râg known as kâlyân, and it is also the basis (but in a different transposition, beginning on G^b) for the unpublished *Essay*, which Foulds entitled "Egoistic". Although all the pieces have "character" titles, it's clear from these two that Foulds wasn't implying that each mode was simply suited to expressing just one mood. The main tune of "Egoistic", too, is closely related to that of "Strophic", but this time its character is vaunting and declamatory, aggrandized by towering, monumental chords. The final *Essay* of the published volume, "Prismic", is built on the mode D–

Ex. 31

Ex. 32

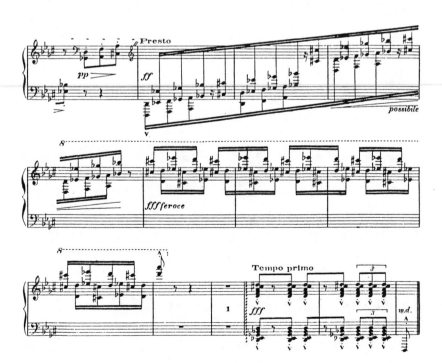

The opening of *Dynamic Triptych* , from the autograph full score. (By courtesy of the Trustees of the British Library. Copyright © 1980 by Musica Viva and the Estate of John Foulds.)

E♭– F– G♭– A– B♭– C#. This frosty, percussive piece possesses something of the mood of a fantastic, leaping oriental dance. Its restless figurations turn in upon themselves like reflections in a prism, and the piano writing has a brittle, crystalline quality. Its final, dissonant, mirror-image chords (Ex. 32—page 61) bring to an end an astonishing and individual cycle of pieces whose harmonies could well have helped lead the young Messiaen into the ways of modal composition.

For all their formidable difficulties, Foulds seems to have had no problem in getting the *Essays* published—in France. Yet another virtuoso piano composition written at the same time, a *Scherzo Chromatico*, did not fare so well when sent for publication in England. Apparently it was accepted by Paxton's; but in August 1928 Cyril Neil, one of that firm's directors, was writing to Foulds: "The Scherzo I have not yet given out, as it is a very difficult work, and while things are somewhat quiet in this field, publication would not do any good." This timorous attitude did Foulds no good, either. The work was never issued. Paxton's went out of business in the early 1960s, and the manuscript has disappeared.

Among the sketch material for further *Essays in the Modes* there is one that clearly cost Foulds much effort, but which began to develop into something altogether bigger. Although we lack some of the intermediate stages, there is no doubt that this particular unfinished piano piece led on to the first movement of Foulds's *Dynamic Triptych* for piano and orchestra, completed in 1929 and really a splendidly virtuosic Piano Concerto in all but name. This is a first-rate work, one of Foulds's most important, full of strong personality and calling for an interpreter of international stature.

Its first movement, "Dynamic Mode", is a bravura toccata-like structure based on the mode D– E#– F# G– A– B#– C#, delineated by the piano in a cadenza-like stream of figuration just after the opening. As in the solo piano pieces, modal composition quite naturally encouraged Foulds to a high level of dissonance, and this movement—in succinct sonata-form with a big pounding cadenza—is an exciting display-piece, crackling with electric energy. Its bold, wide-ranging main theme is a highly characteristic example of Foulds's athletic modernism (Ex. 33).

The title of the slow movement, "Dynamic Timbre", refers chiefly to the kaleidoscopic nature of its scoring, which includes the use of quarter-tones and Foulds's "counterpoint of timbres". The music is, however, often simple and direct in its appeal. After a shimmering *organum*-like introduction on the strings of parallel fourths and fifths moving in quarter-tones, the piano enters with a most beautiful melody—Ex. 35, next page—which is developed throughout the rest of the movement, with a breathtaking range of color and instrumental resource, rising eventually to one of Foulds's grandest and most opulent climaxes, and dying away in what Foulds described as "rainbow hues" of quiet cluster-harmony on the piano. The finale, "Dynamic Rhythm", is another brilliant toccata with rondo-like features. It is founded on an insistent rhythm—

—which persists for the whole of its length, however much it may sometimes be disguised by the predominance of other time-signatures. Before long the mask of grim, percussive modernism has dis-

Ex. 33

Ex. 35

solved into a joker's grin as the music is transformed by sleight-of-hand into a deliciously lilting waltz. This gives way in turn to an emphatic march, in which Foulds achieves a tangy, resonant effect simply by harmonizing every note of the tune with its own second-inversion triad (Ex. 36, facing page).

This tune is soon swathed by the piano in quasi-Bartókian bitonal arpeggios; the waltz brings a hint of Rachmaninoff; the rhythmic insouciance is reminiscent both of Stravinsky's *Petrushka* and Ravel's G major Concerto. But I invoke these parallels simply in an attempt to "fix" this ebullient music's sound-character; there is no plagiarism anywhere, and no sense of stylistic incongruity except that which Foulds's sense of humor has calculated to a nicety. The riotous climax (complete with mock-sinster trombone pedals) and rhythmically exciting

Ex. 36

coda ought to bring the house down in any live concert performance.

Another important creation of Foulds's "French period" is the set of *Three Choruses in the Hippolytus of Euripides*, which constitute the climax of his imaginative involvement with the use of Ancient Greek modes to evoke the atmosphere of Classical Antiquity. The work doubtless grew out of his incidental music to Euripides's play (with which it shares an opus-number, and Gilbert Murray's translations of the texts): and Foulds originally envisaged it as a large cycle for solo and mixed voices in five movements— *Songs and Choruses from the Hippolytus of Euripides*—which would have included a male-voice "Chorus of Huntsmen" he had written for the theater score.

However, the triptych of female-voice choruses which he completed at St. Gobrien in the Loire Valley in September 1928 is musically unrelated to the austerely modal style of the theater music. Each of them certainly begins in an ancient Greek mode, but they continually expand their harmonic horizons to arrive at Foulds's most vibrantly mystical pandiatonic idiom. Foulds wrote them (according to a rapidly-pencilled draft of a program-note found among his sketches)—

> ...not with any idea of approximating to what we know of Greek music, or of obtaining a spurious antique atmosphere, but simply because, having a strong predilection for modal writing, & having steeped myself in the Euripidean [here he leaves space for a word that was never filled in: he clearly did not want to repeat "atmosphere"], this modal type of treatment occured to me most naturally (frequently indeed spontaneously) on reading the choruses themselves.

The choruses themselves, in the general manner of Greek tragedy, arise out of the specific dramatic situations of Euripides's play (the incestuous love of Phaedra, wife of King Theseus, for Theseus's son Hippolytus) but respond to it in more generalized, lyrical terms. It was therefore perfectly possible for Foulds to choose choruses which would make a satisfying independent choral suite with a shape and logic of its own. The first, longest, and most overtly dramatic of the choruses, "There riseth a rockbourn river", is the only one to refer directly to the Queen languishing under the effects of her guilty passion, and it climaxes in a remarkably impassioned appeal to Artemis, the "Helper of Pain". Foulds seldom wrote music more ravishing than this chorus, which seems imaginatively to have penetrated to the archetypal atmosphere of Classical antiquity. Equally spellbinding is the contemplative second movement, "Refuge", which forms the still center of his design and speaks longingly of retreat from the world in triadic harmonies that melt into one another as into an ever-retreating, shimmering haze. The final chorus he called "Aphrodite Triumphant": the goddess of love is here evoked under her title of "Cypris", and this most diatonic movement of the choral triptych produces a fast and jubilant finale.

The three choruses appear to survive only in vocal score, with piano accompaniment—and though never heard in his lifetime, they have recently been performed in this form with great effect. But the composer had planned several alternative instrumentations ranging from solo harp, harp duet, string octet, woodwind septet with double-bass, and others all the way up to large chamber orchestra. One hopes that he did, in fact, complete one or more of these versions, and that the manuscripts may one day see the light.

45ᵗᵉ rue des acacias. paris XVII
July 11ᵗ. 30.

Dear Mr Hawkes,

Herewith the article duly corrected. I could not pass it for publication as it stood & I hope my emendations will go in as They are indicated.

I have been detained abroad longer than I expected, and I have not with me here a list of my published works. If, as I hope, this article is not to be published until Sept. or Oct., it is extremely likely that I shall have returned to London & can get the information you ask for. In fact, the moment I get back I will post the list to you & hope this will do.

Recently I have been amusing myself "re imagining" Schubert's very dramatic Quartet "Death & the Maiden" for full orchestra. It is of course of symphonic length. & character.

Would this interest you for publication?

Yours sincerely

John Foulds.

P.S. I met the other day in Bruxelles my old friend
M. Verbrugghen, now & for some years past the conductor of the
Minneapolis Symphony Orchestra. He authorised me to ask you
if you will be good enough to have sent to :—

   The Librarian
   Minneapolis Symphony Orchestra
     Minn. U.S.A.

the following parts of my "Keltic Suite" 8.7.5.5.4.
He also asks for a <u>score</u>! Alas we have no such thing I
fear. so perhaps the p. forte conductor part must do. Unless you
think it worth while to have a m.s. score drawn out.

Account enclosed with the music will be met in the usual way.

    J. F.

A letter written by Foulds from Paris to the publisher Ralph Hawkes.
(Courtesy of Boosey & Hawkes Music Publishers Ltd.)

A page of Foulds's orchestral transcription of Schubert's *Death and the Maiden* Quartet.
(Copyright © John Foulds Estate.)

10. Back in England (1930-35)

Foulds returned to England in the Autumn of 1930, bearing with him, among other things, his recent transcription of Schubert's *Death and the Maiden* String Quartet as a symphony for full orchestra.[29] He set great store by this *tour-de-force* of his arrangers's skill, but was unable to interest publishers or orchestras in it. Maud had established a clinic for "phono-therapy" (a technique she had discovered for curing nervous complaints by the effects of sound — apparently a forerunner of contemporary forms of music-therapy) at the Abbey Road house, and Foulds therefore spent less of his time there than at a studio he retained in Adelphi Chambers, York Buildings, WC2, and later in rooms at St. James's Place, SW1. He was also an habitué of the Savage Club, long famous as a haven for artists, writers, and musicians, where his friends included Vaughan Williams and the pianist Mark Hambourg.

It seems that his reputation had lost much ground in the period that had elapsed since the *World Requiem* performances came to an end. In the next few years he appears to have made a sustained attempt to re-establish himself as a composer of serious music, especially by trying to promote performances. In this endeavour he had only a qualified success. He was uncomfortably aware that he was pigeon-holed in too many minds as a "light-music composer"; and the fact that the "light" portion of his output continued to be regularly performed hardly helped to correct that impression. A draft of a letter in Foulds's hand (possibly intended for Sir Thomas Beecham) speaks of the "galling situation" that "the BBC, which I have approached, does not apparently wish to perform any of my major works (while broadcasting my light music and theatre music every week)."

It was, nevertheless, the BBC — now an important musical power in the land, compared to the embryo organization of the 1920s — to which he directed his main efforts. The formation of the BBC Orchestra under Adrian Boult in 1930 (around the nucleus of Henry Wood's old Queen's Hall Orchestra) had attracted players from all the other British orchestras, weakening their ability to perform new and taxing compositions — while making the BBC itself the chief arbiter of the repertoire to be broadcast throughout the nation. And through resilience and tenacity he did secure a few performances. The suite *Hellas* for double string orchestra, harp, and percussion — the ultimate form of the *Recollections of Ancient Greek Music*, completed in 1932 after seventeen years' gestation — was broadcast from Birmingham the following year by the Birmingham Philharmonic String Orchestra under Foulds's direction. The orchestral version of *April-England*, which also dates from 1932, was premièred in 1934 in a BBC Orchestra broadcast, conducted by Boult's assistant Aylmer Buesst.

Foulds was luckiest, however, with the *Dynamic Triptych*. The distinguished pianist Frank Merrick, Professor at the Royal College of Music, became an enthusiastic exponent of the work. He gave its première in Edinburgh in October 1931, with the Reid Orchestra, under Sir Donald Tovey's baton. The performance had in fact been scheduled for a later concert, but Merrick agreed to appear at short notice when another soloist, due to play another concerto, unexpectedly fell ill. Because of this switch of programs, Tovey had no opportunity to give us an "Essay in Musical Analysis" about it. Instead he merely printed Foulds's own program-note on the work,[30] prefacing it with the comment that he would write about *Dynamic Triptych* at a later date, for it was such a splendid piece that the Reid was bound to repeat it in a few seasons' time. Alas, it was not to be. There were, however, further performances in Birmingham and Bournemouth, conducted by Leslie Howard and Foulds, respectively; culminating in a BBC broadcast on 4 August 1933 conducted by Sir Dan Godfrey, in a program of that conductor's own choice, which also included Weber's *Oberon* Overture and Vaughan Williams's *London Symphony*. Hamilton Harty, too, looked over the score, and though unable to program it, he wrote to Foulds on 17 June 1933 "Needless to say I found it the work of a first-class composer". The broadcast aroused some interest: in the September *Musical Opinion* the editorial column "On the Other Hand" (written by the composer Havergal Brian,

---

29   See Appendix, No. 4: "Orchestrating 'Death and the Maiden' (1930)".

30   See Appendix, No. 3: "*Dynamic Triptych*: Program Note (1929)".

who had known Foulds in Manchester before the war) commended *Dynamic Triptych* as "a major work by a composer of daring originality". This was, however, to be the last occasion on which it was to be heard in Foulds's lifetime, or for a long time afterwards. Only in 1982 was it revived for a modern LP recording by Howard Shelley and the Royal Philharmonic Orchestra, conducted by Vernon Handley, which has won it new friends and considerable critical praise.

A few days after the broadcast, on 16 August 1933, Foulds wrote a long letter to Adrian Boult,[31] forwarding the score of *April-England*. He concluded thus:

> Within the last two years I have submitted four works to the B.B.C. These in my opinion contained some of my most valuable work. In each case they were rejected by your Selection Committee. [It is not known which four works these were. –MM.] The position, therefore, is that while my principal serious works have received the approval of some of the greatest names in the musical world, and also of practical conductors it would appear, judging from past experience, that any serious work of mine has a poor chance of winning approval of the B.B.C. Selection Committee.
>
> In the meantime my light works are continually broadcast. These... number a dozen or so, as compared with the total of 50 of my serious works. This state of affairs, I think you will agree, is rather a galling one for a serious artist.

Foulds's plea was successful, at least to the extent that it seems to have led to the performance of *April-England* noted earlier. But it could not be said that he did much in other ways to divest himself of the mantle of the "light-music composer". He simply could not afford to. Within a couple of months of his return from France, in December 1930, he had been offering the publisher Ralph Hawkes a new *Keltic Overture*, "one of my very best things in this genre," in response to Hawkes's repeated request for "another *Keltic Suite*." Hawkes's verdict, after considering the score, showed a strange inconsistency:

> I will admit that the work contains a very fine melody and some brilliant orchestration but

on the other hand there is sufficient Scottish music on the market at the moment to meet any requirement and after all a Keltic Overture is a style of work which is only understood in certain parts of the world.... Owing to the difficult conditions with which we have to contend today it is quite impossible to consider any publication unless there is a reasonable chance of its being a "money maker".

A "money maker" was precisely what Foulds had tried to produce, of course; but Hawkes clearly felt that he had already saturated the market. The *Keltic Overture*, a stirring and highly professional little piece, which could well be described as an updated essay in the manner of Hamish MacCunn's *Land of the Mountain and the Flood*, was eventually taken on by Bosworth & Co., but never seems to have atained the popularity its composer hoped for.

It was also during this period that Foulds produced a large number of so-called "Fantasies" — very much routine pot-pourris for orchestra on well-known themes from Mendelssohn, Schubert, Tchaikovsky, and others. These were surely intended merely as "money-makers" (probably successfully, since he wrote several of them in quick succession), and they certainly occupy the humblest position amongst his compositions. Nevertheless, they performed a function in introducing famous melodies to audiences of unsophisticated musical taste, and they have proved surprisingly long-lived; even today, Performing Right returns shows that they are occasionally performed or broadcast in out-of-the-way parts of the globe.

Foulds continued to compose and conduct theater music. He seems to have set some store by the music he wrote for an Arts Theatre production of Maurice Rostand's *Le Masque de Fer* in early 1931, but this has entirely disappeared, and only sketches remain of a score for J.M. Barrie's *Dear Brutus*. The new genre of music for the cinema also attracted him, and he eventually wrote music for about a dozen documentaries and short feature films. Foulds seems to have relished the challenge they presented to his professionalism. Ray Foulds told the present writer that he remembered his father sketching out the music for a little film called *Ten-Minute Alibi*: it took him precisely ten minutes!

---

31 Reproduced in full in *From Parry to Britten: British Music in Letters 1900-1945*, edited by Lewis Foreman (London: Batsford, 1987).

As for his more serious works, by far the most noteworthy was the *Quartetto Intimo*, Op. 89. This large-scale, five-movement quartet (his Ninth), lasting about 34 minutes, is perhaps his most important piece of chamber music; it has been greeted with general acclaim since its first performance in 1980, and deserves an extended examination.

The *Quartetto Intimo* was completed in January 1932 in London. Foulds never heard it performed, although according to the letter to Adrian Boult quoted above, his old friend Arthur Catterall had promised to perform it "when opportunity permits". He was justly proud of it and used several examples from it to illustrate various modern techniques in his book *Music To-day*. Why *Intimo*? The quartet is hardly "intimate" in expression — it is forceful and exciting, and wears its passion brazenly on its sleeve. Maybe it had a personal, hidden meaning for the composer — there are certainly some musical allusions in it to which we lack the key. On another level, the title may be meant to suggest the power of inner inspiration, of inward excitement bursting forth into the outer world. Be that as it may, the quartet is one of Foulds's most "advanced" works, and a spendid demonstration of his ability to remain full-bloodedly romantic at the same time. There may be passing similarities to Bartók, Stravinsky, Ravel and Debussy, but Foulds's personality is entirely distinctive, and the work is completely original in conception. It is very consistent and tight-knit, though it combines a great variety of different *kinds* of music within the various movements, and deploys a dazzling repertoire of *ways* of writing for string quartet.

Quartetto Intimo begins explosively with a re-iterated chord (Ex. 37i) and a hectic flood of triplet figuration. The chord crystallizes Foulds's harmonic language throughout the work. The quartet is "in C", because C is the cello's lowest note and becomes therefore the fundamental tone of a theoretically endless chain of vertically superimposed thirds — a

Ex. 37

A page from Foulds's autograph score of the *Quartetto Intimo* ("Pasquinade" movement). (By courtesy of the Trustees of the British Library. Copyright © 1980 by Musica Viva and John Foulds Estate.)

vastly-expanded C major in which complete triads of other keys (here, G and D) are felt as subordinate "regions". In such harmony, 7ths and 9ths have equality with "softer" intervals and give the music its bite and zing; also, Foulds can move at will into bitonality and polytonality without relinquishing the overall "monotonal" sense.

The first movement is a foreshortened sonata-design, merging development and recapitulation: its principal materials are set out in Ex. 37*ii-vi* (page 71). The old love of contrary motion now brings forth bold gestures of whole-tone clusters and glissandi, while Ex. 37*vi* presents cadential chords elaborated from the premises of the original chord 37*i*. These chords, and the cell *a*, continue to develop in subtle and far-reaching ways throughout the entire quartet.

The first movement's development is highly imaginative. The music's vigour begins to be undercut by pensive, other-worldly sounds, such as the cello's ethereal augmentation of Ex. 37*iv*'s first few bars in harmonics. A vehement return to the mood of the opening, and an elaboration of chord 37*i*, lead again to a torrent of triplets in all four instruments — which suddenly turns aside into a weird, soft, totally chromatic groping that steers into an eerie region where spectral fragments of exposition material flit across the scene in a texture compounded entirely of harmonics, pizzicati and slow glissandi (recalling 37*iii*). From this shadow-land we emerge into daylight when the "second subject" tune 37*v* reappears on the cello: it leads the way towards a turbulent coda that harks back to the start of the move-

ment with inventions on the chord 37*i*. A *fortissimo* version of it, rhetorically decorated with trills, is the penultimate harmony; the movement ends brusquely and unexpectedly with a *sforzando* C major triad, first inversion on E — the note which 37*i* has always lacked.

The slow movement, marked *Lento introspettivo*, is based on two themes.

The first (Ex. 38*i*) is grieving and highly chromatic; it begins with a distorted image of cell *a*, and its continuation (not quoted) proceeds from phrase to phrase with a sobbing portamento, and turns a^3's falling seventh into a written-out glissando. The accompaniment is sparse, in hollow bare fifths, but continues to suggest a root tonality of C. The second theme (Ex. 38*ii*) is in complete contrast — diatonic, warm, fervently romantic and gutsily harmonized. Mounting steadily, key by key, it carries all four instruments up to stratospheric registers before a glacial descent takes the music into another ghostly inner world. When theme 38*i* returns, on viola, it is to the unsettling accompaniment of quarter-tones and glissandi pizzicato chords in the cello and slow written-out glisses in the violins. Theme 38*ii* makes another bid for positive, full-blooded romanticism, but the movement ends in a numb emotional no-man's land of quarter-tone harmony, combined with arco and pizzicato harmonics.

If the first two movements have their bizarre moments, the third, a scherzo entitled "Pasquinade", is stranger yet. A "Pasquinade" is usually defined as a satire, squib or lampoon (from the Roman custom of

Ex. 38

affixing rude verses to public statuary),[32] and Foulds's movement *may* be intended as a satire on various aspects of musical modernity: if so, it transcends any such function—it is a brilliant study in thematic and harmonic acerbity, full of wit and fantasy.[33] The spikily rhythmic first theme:

Ex. 39

which appears at first to be an elaboration of a descending scale, is violently juxtaposed against stabbing, rapidly repeated cluster-chords derived from Ex. 37*iii*. But before long Ex. 39's archetype is revealed as the *"Dies Irae"*, heard first pizzicato, *ff*, on violin I and cello in extreme high and lower registers against pulsing chordal inner parts. (Foulds's use of pizzicato is especially lavish in this movement, and includes "slap-pizzicato" and rapid non-arpeggiated chords played with two fingers.) The *"Dies Irae"* is treated in diminution, in augmentation and stretto along with a gaggle of related, highly rhythmic motifs. Magnificently conceived for strings, the music nevertheless makes no concessions to the players: all four must play rapid streams of double-stopped parallel fifths, a fact unlikely to endear the movement to faint-hearted violinists. The harmony breaks into genuine polytonality (A flat, E and D major) for the presentation of a sweetly contrasting *amabile* second theme, distantly related to a^4; by means of accents and phrasing the passage superimposes rhythmic patterns also, in a manner reminiscent of the March from Stravinsky's *The Soldier's Tale*. At the center is another icy, enigmatic withdrawal, recalling similar manoevers in the previous movements; then an even wilder review

of the previous material, and a bizarre coda based on Ex. 39 (in contrary motion) with a zanily dissonant final cadence that lands on a unison *ffz* pizzicato C.

The fourth movement, entitled "Colloquy", functions as an extended introduction to the finale. It begins, muted, with a slow, mysterious, chorale-like progression—none other than Ex. 14, from the *Aquarelles*, at the same pitch but fitted now, in minims, to a 5/2 metrical scheme. In fact this idea, which Foulds may be using here as a personal "trademark", has a complex history throughout his *oeuvre*. Here he uses it—each repetition varied in texture, register, key and ultimate harmonic direction—to "frame" unbarred sections where the individual instruments establish their separate personalities with dream-like reminiscences of the main themes of the first three movements. At length the first violin breaks into an agitated cadenza which soon brings forth a new, boldly ascending *passionata* idea. The "Colloquy" draws to a close with a final husky development of the "chorale" in close harmony, each chord separated by silences, squidging its central point (*x* marks the analogous spot in Ex. 14) into an ever smaller and nastier cluster: at which point a kinship to Ex. 37*iii* becomes clear. The movement concludes on a serene triad of F sharp major, five octaves deep, and the finale begins *attaca subito* in a G-inflected C with Ex. 40*i* (next page), developed from the *passionata* idea mentioned above.

The 5/4 meter (Foulds adds a note: "not 3 and 2, nor 2 and 3, but 5!") persists for most of the movement and gives it a curious loping inevitability that is very exhilarating. All the doubts and hesitancies that had beset the other movements have been overcome. Otherwise the layout of the finale echoes the first movement at many points. The first subject has two main themes—Exx. 40*i* and *ii*, whose organic connection parallels that of Exx. 37*ii* and *iv*—and a dissonant chordal idea, Ex. 40*iii* (paralleling 37*iii*); moreover the

---

32 Foulds had a fixation with this title in his later years (he possibly first encountered it when he made an arrangement of the *Pasquinade* for piano by the 19th-century American composer Louis Moreau Gottschalk). The *Puppet-Ballet Suite* (see p. 76) was orginally conceived as including "several Pasquinades": three at least were sketched, and one became the original fourth movement, only to be discarded at a late stage in the composition (Foulds's full score of it is missing; it survives in a virtually complete piano-conductor form). Another of them progressed no further than a brief sketch marked *Allegro sardonico*, but then became the starting point for the first movement, "Ironic", of the set of 3 *Pasquinades* for orchestra (?1934-35) which I have suggested (p. 55n) should be re-named *Sinfonietta*. He also produced the *Pasquinades Symphoniques* for orchestra (1935); the (lost) scherzo of his *Quartetto Geniale* (1935), which was entitled "Pasquinade" (or, on one list of movements, "Gasconade"—not exactly an equivalent term, as this would be less a satire than a show of bravado); and a *Pasquinade* for woodwind quartet (?1936—only a sketch survives).

33 Foulds seems never to have written a program-note for *Quartetto Intimo*, but a scrap of paper bearing its movement-titles also carries the pencil scrawl: "The listener may drawn his own conclusions as to what (whether persons, methods or,—himself) the composer lampoons in this not altogether bitter.... 'pasquinade'."

Ex. 40

seed chord 37*i* itself reappears in jubilant reiterations.[34] There is also a distinct "second subject", based on a descending scale harmonized entirely in triads, which (analogous to the first movement's Ex. 37*iv*) is a further transformation of Ex. 40*i*, derived from its last two bars. If anything, however, the diversity of the material presented in the finale is even greater than in the earlier movements. Other features include a Bartókian "folk-like" passage combining *tastiera* with *ponticello* playing; a voluble cadenza-like effusion for first violin over rich, heavy chords which on inspection turn out to be virtually Ex. 37*vi* in different spacing; and the return of more first-movement elements — notably a^3, which is no less at home in a 5/4 waltz than a 3/4 one. Foulds welds all together with masterly structural control.

Once again there is a development which fragments and retreats into elusive introspection. But this time the music does not linger there; it fades out in a shimmering summer haze of trills which evaporate as they rise, leaving one high sustained C exposed on first violin. The time changes to 4/4, and a rhapsodic

cello solo, *con dignitá*, reshapes Ex. 40*i* in more measured tempo. This has the function of a recapitulation, but it develops instead into a gorgeous apotheosis that combines the trills, the work's opening chord, and most of Ex. 37*iv* into a grand polyphonic fantasy where the main melodic burden is carried by a soaring augmentation of Ex. 40*ii*. The meter broadens to 6/4, the sonorities take on an orchestral opulence, and the vast melodic span, superbly constructed, yearns and exults with an ecstatic passion that puts it between Schoenberg's *Verklärte Nacht* (1899) and Strauss's *Metamorphosen* (1945) in more than just date. It concludes in an intensified statement of the dissonant Ex. 40*iii*, and a series of exultant, granitic chords (Ex. 41, massively developed from 37*vi*), like a proud statement of a personal harmonic credo, cadence into C and the coda.

The coda is a whirlwind even-quaver development of 40*i* and an exuberant orgy of triple- and quadruple-stopped iterations of the quartet's first chord, 37*i*; it finally issues in what is possibly the work's only tonally significant root-position C major

Ex. 41

---

34   Ex. 40*ii* may be traced back to *Mantra I*, where an early form of it is the continuation of the theme I have quoted as Ex. 25*a*; the chordal idea 40*iii* is similarly developed from a cadential formula in that work.

triad, *fff*, before a last upward scamper to a resounding octave C.

After some years' familiarity with the score, I feel justified in regarding *Quartetto Intimo* not only as John Foulds's masterpiece in the field of chamber music, but a masterpiece by any standards: one of the greatest string quartets by a British composer.

It seems inevitable that Foulds's work should be compared with its near-contemporaries, the late quartets of Frank Bridge, so recently reappraised and accorded eminence. Bridge's quartets are now much admired for their technical sophistication: Foulds seems to me at least his equal in that, and he goes beyond Bridge in the sheer range of sonority, texture and effects that he produces. The language is just as "modern", if that is your critical yardstick, though it inclines more in the direction of Bartók than the Second Viennese School. But the composers' creative characters are very different, as different as the souls of their respective instruments, viola and cello. I find myself preferring Foulds. His inner world may not be so somber, haunted, or emotionally ambivalent, but it is not therefore less interesting or complex. Nor is his romanticism a pose or his optimism shallow or easily-won; and the intensity of emotion and many-layered associations generated by the final climax of *Quartetto Intimo* makes most of his contemporaries sound rather thin-blooded. (Likewise his successors, though some reviewers of the 1981 record of Foulds's quartet were quick to claim it as a forerunner of Benjamin Britten's.)

This magnificent quartet was by no means Foulds's only attempt in the "serious" music field in the early 1930s. Among various other scores, two are worth singling out. *The Seven Ages*, a "monologue for baritone and orchestra" written in early January 1932 hard on the heels of the *Quartetto Intimo*, is a setting of Jacques's famous speech from Shakespeare's *As You Like It*:

> All the world's a stage,
> and all the men and women merely players.
> They have their exits and their entrances,
> And one man in his time plays many parts...

If we remember Foulds's long association with the theater, and his penchant for "playing many parts" in his music, it may well be that this monologue has an element of personal testament in it. The orchestral material is missing, but the work survives in Foulds's transcription for baritone and piano, which has been performed in recital and on radio with success in recent years. One veteran accompanist, while rehearsing for one such broadcast of it in 1984, described it to me as "an absolutely masterly conception".

The singer requires as much dramatic and histrionic talent as any actor to project the various stages of human life, which Foulds has crisply and vividly characterized in the monologue's seven sections. These are bound together by a characteristic "motto-theme" of fanfaring triads, closely related both to *Saint Joan*'s "voices" motif and the main theme of the modal essay "Egoistic". Into a brief compass of barely five minutes, the composer has compressed brilliantly evocative vignettes that range from the tumultuous battle-scene for the "Soldier... seeking the bubble reputation even in the cannon's mouth", through the wittily well-rounded harmonies for the full-bellied Justice and the pathetic comedy of the "lean and slippered Pantaloon", to the comfortless cold tremolos of the last scene, "sans teeth, sans eyes, sans taste, sans every thing". That so-familiar speech has found its ideal composer: surely no other setting has penetrated to its heart so economically, so entertainingly, or with such dramatic truth.

A very different, more whimsical creation is the five-movement *Puppet Ballet Suite*, for orchestra, completed in 1934. Like Maud MacCarthy, Foulds was interested in the possibiiities of puppet theater (and had written some music for at least two of her puppet plays); but as far as we know this ballet suite was conceived entirely as a concert work, not as extracts from any actual stage production.[35] No scenario has come to light, but in drafts and rejected titles for some of the movements it is clear that the composer's imagination was stimulated by the figures of the Italian *commedia dell'arte*—the puppets whose characters are depicted in the music include Pulcinella, Columbine, and Sgnarelle: indeed the opening Prelude was originally entitled "Grand Entrada—Sgnarelle and Retinue". In fact this Prelude was probably written last, to replace a longer one which Foulds turned into an independent work, his *Carnival* for orchestra.

Foulds views his puppets through slightly French-tinted spectacles, producing a score with some af-

---

35 As far as we know Foulds never did write a ballet to an existing scenario, but his short orchestral piece *Isles of Greece* was performed in London as a ballet in 1932, and there are sketches for an *Indian Ballet* from about 1936.

finities to Debussy's children's ballet *La Boîte à Joujoux* and also, in its occasional touches of archaism, to Ravel's *Le Tombeau de Couperin*. Broadly speaking the rumbustious, full-scored Prelude and concluding March (which wickedly parodies Elgar's *Pomp and Circumstance No. 4*) frame three gentler, more delicate dance movements. There are however many compositional subtleties going on beneath the apparently simple, uncomplicated surface, and a considerable amount of discreet cross-reference—perhaps indicating that certain themes were associated with particular characters in the ballet taking place in Foulds's mind. The second theme of the Prelude crops up again in the March, and an idea in the "Puppet Love Scene" (originally entitled *"Scène d'Amour"* and more than a little reminiscent of Fauré) is varied in the ensuing cool, statuesque *"Passepied"* (with its echoes of Ravel). But the beguiling second strain of the "Dream-Valse" is a self-quotation—of Ex. 37*a*, the heady waltz-motif from the *Quartetto Intimo*!

Foulds had several other projects under way during this period. A symphonic "ode for orchestra" entitled *Sappho*; his *Indian* and *Chinese* Suites; a set of *Pasquinades* for two pianos for Mark Hambourg and his daughter Michal; and probably the final set of "Music-Pictures", *Indian Scenes* for orchestra, were all begun between 1932 and 1934. But the other principal achievement of these years was the publication in 1934 of Foulds's book: *Music To-day: Its Heritage from the Past, and Legacy to the Future*.

Foulds was now in his early fifties, and had 40 years of practical music-making and consuming interest in contemporary developments to draw upon and communicate to his readers. *Music To-day* is a fascinating volume, therefore—too discursive for an artistic credo, but a compendium of much that Foulds had done and heard and thought and felt during his professional life. Like his best music, the book gives the impression of a mind open to all fruitful influences, unafraid of new experiences, brimming with ideas. If not an impeccable stylist, Foulds was a fluent, entertaining and characterful writer; and he is never boring. He discusses, with great gusto, public distrust of modern composers, the significance of musical mysticism and mystical inspiration, occult influences in composition, ancient Greek modes, Indian music, "atonality", quarter-tones and microtones, new techniques of orchestration, the therapeutic effects of music, the connection of music with color and light, musical aesthetics, music criticism, music and nationalism, music and sex, music and spirituality,

light as against serious music, the effect of the gramophone and radio, improvisation, various kinds of tuning, and the achievements of 30 or so contemporary composers. The whole leavened with many passing *aperçus* and anecdotes from his eventful musical life, and embellished with music examples drawn from a very wide range of past and contemporary music, including his own works, reproduced in his own beautiful script.

However one may agree or disagree with much that he says, *Music To-day* is one of the most stimulating books on music—music seen as part of, not apart from, life—in the English language. Foulds's "vignettes" of his contemporaries are fascinating, for what they tell us of the author as well as of his subjects. He clearly dislikes Schoenberg, but greatly respects him; Bartók he admires perhaps most of all among living composers; Scriabin most among the recently dead. He has trenchant and illuminating reactions to Hindemith, Honegger, and Sibelius; the essay on Busoni is both perceptive and moving. Foulds's sympathies are not unlimited: strangely, he draws the line at jazz—for rhythmic banality!—which makes one wonder what he might have said about the pop music of a later age. He is scathing about composers (such as Bantock, presumably, though Foulds does not mention him by name) who use generalized "Oriental effects" merely for coloristic purposes, without real knowledge of Eastern music. Maud MacCarthy, incidentally, disliked the book, as much of its material on inspiration, deva-influence and phono-therapy was derived directly from her own writings (as Foulds was forced to acknowledge in a postscript)—and, according to her, was garbled in the process. Nevertheless, *in toto*, the book is a sympathetic and revealing document, and highly enjoyable for the general reader.

Although Foulds had probably intended that *Music To-day* should help to bring his name before a wider public, and form an important stage in reviving his reputation, events conspired to change his plans. Not long after the book's publication, he left England for what proved to be the last time. In the course of her "phono-therapy" work, Maud MacCarthy had a chance meeting which led her to discover a laborer in the East End who possessed remarkable powers as a medium—William Coote, known to her and her circle as "The Boy". He proved to be extraordinarily receptive to inner-plane contacts (*devas*, in Maud's terms) who identified themselves as "The Brothers"—even to the extent of altering his facial features while he was in trance. Speaking freely through "The Boy", "The Brothers" began to communicate a prodigious amount of occult teaching; and they also began urging Maud to return to India to continue their work there.[36] Foulds accepted her guidance in this, not least because he had long wished to visit the subcontinent for himself; and he appears to have negotiated a contract with the publishers of *Music To-day* for a follow-up volume to

be devoted specifically to the music of India. On 25 April 1935, therefore, the Fouldses, their two children, and "The Boy" sailed for India. John Foulds's musical career was beginning its last phase, and already he was looking in new directions: the *Indian Suite*, an orchestral work based on authentic folk melodies, was completed on shipboard in Port Said before he ever saw the land to which his thoughts had so often travelled in *Music To-day*.

Above: John Foulds in the early 1930s, with his son
Patrick and his daughter Marybride. (John Foulds Estate.)
Facing: An advertising leaflet for Foulds's book *Music To-day:*
this leaflet seems to be the only place where the form
"Today" is used in the title. (Author's Collection.)

---

36   Since I am concerned here only with Foulds and his music, I omit the details of this strange story. Maud MacCarthy, writing as Swami Omananda Puri, recounted the whole much later in her autobiographical *The Boy and the Brothers* (Gollancz, 1959; 2nd ed. Neville Spearman, 1967).

MUSIC TODAY BY JOHN FOULDS

I N this book we offer to music-lovers of all types an interesting, not too technical, yet intensely stimulating and informative commentary upon almost every variety of music today.

Where experience is the only safe guide John Foulds speaks with the authority that results from participation in upwards of ten thousand public performances, either as conductor or performer.

His views on the orchestra result from intimate acquaintance with every branch of it and prolonged study with conductors of the eminence of Hallé, Richter, Nikisch, Mahler, Lamoureux and many more, in all the chief music-centres of Europe and America.

His commentaries on the many composers whose work is estimated are not those of a *dilettante*, however enthusiastic, nor of a musicologist, however learned, but of a composer whose own major works comprise opera, oratorio, concert-opera ; orchestral, choral and chamber-music ; songs, theatre music, etc.

Recherché subjects of today and perhaps tomorrow, such as Quarter-tones and A Greatly Extended Model System in which this composer is a pioneer, are also fully treated.

But it is not alone in these particularised fields that vital thoughts and helpfully critical views are proffered ; for in the realm of Aesthetic—of the evaluation of beauty—chaotic as our present attitude is, a definite and boldly constructive schematization is offered which appears to be of great value.

Whilst in such sections as those dealing with The Rationale of Inspiration ; The Ensouling of Music ; Colour and Music ; Its Therapeutic Effects and Mystical Inspiration ; veritable New Vistas are opened, and profound and helpful views formulated which are not to be found elsewhere in musical literature. A claim which a careful reading will be found to substantiate.

Copious musical illustrations enhance the clarity of the arguments, and no music-lover should delay in possessing himself of the unique and valuable knowledge offered him in *Music Today.*

CONTENTS.

PART ONE

BY WAY OF INTRODUCTION.

Apologia—A Clear Vantage-ground—Viewpoints— Musical Patriotism—More Intelligent Listeners— Occult and Overt—The Rationale of Inspiration— The most Important Aspect of Music Today.

PART TWO

A SURVEY OF MUSIC AT THE PRESENT TIME.

PART THREE

TOWARD A MUSICAL ÆSTHETIC.

PART FOUR

MODERN MASTERS AT WORK.

PART FIVE

NEW VISTAS.

IVOR NICHOLSON AND WATSON LIMITED, 44 ESSEX STREET STRAND W.C. 2

Part of the double sheet of Indian tunes described on p. 81. (John Foulds Estate.) It was almost certainly this occasion that Foulds recalled in his 7th "Orpheus Abroad" talk: "...up in the Punjab not long ago. A couple of shanai players and a drummer who had probably heard that we were a family of mad English who were actually interested in Indian music, sang and played for us on the verandah. I noted down the music at the time."

11. India (1935-39)

A few months after Foulds left England, Bernard Shaw sent him a postcard. It said simply "What the devil are you doing in India?". The move can hardly have aided Foulds's career and reputation, for out of sight was out of mind as far as the British musical establishment was concerned. A representative of Boosey & Hawkes who visited him in 1938 in Delhi wrote afterwards in terms of Foulds "hiding here" as if in a backwater. He knew this well, and must often have felt the frustration. "I feel an exile—I *am* an exile", he wrote to Maud from Calcutta in the last days of his life. Yet his last four years were full of activity, more than enough to absorb his energies.

He taught composition and piano. He gave some public lectures in Lahore. He contributed essays and music-criticism to Indian newspapers, speculating upon the possibilities of combining Eastern and Western musics. Always a keen amateur painter, he now produced beautiful watercolors and miniatures irradiated by the exotic light effects which he encounted on his travels. (Some of these still remain in the possession of his family.)

But as already mentioned, Foulds's primary professional reason for visiting India was to study its music at first hand; and he did, indeed, spend much time doing so in the northern part of the subcontinent, especially in Kashmir and Punjab, during 1935 and 1936. His studies continued in the following years, if less intensely; the last identifiable "gathering" being a group of snake charmer's tunes noted in Delhi in January 1939. Generally, to judge from the manuscripts that survive, Foulds jotted down songs and instrumental pieces that he heard on loose pages of music-paper—sometimes unidentified, more often furnished with date, place, and other details, and at first still feeling his way with the unfamiliar dialect names.

A double sheet headed "Shahnai Tunes", for example, is dated "On verandah Sep.18 35 Holta Punja India" and records ten tunes performed by Pahari men on two Shanai (an oboe-like instrument of conical bore), voice, and drum. Above one melody, which Foulds identifies rather doubtfully as "Artki jai ju(n)k", he notes that the pitch G is always quarter-sharp when descending but full sharp ascending; he also notates the basic drum rhythms only, adding "these alternate & there is an occasional quaver rest.

Also an occasional *ff* thump at odd beats." But it is clear that this one sheet has been re-used on at least three other occasions to notate tunes from other sources, and some of his own compositional sketches appear in odd spaces and edges. This continual re-use of available paper is typical of Foulds, especially in these last years, and it makes a systematic examination both of his original music and his folk-music studies very complicated. In any case, the proposed book for Nicholson & Watson was never written. Instead, he put what he learned to other, more immediately practical uses.

The India in which Foulds had arrived was a land caught up in a rising ferment of political change. That precise period of Indian history—in the final decade of British Imperial rule, just before World War II and Independence—has been chronicled in the novels of Paul Scott and given glamorized portrayal in recent television series such as *The Jewel in the Crown*. Foulds himself seems to have taken no active part in the politics of the time, although Maud is known to have met both M.A. Jinnah, the "father" of the future state of Pakistan, and Pandit Nehru. While continuing to pursue her occult work with "The Boy", Maud was active as a free-lance journalist under the pen-name of Tandra Devi, published a number of books, and eventually created and directed a successful hand-weaving business in Kashmir. The divergent paths of their careers meant that she and Foulds were quite often in different parts of the country.

This was also a time of revolutionary change in Indian music itself. Western influence—in the shape, especially, of the harmonium—was having a profound and, in Foulds's eyes, baleful effect. First introduced by Western families and missionaries, cheap to acquire and needing small skill to play, the portable harmonium was starting to oust traditional Indian instruments as the preferred accompaniment for songs. (This doubtful practice has continued to the present day, especially among singers feeling the need of strong melodic support.) Foulds felt keenly that the Western keyboard instrument, with its rigidly even-tempered scale, strait-jacketed the microtonally inflected traditional songs; and that by its very ubiquity it was ruining the Indians' ear for pitch, especially for the smaller intervals, the *srûtis*, of their own musical culture. Dubbing it the "Harm-

STATESMAN SATURDAY, MARCH 19, 1938.

COMBINED MUSIC

VICEROY'S PATRONAGE OF DELHI CONCERT

Under the patronage of Their Excellencies the Viceroy and Lady Linlithgow a unique concert of combined Indian and European music in aid of the King-Emperor's Anti-Tuberculosis Fund is to be given in the Regal Theatre, New Delhi, on Monday, March 28.

For what it is believed to be the first time in the history of music Indian and European musicians will take the stage together and will combine in music specially written for the occasion by Mr. John Foulds, the well-known composer, who is in India studying Indian music.

On one side of the stage will be a band of Indian artists who will be playing from manuscript instead of memory, while on the other side of the stage will be members of H.E. the Viceroy's orchestra, which is being lent for the occasion.

The concert is described as "an Indo-European Orchestral Concert". It will open with an Indo-European March, the first part being played by Europeans, the second by Indians, while the third and concluding movement will see both sets of musicians joining together proving that there is much in common between the two styles. Other examples in the programme of the links between Indian and European music will be Padraic Colum's "Mantle of Blue" and "Eileen Aroon," and Longfellow's translation of "Allah gives Light in Darkness."

Further Indian items include a Kashmiri Boat-song, an Afghanistan Dance, a Kashmiri Wedding Procession and a Pahari Melody (which will be played upon Indian instruments.)

Their Excellencies the Viceroy and Lady Linlithgow will attend the concert.

Tickets and plans of the seating accommodation yet unbooked may be seen at the Regal Theatre and at Messrs. Ramesh Ltd., in Connaught Place.

The announcement of one of Foulds's orchestral concerts, from the Indian newspaper *The Statesman*. (John Foulds Estate.)

John Foulds in Delhi, photographed at an A.I.R. reception, Christmas Day 1937. (John Foulds Estate.)

omnium",[37] he inveighed against its use (and against all crude, ill-conceived Westernization of Indian music) in articles in newspapers and music magazines.[38]

A secondary "revolution" taking place was that the traditionally wide variety of Indian plucked and bowed string instruments was narrowing. The esraj, sarod, dilruba, sarangi — and notably the noble, mellow-toned vina which Foulds himself had learned to play — were beginning to give way not only to the harmonium but to the sitar, which until this time had only been one among many instruments of its family, rather than, as we in the West now tend to consider it, "the" Indian instrument *par excellence*.[39] This trend, too, Foulds deplored, maintaining that the individual sonorities of the various instruments constituted a wealth of timbre as valuable as the European symphony orchestra.[40]

Early in 1937, Foulds secured the post of director of the embryonic European Music Department at the headquarters of All-India Radio in Delhi. Although an English-language station, A.I.R.'s music broadcasts were mainly Indian music for the indigenous population, who in the late 1930s numbered around 350,000,000 as against some 55,000 British residents. Here, once more, Foulds's organizational abilities were put to good use. His duties included giving solo piano recitals; accompanying most of the broadcast vocal recitals; providing music for comedy programs, plays and dance sessions; devising and introducing record recitals; and giving weekly talks on musical subjects.[41] Moreover, he set out to provide live orchestral music. With the support of A.I.R.'s dynamic Director, Lionel Fielden, he formed "John Foulds's Instrumental Combination", which gave its first broadcast (including two new Foulds works on Indian themes, *Kashmiri Boat Song* and *Kashmiri Wedding Procession*) on 18 March 1937. By 23 July it had

been expanded to "John Foulds's Chamber Orchestra", on which date he was able to give his recently-completed *Hebrew Rhapsody*; and by 17 October he had a full Radio Orchestra. From then on until 1939 he gave broadcast concerts from Delhi several times a week. The programs, inevitably, had to be fairly light in tone, but he performed a prodigious amount of "middlebrow" music of the 18th, 19th and 20th centuries, and was able to include much of his own output in that field. It appears that he established the basis of a library of Western music, writing to his various publisher acquaintances and soliciting donations of suitably easy-on-the-ear music from their catalogues. Boosey & Hawkes, for instance, sent him a large parcel in July 1937, including music by Haydn Wood, Armstrong Gibbs, Eric Coates, and similar repertoire.

During March-May 1937, Foulds gave on A.I.R. an ambitious series of twelve radio talks under the general title "Orpheus Abroad". All but one of the scripts have survived: they amount to a survey of the distinguishing characteristics of Oriental and Occidental music, and a tentative program for combining them into a viable artistic unity. From the music of India, he suggested, Western composers could learn precious lessons of melodic purity and rhythmic emancipation, new methods of tuning, the expressive use of micro-intervals, new timbres, and the value of meditation, timelessness, and spontaneous improvisation. And Indian music in its turn, if it was to develop rather than ossify or merely be corrupted, could capitalize upon its melodic riches by learning the Western arts of polyphony and ensemble playing. Illustrating the talks with examples played both by himself and by Indian musicians, he proposed the formation of ensembles that would comprise the whole range of traditional instruments, and which could play together as an "orchestra" while still

---

37 In an article "The Harm-omnium", published in *The Indian Listener* on 7 July 1938 which was later translated into Urdu, Hindi, Gujurati, and Marathi. As a direct result of this the A.I.R. (All-India Radio) Bombay station began to pay higher rates to musicians who sang without the aid of a harmonium!

38 See also Appendix, Nos. 6-9.

39 The vina is an instrument with a 3,000 year history. During 1986 the BBC's World Service broadcast an interview with an Indian vina-player who stated that he knew of only two other people on the subcontinent who still specialized in his instrument. This was undoubtedly an exaggeration; but it is reminiscent of Foulds's own testimony (in a 1937 A.I.R. broadcast talk, the fourth in the series "Orpheus Abroad") that "one of the things that has been rather depressing me since reaching India has been to notice how rarely one can meet a vina player — and to hear upon all sides that it is dying out."

40 See Appendix, No. 8: "An Indo-European Orchestra".

41 He was even found, on 15 February 1938, providing a running commentary on the first All India Cattle Show!

The third movement of the *Indian Suite*, seen here complete in Foulds's manuscript "piano conductor" reduction. (Copyright © 1982 by Musica Viva and the Estate of John Foulds.)

retaining the integrity of each particular râg by restricting its harmonies entirely to the pitches of that râg. This was a clear development of Foulds's own creative practice in the *Essays in the Modes*. But he went further, proposing as the final goal an "Indo-European Orchestra" that would combine European and Indian instruments to achieve an unparalleled range and flexibility of timbre.[42]

Foulds's own compositional endeavors continued unabated throughout his "Indian" years. At first in two streams: the further refinement of his personal "European" language at its most highly developed, in successor-compositions to the *Dynamic Triptych* and *Quartetto Intimo*; and (secondly) a series of works more closely based on Indian folk sources. A third stream, that of his "light music", was reduced to a mere trickle in 1935-36 (though it probably never dried up entirely); but in 1937, as soon as Foulds obtained his A.I.R. appointment, it started flowing with renewed strength as he began to create a new repertoire for his at first quite limited orchestral resources. There was to be a fourth stream before the end — of music created especially for Indian instruments — but more will be said of that in the proper place.

The first three types at times coalesce, making only the roughest categorization possible. For example, the Indian influence invades some of the lighter music, and also has effects on the harmonic and melodic character of some of the overtly "European-classical" scores. Similarly the distinction between "light" and "serious" is in places very finely drawn. The orchestral *Chinese Suite*, Op. 95, for example, is on one level a continuation of the picturesque series of *genre* suites begun long ago with the *Holiday Sketches* and *Suite Française* — yet its scintillating, percussive, hard-edge scoring and its sonorous unsentimental pentatonic writing (so different from the pentatony of the *Keltic Suite*) bring it close to the intellectual world of Foulds's more abstract and sophisticated orchestral pieces.

Similarly, the short "oriental nocturne" for small orchestra with obbligato violin and cello which Foulds eventually titled *An Arabian Night* seems altogether too intense in its expression to be merely for entertainment. Its inspiration is undoubtedly In-

dian — it originated in sketches for a work called *Shalimar*, intended as one in a whole series of brief orchestral movements with the collective title of *Nature-Notes*. Completed members of the sequence included the *Kashmiri Boat Song (on the Jhelum River)* and the *Kashmiri Wedding Procession*, based upon tunes Foulds himself had noted down "in the field". An equally evocative little composition is the *Song of Ram Dass*, founded on a tune in Indian style provided by Maud MacCarthy — a tranced Adagio with something of the haunting exotic quality of the slow movement of Rodrigo's *Concierto de Aranjuez*.

The five-movement *Indian Suite*, although completed before Foulds arrived in India, really belongs to this period too, and indeed sets some of the pattern for his treatment of Indian materials. The title page of the manuscript proclaims that it is "Based on authentic Indian Melodies from the collection of Maud MacCarthy" — her still-unpublished collection made in the first decade of the century. The layout of the suite is to some extent symmetrical: its comparatively elaborate and fully-scored first and last movements, both based on classical Hindu songs from South India, enclose two shorter, scherzo-like movements which themselves flank a brief, still central slow movement for only a small number of instruments.

The first movement is founded on *"Bhavanutha"*, a song to Shri Rama composed in the early 19th century by the Indian saint-musician Tyagara (c.1800-1850). The tune (Ex. 42, page 86) was a favorite of Maud's which she often sang in her lecture-recitals, and Foulds had apparently produced at least one earlier instrumental version of it, although this is lost. In the Suite he builds upon it an orchestral movement striking for the respect with which it treats the song material. The bareness, or indeed absence, of harmony except that derived from the tune itself results in a sound-world quite different from conventional "Orientalism" — to contemporary ears it may display curious affinities with the work of the Armenian-American composer Alan Hovhaness. Foulds compensates for the harmonic austerity with brilliant and subtle orchestral coloring and an unusually independent rhythmic pulse, often with vigorous tenor-

---

42 Strictly speaking, Foulds seems to have used the term "Indo-European Orchestra" in two different senses depending on the context. The purely Indian ensemble was also sometimes referred to as an "Indo-European Orchestra" on the grounds that it was an orchestra of Indian instruments, playing music Indian in derivation but presented according to European principles. See "An Indo-European Orchestra", Appendix, No. 8.

Ex. 42

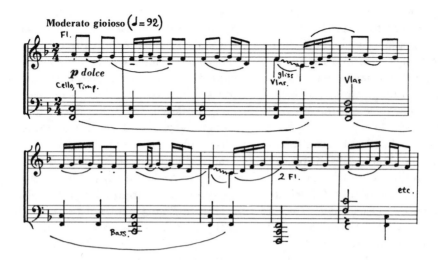

drum writing accented on unexpected beats of the bar.

By contrast, the central "Love Song of Krishna and Radha" (after a Hindu folksong) is a tranced, ecstatic miniature, a floridly decorated duet for clarinet and cor anglais reinforced by bare string harmonies and a few horn and harp notes. The other movements are all quicker-moving, in fact full of rude energy, especially in the raucous, *Allegro vigoroso* second, a gleeful scherzo on a theatrical song from Bombay Presidency. Foulds in this suite succeeds in his intention (declared in a manuscript program-note[43]) of evoking an India that is not so much exotic and mystical, as worldly and affable—a living landscape, peopled with very human figures entwined in an ambience of the melodic riches that have accumulated over the course of centuries.

In India Foulds never commanded the orchestral resources that would have allowed him to perform scores as elaborate and sophisticated as the *Indian* and *Chinese* Suites. His hopes of hearing his even more ambitiously conceived projects—among which were a new string quartet, and several orchestral compositions of at least quasi-symphonic scope—

were clearly even slimmer. Yet there are abundant indications that he persisted with them nonetheless.

But in attempting to evaluate Foulds's achievement in these final years we face a profound puzzle regarding the copious manuscript material that has come down to us. In a notebook which he entitled "Detailed Bibliography, Book I. Major Works"—and which from internal evidence must have been prepared in March-April 1939 in the final weeks of his life—Foulds lists, as if complete, his *Indian Scenes (Music-Pictures Group IX)* for orchestra, Op. 90; the *Pasquinades* for two pianos, Op. 93; *Deva-Music*, a symphonic diptych for orchestra, Op. 94; a string quartet (his tenth), *Quartetto Geniale*, Op. 97; *Pasquinades Symphoniques* for orchestra, Op. 98; *A Symphony of East and West* for European symphony orchestra and Indian ensemble, Op. 100; and two *Symphonic Studies* for string orchestra, Op. 101.[44] The last-named, which is also the most recent, of these items was certainly complete by 26 September 1938, when its dedicatee, the conductor Walter Kaufmann, acknowledged receipt of the score in a letter which still exists; and Kaufmann conducted the work with the Bombay Symphonic Strings on 10 March 1939,

---

43   See Appendix, No. 7: *"Indian Suite*: Program Note (1935)".

44   This "Detailed Bibliography" is a highly selective document. It should be noted that it also lists as complete the *Indian Garland* for piano, Op. 96 and a suite for unknown forces entitled *Poetical Reveries*, Op. 99. All material for the latter is missing; for the former only a couple of sketches have so far come to light. Wholly *un*mentioned are the *Chinese Suite*, Op. 95 (complete and extant); the *Sinfonietta* (or 3 *Pasquinades*) for orchestra, Op. 37 (of this period despite the misleading opus number, and extant in full score although not quite complete); and the Symphonic Ode for orchestra *Sappho*, Op. 91 (possibly never completed but in any case missing *in toto*). We must conclude that Foulds did not consider any of these among his "major works".

afterwards returning the score and parts (according to his recollection many years later) either to Foulds or to A.I.R. But not one note of *Symphonic Studies*— not even the smallest sketch — has come to light so far. As for the rest, with one exception they are represented in the surviving materials that descended eventually to Foulds's daughter only by a couple of tiny sketches (*Indian Scenes*,[45] *Symphony of East and West*) or by a complex tangle of sketches and drafts, seriously incomplete in some respects, and lacking any kind of final score. The exception is the *Pasquinades Symphoniques*, for which sketches, drafts, *and* score all survive — only the score itself proves not to have been finished, although it establishes the vast bulk of the composition in definitive form.

What are we to make of this? There seem to be at least three alternative explanations.

(1) We can choose to believe that the manuscript materials so far located (which came to Maud from A.I.R. in Delhi after Foulds's death) are all that ever existed — that he did not, in fact, complete these evidently major works. But the completion and performance of the *Symphonic Studies*, chronologically the last of them all, is well documented, and thus seriously undermines such a conclusion with respect to the others.

(2) Perhaps the items were completed but the final scores were later destroyed. Maud remained in India until the late 1950s: there is a family tradition that some (unspecified) Foulds Mss. were eaten by rats and white ants during those twenty-odd years.[46] The story appears to be well-founded — on the cover of one well-gnawed printed copy of the *World Requiem* vocal score, Maud has written: "Eaten by rats!" But if these vermin disposed only of the final scores of Foulds's most ambitious Western-style pieces, not the contemporary light and Indian-influenced music, they surely displayed extraordinary discrimination

in their diet — though this may, indeed, account for some of the unfortunate gaps in the sketch-material.

(3) It seems to me rather more probable that these important later scores are missing precisely because they *were* finished, and Foulds had no need any longer to associate them with their sketch-materials (and thus, conversely, that the *Pasquinades Symphoniques* full score is extant precisely because it remained to be completed). It follows that the missing scores could have been separated from the bulk of his musical papers, possibly at the very end of his life; and I shall say a little more about this question when we arrive at that stage in the narrative.

Whatever the explanation, the upshot is that we are seriously hampered in attempting a discussion of the final stages of Foulds's musical evolution in precisely those genres which he set greatest store by. Yet the task must be attempted.

We should note, as preamble, that until this period Foulds had shown singularly little interest in the idea of the Symphony as a form suited to his musical impulses. The first instance of his employing the term in a title does not occur till 1930 — and then only in connection with his transcription of Schubert's *Death and the Maiden* quartet "as a symphony" for orchestra. In *Music To-day* he speaks of symphonic form as "closed", "an outworn matrix which should be outgrown" (p.297).[47] Yet suddenly in his last five years there seems to be a reversal of attitude. *Sappho*, a work that is wholly missing, was described as a "Symphonic Ode" for orchestra. The (largely missing) first movement of the two-piano *Pasquinades* is entitled "*Symphonie*"; *Deva-Music* is a "Symphonic Diptych", or in some sketches "Symphonic Pieces"; *Pasquinades Symphoniques* not only has the symphonic idea in its main title but was originally entitled *Pasquinades: A Symphony in 3 Movements*; and Foulds's "Bibliography" of major works concludes with a *Symphony* of East and West and a set of *Symphonic Studies*.

---

45 However, there is also a highly detailed program-note for *Indian Scenes*, full of descriptions of scoring which strongly suggest that this final suite of "Music-Pictures" was in fact completed. The note also indicates that the bulk of the work was composed in India, and that it was comparable in scope to the *Indian* and *Chinese* Suites, being based — like the latter — on "original melodies couched in the [Oriental] idiom", but making use of *râgâs* and *talas*.

46 According to the recollection of Foulds's son Patrick, two manuscripts which definitely did succumb to the depredations of ants were the *Masse-Mensch* music and the orchestral *Schubert Fantasie* pot-pourri.

47 As a parallel observation, it could be noted that Foulds — though a fluent and masterful contrapuntist when the occasion arises — makes comparatively little use of the stricter contrapuntal forms of fugue and canon, at any time in his career after his very earliest productions. (Among the few exceptions we should note the fugal Modal Essay "Introversive", and the canonic textures of the central part of *Mantra I*.) He seems greatly to prefer a more plastic, freely-flowing polyphonic texture, and indeed he criticizes Hindemith in *Music To-day* (p.262) for having recourse to the "everlasting device" of strict canon, an "old bottle" into which he was attempting to pour "new wine". Foulds does, however, quite often favor the old contrapuntal technique of inventions on a ground bass — though again he seldom writes anything resembling a strict chaconne or passacaglia (there we should cite *Mantra III* as an important exception).

A page from Foulds's "full-score sketch" of *Deva-Music*. (John Foulds Estate.)

Whatever this nomenclature means in detail, in general it implies a late rapprochement with the ideal of large-scale classical symphonic architecture, although this ideal was clearly to be approached from a variety of non-classical angles.

The sketches and drafts of *Deva-Music* are especially tantalizing. No material whatever seems to have survived for the first movement, "Of Gandharvas", prompting the speculation that Foulds had no need to sketch any: it could have been an expanded and fully orchestrated version of his earlier *Gandharva-Music*. But the material for the second movement, "Of Apsaras" (Gandharvas and Apsaras are respectively the male and female forms of the familiar nature-spirits, the Devas, "whose being is music", according to Hindu mythology) is extensive, and include ten pages of rough-draft full score showing music in Foulds's most luminously ecstatic style, apparently a direct descendant of the slow movements of the *Mantras* and *Dynamic Triptych*. Further sketches suggest that the movement was eventually to evanesce into a shimmering halo of free-floating multi-polyphony, each individual strand growing organically onward with no phrase-repetition, in a realization of the idea of "endless melody" (the phrase is written in the sketches).[48]

The string quartet listed in the "Detailed Bibliography" — *Quartetto Geniale* — like the *Quartetto Intimo*, was planned in five movements, the fourth of them a "Colloquy", and the "Pasquinade" scherzo this time coming second. No sketches for the "Colloquy" seem to exist, and only a couple for the scherzo and finale; but with the opening *Animato Assai* and the *Lento Quieto* third movement we are more fortunate. For the latter, indeed, there is a complete sequence of materials extending from a first jotting of its opening theme (against which Foulds has written the words "Intimate melodies from the Beyond"), through several sketches, a pencil draft, and a complete rough copy in ink. On the basis of this the movement was performed and recorded in 1981, and proved to be one of the composer's most beautiful and affecting creations, in a simpler, more direct and yet more refined style than the previous quartet. It is a serene nocturne in A major, with just a hint of strangeness beneath its profound calm, and a sense of veiled anguish at the climax, which finally fades into silence in ethereal harmonics. An Indian tincture is obvious in the intervallic characteristics of the main theme (Ex.43, page 90), but this is subtle, not overt—it has been completely absorbed into the bloodstream of Foulds's own compositional personality.

The second theme, characteristically and mysteriously harmonized in free-floating triads, has a strangely hymn-like character: one reviewer of the 1981 recording likened it to "From Greenland's Icy Mountains". It is indeed a hymn-tune, but one of Foulds's own — he derived the melody from a choric hymn sketched a decade before in his unfinished music for *Veils*, set to the words "This is the Book of God..."

There are only a couple of pages of a comparable ink draft of the *Animato assai* first movement: but a performing score put together by the present writer from the copious and much-disordered sketches in 1986 revealed an ebullient, rhythmically powerful, and witty sonata-design fully comparable with anything in *Quartetto Intimo*. Unfortunately the sketches only extend part-way into the recapitulation section, revealing nothing of the intended coda.

With the *Pasquinades Symphoniques* we possess Foulds's final, though unfinished, full score of the work—perhaps the most substantial and impressive survival among the music of his last years. The composition is a three-movement symphony in all but its eventual name, but a symphony of a rather unusual kind, conceived as a series of commentaries on aspects of symphonic form. The titles of the individual movements—"Classical", "Romantic", "Modernist"—do not denote limitations of style: all three are in Foulds's ripest "Western-modern" idiom. Rather, perhaps, they indicate a certain cool, almost ironic (but not overtly humorous or parodic) handling of the basic material.

The "Modernist" finale, with its pealing ostinato of bells and horns and simultaneous augmentation and diminution of themes, suggests an attitude reflecting geometrical or even Cubist ideas in art—as does its overall form. Although the manuscript, sadly, breaks off abruptly in the middle of a page, there are sketches for part of the continuation and a note to the effect that the movement is to be an exact palindrome.

---

48 This idea was also somehow associated in Foulds's mind with that of modern music learning anew from Palestrina, a composer whom he treats of in *Music To-day* with enormous reverence: "the loftiest, grandest, and purest composer the Western world has ever known.... If you are willing, as so many of you rightly are, to take the *Wohltemperirte Klavier* for your daily bread, take the *Madrigali Spirituali* as your consecrated wine" (pp.175-76). Anticipating our contemporary vogue for Early Music, Foulds called for **[continued]**

Ex. 43

The "Romantic" slow movement is a brilliant exercise in seductive textures, spicy harmonies, and passionate, arching melody over a broad ternary song-form, wearing its heart on its sleeve as blatantly and beguilingly as the slow movement of *Dynamic Triptych*. But the "Classical" first movement is Foulds's largest and most impressive sonata structure.

Here again we find a mingling of different tonal resources, but with a new structural logic and symphonic sweep in their deployment. The opening, building up broadly and mysteriously, solely on the three tones of this rushing ostinato figure (Ex. 44)—

—has an oddly Brucknerian flavor, which is not dispelled by the emergence of the first main theme on trombones and tuba (see Ex. 45, below). Ex. 45 clear-

---

Footnote 48 *(continued)*

a pre-Bach revival. Bach has "come again" of late, and we should be grateful for that, but a closer study of, and assimilation of the methods of those composers whose works and tendencies were epitomized by Palestrina, would do much toward clearing the ground for the next step forward.... A composer may yet arise who will vision a new musical world through the inspiration of Palestrina. (pp.52-53)

Elsewhere (p.283) he speaks of Palestrina as under "constant devic influence"—a suggestive phrase in the context of *Deva-Music*. The sketches for the latter part of this work show Foulds modelling one of his "Endless melodies" as a Cantus Firmus closely derived from a melody in Palestrina's *"Ecce Sacerdos Magnus"*. In the margin he has pencilled the following note:

Free melodies of "form" so-called, as modern poets are freeing poetry of rhyme & lilt. I.e. a melody proceeds onward all the time from beginning to end. It is balanced of course but subtly, not obviously, as are all Classical melodies (since Bach). This is one aspect of the true "back to Palestrina" idea.

ly derives from Ex. 44, with its characteristic fourths, but the very "unclassical" whole-tone segment of Ex. 45's third and fourth bars brings soon enough some thoroughgoing whole-tone writing and a pervasive harmonic instability. The second subject is apparently simple and diatonic, but Foulds is able to combine it with his conjunct-triad harmonies over a 12-note bass (formed from the fourths of Exx. 44 and 45) to produce such passages as Ex. 46 (below).

The upper line here is in fact the second subject of *Quartetto Intimo*'s finale, reshaped for orchestral forces. This theme extends into a magnificently polyphonic paragraph with an almost Elgarian warmth of expression. There is a powerful and complex development (actually cast as a large-scale variation of the exposition — a similar practice is employed in the *Quartetto Geniale*) and in the recapitulation the subjects return in reverse order. Ex. 45, now played in multiple diminution as a thrilling trumpet and horn fanfare, drives the movement to its highly dissonant climax; after which the music fades away on rich brass harmony and the Brucknerian ostinato in shimmering orchestration. This virtuoso symphonic work makes one regret the disappearance of Foulds's other late compositions all the more keenly.

* * *

By early 1938, under the auspices of All-India Radio, John Foulds was beginning to make some progress towards his goal of an "Indo-European" musical fusion. He had begun to work with Indian instrumentalists very early in 1937, in connection with the "Orpheus Abroad" talks; and he developed

these contacts by persuading them to take part with European orchestras and to adapt to Western practices of notation and ensemble-playing. A photograph, dated "Delhi 1937", shows him with the "Nucleus of Indo-European Orchestra" — seven musicians including Foulds himself, who holds a vina. So he must have been trying out his ideas before the end of that year. The first public realization of them, however, seems to have been on 28 March 1938, when Foulds conducted an "Indo-European Orchestral Concert" at the Regal Theatre in Delhi before a large audience including the Viceroy himself. In this concert his A.I.R. radio orchestra was augmented by a small ensemble of Indian instruments. The program consisted entirely of music composed or arranged by Foulds. The symphony orchestra (and a succession of vocal soloists) naturally had the lion's share of the repertoire, but there were solo spots for the Indian ensemble playing some short pieces he had based on folk-melodies (these included specially-arranged versions of the *Kashmiri Boat Song* and *Kashmiri Wedding Procession*). And at the beginning and end of the concert came two performances of a new work for combined orchestra and ensemble, the *Grand Durbar March*.

Although a minor piece by the standards of those discussed earlier in this chapter, this *March* has some importance as a first tentative step towards ideas which were presumably realized on a much more elaborate scale in the *Symphony of East and West*. It is laid out in a conventional march-with-trio form, and the march sections represent, or perhaps even send up, the music of Europe with what seems a zestful excess of swagger. For the concert Foulds had been able

Ex. 45

Ex. 46

In Aid of Her Excellency The Marchioness of Linlithgow's
Appeal for the King-Emperor's Anti-Tuberculosis Fund

Indo-European Orchestral Concert

ARTISTS :

XENIA PATERSON
EILEEN LEETE
GRACE NOCKELS
F. F. C. EDMONDS

An INDO-EUROPEAN ORCHESTRA of
upwards of 50 performers including
His Excellency the Viceroy's Orchestra
(by kind permission of His Excellency)
Leader : Paul Strauss

IN A

PROGRAMME

of compositions by

JOHN FOULDS

(Conducted by the Composer)

UNDER THE DISTINGUISHED PATRONAGE

of Their Excellencies

The Viceroy & the Marchioness of Linlithgow

AN

INDO-EUROPEAN
ORCHESTRAL CONCERT

Conductor

JOHN FOULDS

Programme

Monday March 28

Regal Theatre

9-30 p.m.

Part of the program of the "Indo-European Orchestral Concert" given 28 March 1938. (John Foulds Estate.)

John Foulds in Delhi, 1937 with the "Nucleus of Indo-European Orchestra". From left to right, the instrumentalists are playing a sarangi, a bamboo flute, a sitar, an esraj, a saranda, and a tambura; Foulds himself, at extreme right, holds a vina. (Estate of John Foulds.)

The last known photograph of John Foulds, on a boat in a river in Kashmir, late 1938. (John Foulds Estate.)

Ex. 47

to suborn some musicians from the Viceroy's own band, so the march features elaborate rhetorical fanfares for no fewer than six trumpets. But this Western brashness subsides into a quietly hypnotic trio, in which the Indian instruments emerged[49] with a plangent, repetitive dance-melody (in the râgâ Pilu) from the Punjab. This fades: the fanfares return, and with them the "European" march with its echoes of Meyerbeer, Elgar, and the Grenadier Guards. But at the climax Foulds, by deft compositional sleight-of-hand, superimposes the Indian melody upon the march-tune in a cheerfully dissonant, skirling polytonal melange.

Reviewers of the concert in the local press were somewhat bewildered: it was generally felt that the Indian ensemble had tended to be swamped by the symphony orchestra. But the pieces for the ensemble alone were better received. The critic of the *Lahore Monday Morning* praised Foulds's version of a *Pahari Hill Tune* as

> entrancingly arranged... heard in Kangra Valley played by a mule driver as he walked briskly beside his mule.... It was exquisite and brought down the house.... This is the kind of music India must develop—to add to her rich melodic art, but not, of course, to supersede it.

Foulds now pursued his idea of an enlarged Indian ensemble that could function as an "orchestra" in its own right. He must have spent much of the summer of 1938 in the organization of this enterprise; and considering that he was attempting to create two musical traditions quite new to Indian musicians—the discipline of ensemble playing, and the ability to read musical notation—he was undertaking a herculean task. He must have had to evaluate many musicians for the personnel of the ensemble, and every one of those he eventually chose he personally, with great patience, taught the principles and practice of Western notation. This was vital because the pieces he was writing for the ensemble were *composed*, not improvised—although at certain "cadenza-like" points improvisation was allowed for.

Finally in September 1938 this "Indo-European Orchestra" (of Indian instruments blended in European ensemble style) began to broadcast on the Delhi station of A.I.R., and was featured regularly each week until March 1939. The basic complement seems to have been eight instruments—bamboo flute, vina, esraj, sitar, sarangi, saranda, tabla, and tambura—but it expanded on occasion to about a dozen with the addition of ghungharu, sarod, dilruba, jiltarang, and occasional doubling of one or more instruments.[50]

His bowed instruments were the Esraj (the long-necked fiddle of Bengal), Dilruba (a fretted fiddle with a skin soundtable, found throughout North India), Sarangi (a short-necked fiddle used in Hindustani classical râgâ music), and the Saranda (which I take to be the instrument more commonly called the *Surinda*, a double-chested fiddle from West Rajasthan). The plucked instruments were the Sitar, Sarod (double-chested fretless lute from North India), Tambura (a long-necked drone lute, occuring in various sizes), and the Vina. This last-named term has historically sometimes been extended to include practically all Indian instruments of lute form, but photographs show Foulds holding an instrument that is almost certainly the large long-necked plucked lute of Southern Indian classical music, the *sarasvati vina*. Percussion was provided basically by the Tabla (the common small tuned hand-drums of North and Central India), augmented at times by the Jaltarang (a percussion instrument of bowls of water played with bamboo sticks), and an instrument which Foulds calls the "Gunghuaru", by which I conjecture he meant the *ghunghru* or small metal ankle-bells of Rajasthan, usually employed by dancers.

The repertoire—entirely provided by Foulds—consisted mostly of arrangements of folk-tunes, plus some short original compositions for the ensemble, and a few transcriptions of European music. (It is rather droll to notice that this latter category included an arrangement of Rimsky-Korsakov's *Chant*

---

49 The instrumental parts for the Indian instruments have not survived, but they are cued into some of the Western instruments to allow performance by European orchestra only; and in this form the *Grand Durbar March* has been successfully revived at some concerts in the 1980s, by Raymond Head, for instance in a concert in July 1987 to mark the opening of the Clive Museum at Powis Castle in Wales.

50 I have adopted Foulds's spellings of these instruments' names, although in one or two cases his chosen forms now cause slight confusion in identifying the precise instrument he intended. As he had forecast in his "Orpheus Abroad" radio lectures, the ensemble consisted of families of bowed and plucked instruments, supported by a small amount of percussion and wind—in practice, however, the only wind instrument used was the bamboo flute, although in "Orpheus Abroad" he hoped to make use of "one of those long trumpet-like brass instruments... from Nepal I think", and the Shanai.

Hindou.) In all, 27 items have been identified. However, no final scores for these pieces have come to light, although in this case it must be doubted whether any such scores existed. With a tight broadcasting schedule to meet, Foulds almost certainly worked straight from drafts into the realization of individual parts for the players (a practice he was familiar with from his theater-music experience). The extant materials among Foulds's papers are scattered individual parts, rough draft scores (mainly unfinished), and sketches—enough to reconstruct two or three pieces at most from the broadcast repertoire. Enough survives, certainly, to show that at this stage he was still composing with the limitations of his players very much in mind—the textures remain fairly simple, the polyphony tentative, the bass instruments generally providing only a drone. Some idea of the result may be gained from Ex. 47 (p. 94), an untitled eight-bar fragment which I have fair-copied from Foulds's roughly-pencilled manuscript: a comparatively rare example of his writing for the ensemble in a "full score" layout. It must be stressed, in any case, that these little compositions were in Foulds's eyes merely a first step: to acclimatize Indian players to an idiom and to present Indian and European listeners with an idea.

Certainly the *sound* of the ensemble must have been remarkable; and there is ample evidence that its broadcasts were extremely popular. Foulds's papers include a large file of extracts from letters received from listeners, all uniformly laudatory. Interestingly enough, the vast majority were from Indians. Despite this success, it seems likely that Foulds's activities with the ensemble ran into some opposition at the Delhi station. A revealing side-light upon the conditions under which he was operating is cast by a short note he scribbled on some blank staves of the draft for an original composition for the ensemble entitled *Golconda*.   The note is headed "ONE WEEK WOE I-E"....

Sunday. Studio repairs after rehearsal starts.
Monday. Vina car "sent somewhere else".
Tuesday. Sarangi string breaks. "Been asking
　　for strings 6 days".

Wednesday. Tambura "being used for audition".
Thursday. Sarangi rude to A.A.A. ?sack him?
Friday. Studio still occupied by Drama rehearsal at 11.10. May be free at 11.35. Transmission Indian 12.15.
Saturday. Car not available for Mr. Ramchandra.
Sunday. Dilruba accident. Sitar summoned to court: no rehearsal.
Monday. Back from Kashmir. Ramchandra accident. No Vina.

("A.A.A." is unidentified—in fact the names of most of the Indian players Foulds worked with are now unknown.[51] Some lists survive in his handwriting, but they seem to date from the period when he was auditioning for the ensemble, rather than when it had become established.)

Although the "Indo-European" project had consumed much of Foulds's energies, there are some indications that he felt it necessary to keep his career options open. "The scope in India is absurdly small" he wrote to Ralph Hawkes on 25 November 1938, "and, so far as I can see, not likely to increase much, if at all. Political, financial, racial, and cultural reactions all combine to cause this state of affairs." In the same letter he askes if Hawkes might be interested in publishing some of his arrangements of Indian material. If there was any response to the request, it was negative: but he seems to have petitioned several London publishers on this subject at the same time, and had already succeeded in selling the *Kashmiri Boat Song* to Paxton's; and in September 1938 managed to interest Hinrichsen Edition in a suite for piano and small orchestra. Several sketches and drafts survive for portions of this latter work, *Indian Melodies*, which was to have been his Op. 102.

(In view of this renewed contact with British publishers—Hinrichsen Edition is perhaps especially significant, since they had never published anything of Foulds's before—I consider it a possibility that he may have sent the completed scores of the missing "major works" to England for consideration. As yet, however, no documentation has been discovered that would confirm this theory.)

---

51 "Mr. Ramchandra", however, is likely to have been the same "Mr. Ramchandra from Madras—a deep student of the art and an artist on the *vina*" who provided some of the musical examples for Foulds's fifth "Orpheus Abroad" talk in early 1937. As already noted, Foulds also played the vina; it is not clear whether he generally conducted the ensemble or played with them when Ramchandra was unavailable. It is possible that on a few occasions both of them played, as in the tenth "Orpheus Abroad" talk (see Appendix) Foulds foresees a need for a second vina, and two surviving photographs of the ensemble broadcasting from a studio show Foulds conducting, with a vina at his feet.

Also towards the end of 1938, Foulds was again in communication with George Bernard Shaw. It was proposed to make a film version of *Saint Joan*; and Shaw was adamant that only Foulds could compose the music for it. He proposed to Foulds that he use the substance of the original theater score, but expanding and weaving it into a continuous symphonic tapestry, with new elements added. Foulds was fired with enthusiasm; but negotiations for the film dragged on and on, and a filmed *Saint Joan* was not to appear until the 1940s. By then, it was too late.

So successful had Foulds been at All-India Radio in Delhi that on 15 April 1939 he was transferred to take charge of the newly-opened Calcutta station and perform similar organizational miracles there. Maud, in Lahore at the time, had forebodings and warned him not to accept this post, although it was a promotion. Nonetheless he went to Calcutta. But he was destined to serve there for only a few days. The end came very suddenly in the small hours of 25 April. Maud MacCarthy described the circumstances in a letter to Ralph Hawkes from her ashram in Srinagar, Kashmir dated 17 May 1939:

> No-one knows how he had contracted cholera. He had gone to Calcutta in the awful heat, against the wishes of his family including myself. We all feared for his health and even life there. He took a small flat close to All India Radio, & within three days of moving into it, he died. He had been well all day, & in the evening he was met by the Chief at All India Radio 9.30 p.m. He was feeling sick, & asked to leave to go home. One of the gentlemen there took him back in his car. On the way he chatted happily & seemed quite himself again. He had told the Chief not to bother to come round after closing down, & the Chief very reluctantly decided not to go. So my husband was alone in his flat. There was not even a servant there. At 2.a.m. a lady in the next flat heard his cries. When she reached him he was in the last stage of Asiatic Cholera. He was taken to hospital & died there after a few hours.
>
> I was in Lahore with our family. No friend was near him....
>
> The shock of this has been almost too much for us. My husband had been giving so much happiness to hundreds of thousands of listeners.... especially it was felt that at Calcutta he would be able to do better with his Indo-European Orchestra (the dearest wish of his heart) than it had been possible, under severe departmental restrictions, to do at Delhi.... Really one might say that he laid his life down for his dream of creating that orchestra along certain lines which his great sympathy with *genuine* Indian music & his able musicianship combined, made him so uniquely fitted to follow.

25 April 1939 was the eighteenth anniversary of the completion of the *World Requiem*. Foulds was 58 years of age. He was buried that day in the English Cemetery above Calcutta. His manuscripts and other effects were sent to Maud from Delhi, but she had no way of knowing if they were complete—and there seems to be no way, at this distance in time, of determining whether the materials Foulds would have taken with him to Calcutta (which just might have included the missing full scores of his last major compositions) were ever reunited with them. All she could do was keep the music safe, throughout the many years she remained in India, most of the time in severely straitened circumstances.

The Second World War was at hand. Patrick Foulds, who had shown early promise as an artist, went into the army instead, eventually rising to the rank of Major. Marybride Foulds remained some years more with her mother before embarking on a globe-trotting existence that took her to Fiji, New York, back to England, and finally to the West coast of Scotland. Maud continued working with "The Boy", whom she married in 1943, and later became a sannyasa of the Puri Order of Vedanta under the name Swami Omananda: the first woman ever admitted to full sannyasa rank. In the late 1950s, now widowed for a second time, she returned to Britain, where she published two books of occult teachings; and died in the Isle of Man in 1967. By this time John Foulds was almost entirely forgotten in his own country, and his music had descended into the obscurity of silence. His manuscripts, which Maud had kept safe against a possible revival of interest in his music, were bequeathed to her daughter Marybride, who preserved them in her turn while attempting to codify and publish more of her mother's work. Had they not done so, it is highly likely that Foulds would have remained forgotten—and his distinctive achievement at worst unnoticed, at best misunderstood.

12. New Beginnings

No new possibilities! Think of that....
— *Music To-day*

When I came to write the concluding section of the previous version of this book in 1975, I felt it incumbent upon me to be circumspect and tentative in my summing-up. The testimony of the scores themselves indicated that John Foulds had written an ample body of music of considerable interest, originality, and beauty, and that he had in fact been a very different, and far more substantial, composer than was conveyed by the few scanty and inaccurate references to him in the various current musical encyclopedias.[52] But at that time even I had heard none of his important works played, and it was impossible to foresee how performers, listeners, and the musical press would receive them — or indeed to what extent performances would prove possible to promote. I therefore concluded with a suggested list of pieces which seemed clearly to be worth hearing, and a plea that the composer's output should be rescued from the silent limbo into which it had fallen.

In the event — beginning with personal attempts to interest leading musicians in the smaller and immediately available pieces, and using the publicity generated by the first few performances to attract the attention of grant-giving bodies, orchestras, record companies, and the BBC — the revival of Foulds's music has already achieved much more than I would have dared to hope. His name remains unfamiliar to many music-lovers, of course; but few of those who take an especial interest in 20th-century British music are now wholly unaware of his existence or his potential importance. A wide range of Foulds's output has been played — many pieces for the first time — either in public concerts or studio broadcasts. Four LP records (one already reissued on compact disc) have been made to date, encompassing a total of 11 different compositions, and these have been sold and broadcast throughout Europe and the USA. Players have tended to find the music absorbing and rewarding, audience response has been very warm, and the response of critics and musicologists, though certainly not undivided, has been gratifyingly positive. This process shows every sign of continuing; and the detailed and relatively well-informed assessments of Foulds now enshrined in the current editions of *Baker's* and the *Oxford Dictionary of Music*, the inclusion of the *Quartetto Intimo* in a recent book-length history of the string quartet, and Lewis Foreman's verdict in his history of British music in letters — *From Parry to Britten* (1987) — that "his output is a substantial and important one; it is not possible to form a balanced view of British music in his time without experience of it," are welcome signs that Foulds's music is starting to take its place alongside that of his contemporaries as an important field of study. I therefore feel considerably less need for caution in expressing my conviction of its worth — although, of necessity, this still remains an interim judgment.

The "Foulds Renaissance" may be said to have begun on 29 September 1975, at the Purcell Room, London, when Moray Welsh (cello) and Ronald Stevenson (piano) performed the Op. 6 Cello Sonata. As far as is known, this was the first occasion on which the Sonata had ever been publicly heard in the composer's native country, and its first documented performance anywhere for 45 years. The occasion was unheralded by any fanfare of publicity, but the composer Hugh Wood was moved to write of this "startlingly impressive piece" in *Tempo* magazine that "It is one of these very rare unknown works whose sheer vitality and natural musicality make one wonder, after all, whether there is not an element of blind capriciousness in the winnowing process of Time, which sweeps so many composers away...." A broadcast of the Sonata was followed by other performances of short works, but it was only in the centenary year of Foulds's birth, 1980, that it was possible to put before the public a reasonable cross-section of his output in the chamber and instrumental fields. The Bromsgrove and Bracknell Festivals both featured Foulds in that year — the former including the world première of the *Quartetto Intimo* by the Endel-

---

52 The 5th Edition of *Grove's Dictionary of Music and Musicians*, for example, sported a two-paragraph entry on Foulds by Eric Blom which omitted almost every interesting detail of his career and made five errors in a highly selective list of a mere 18 works. I offered to revise this entry for the new edition then in preparation, and sent a copy of the 1975 book to assist any editor; but all that transpired was that the *New Grove* has reprinted Blom's entry verbatim, uncorrected, with the sole addition of a one-entry bibliography!

lion Quartet and the latter a complete performance of the *Essays in the Modes* by Peter Jacobs; and the actual birthday was signalized by concerts in Manchester and London.

"Foulds does not write like a persecuted man," commented Hugo Cole in the *Guardian*. "It seems more likely that his own restless taste for experiment debarred him from worldly success. Yet the few pieces... I've heard during his centenary year have all impressed me by their clarity, sense of direction, professional expertise combined with a turn of invention that does not follow the expected line."

Paul Driver in the *Financial Times* made the *Essays* the principal item in his report from the Bracknell Festival, commenting that "these pieces... establish something like a Debussyan sophistication of means upon the unobtrusive anchorage of his Englishry.... How many pianists do not know what they are missing!"; he also praised the "sweet but supple" piano piece *English Tune with Burden*, the original version of the third *Aquarelle*.

"Listening to a couple of hours of his music, I was impressed by a richly endowed musical personality," wrote the Manchester correspondent of *Musical Opinion*. "I was deeply sceptical when I walked into the Foulds centenary concert," admitted Michael Kennedy in the *Daily Telegraph* —

> What I heard, however, convinced me that his advocates have a good case... his music is not only as good as they say, but impels one to ask passionately why it was neglected.... The Cello Sonata is a fine example of youthful romanticism but, unlike many English works of the same period, it does not run to seed because its structural plan is so well laid out and adhered to.... *Mood-Pictures* and the *Essays in the Modes*, far from being the usual mish-mash of eclecticism, struck me as not only well-written but having a clear sense of purpose and direction.... "The Reed Player", which employs both speaking and singing wholly convincingly, is a brilliantly original and haunting song.... One could detect individuality of utterance, a real composer, not a sham.... A nation which can neglect music springing from the genuine inspiration heard during this brave concert deserves all the phoneys who have queued to take its place.

David Murray, also in the *Telegraph*, praised the "richly inventive and melodious" *April-England*; David Fanning (*Guardian*) commended the "impres-sively resourceful" *Essays*: "the music is quite the opposite of parochial or timid."

But it was the *Quartetto Intimo*, in that year's live performances, the subsequent radio broadcasts, and finally on the first LP record of Foulds's music ever made (a string-quartet recital by the Endellion Quartet financed by the Ralph Vaughan Williams Trust and the British Music Society) that drew especially unstinted admiration. "Firmly establishes Foulds's importance," wrote Edward Greenfield in the *Guardian*, "...the striking thing about the *Quartetto Intimo* is its confident cosmopolitan voice. Of Foulds's contemporaries only Frank Bridge was writing quartet music to compare with this." To Robert Henderson in the *Daily Telegraph* the work was "fiercely undogmatic, except in its belief in the creative spirit... a work of vividly decisive character"; Paul Griffiths in the *Times* was "entirely unprepared for the shock of the *Quartetto Intimo*.... I can think of nothing at all like it... must count among the quartet masterpieces of the Thirties." Paul Rapoport in the U.S. record magazine *Fanfare* fond it "a real discovery, with wonderful music from the first page to the last, unforgettable in the richness of its ideas and the tremendous skill and flair with which they are developed and related." The recording won the coveted and rarely awarded Rosette of the *Penguin Record Guide*, given only to discs of unique artistic excellence.   When it was reissued on compact disc in 1987, the applause continued: "*Le* Quatuor Intime... *n'est rien d'autre qu'un chef-d'oeuvre*," according to Jean-Yves Bras in the French music journal *Diapason*.

Later performances and recordings, with some of the orchestral works finally being heard, brought further plaudits. Martin Anderson found that *Hellas*, revived by the Govannon orchestra under Raymond Head 50 years after its Birmingham première, "shows Foulds to be an outstanding adherent of the great English tradition of string writing.... It oughtn't to wait another five decades for its next performance"; the *Indian Suite*, premièred in the same concert, presented "its simple ethnic and traditional materials with notable resource" (*Tempo*). Robert Briggs praised the "boundless energy and great strength" of *Pasquinade Symphonique No. 1* as recorded by the Luxembourg Radio Symphony Orchestra under Leopold Hager; Michael Oliver in the *Gramophone* preferred *Mirage* for "the real Foulds... in the shimmering, fleeting, enigmatic section that gives the work its title, in the impressive, reserved power and mystery of the opening and closing pages." Steven

Draper in the *British Music Society Newsletter* found the *Dynamic Triptych* "a really exhilarating piece.... Foulds's style is totally his own... the short finale is a complete tour-de-force"; Edward Greenfield praised the work for its "wildness mixed with poetry... arguably too full of ideas, but they are sharply memorable... a work to treasure."

Lance Tufnell, whose "most stunning musical experience" had been the first hearing of the Endellion Quartet's Foulds record, hailed *Essays in the Modes* on Peter Jacobs's disc of Foulds piano music as "one of the most important works for solo piano by a British composer... concert pianists will be hard pressed to find many better sets of twentieth century piano music.... At his best, John Foulds was a fabulous composer" (*BMS Newsletter*). In *Tempo*, David Brown agreed: "I find it difficult to think of a greater work for the piano by an Englishman.... Foulds's genius is to find, in what might seem almost a game, the perfect vehicle for the subtlest expressive purposes"; he found *Gandharva-Music* "perfect and insubstantial as a breath of air," and *April-England* a "knockout of a piece."

I have dared to parade these examples not merely because they are excellent reviews by any standards, and not because I think they are indisputably valid from an objective point of view (though obviously I would agree with their general tenor). The point worth making, I believe, is that they are a useful in-dicator of how Foulds's works have struck contemporary listeners, often on first hearing. Moreover, they are better than most of the reviews Foulds received in his lifetime: it may be that the climate of critical opinion is just now catching up with his music.

Despite the recent airing of a goodly proportion of Foulds's output, much remains to be heard and assimilated, and the chief direction and thrust of his life's work, though much clearer than in 1975, remains difficult to grasp. In part this is due to the complicating circumstance — which in reality is an essential aspect of his musicality — that Foulds worked willingly in very diverse forms and idioms, and at deliberately varied levels of sophistication. In an age which even then was tending towards musical specialization, Foulds was a conscious all-rounder, and proud of it. Partly because of that, his surviving *oeuvre* has at first sight an untidy appearance, with many pieces which remain hard to categorize. Another circumstance is the simple fact that Foulds died unexpectedly, in the prime of creative life, half-way around the world from the European concert scene, with many projects unfulfilled, scores unfinished, and others doomed to be lost. Furthermore, his Indian sojourn itself, though entirely logical in terms of his developing interest in the music of that part of Asia, seems superficially like a radical change

John Foulds with the "Nucleus of Indo-European Orchestra", Delhi, 1937. (John Foulds Estate.)

of direction as far as the development of his own compositions was concerned.

Indeed, it has been put to me that in embarking upon his "Indo-European" projects Foulds had entered a blind alley, irrelevant at once to the mainstream of European music, to the needs and nature of Indian music, and to his own deepest gifts. However, I do not see that we are in any position to pass such a judgment. Foulds's work with the "Indo-European" ensemble was—as he himself made clear—only a first small step towards a much larger goal. If we possessed the finished score of the *Symphony of East and West*; if he had lived another decade or so; had history (political as well as musical) moved in a different way—the verdict might be very different. It is maybe arguable that Foulds was too easily swayed by the idea that European listeners had not the patience to enjoy classical Indian music in its traditional forms. He might have been very surprised by the reverend attention which London concert audiences nowadays extend to the recitals of celebrated musicians such as Ravi Shankar and Imrat Khan. But he may also have felt that those audiences' attitude threatens to consign Indian music into as much of a "museum culture" as our current European concert repertoire. In his ensemble pieces Foulds was trying to point out a *future* direction for music in India, capitalizing on her own rich and varied instrumental traditions—which have instead continued to shrink between the sitar's dominance and the impact of Western instruments. The few European or American composers who have written for the sitar in combination with Western instruments are, unconsciously, carrying on Foulds's work—but on a far more limited scale than he himself envisaged. Foulds's little ensemble works are a signpost to a way not taken.

Foulds's commitment to Indian music was not merely practical or ethnomusicological, of course. It was closely related to his spiritual search—to his involvement with Theosophy, which provided him with an occult frame of intellectual reference that looked towards the East, and especially India, as the ultimate source of an ancient and Higher wisdom.[53] This is not an aspect of Foulds which every reader can be expected to contemplate in sympathy. But it is one with a distinguished tradition in the arts, and is manifested in much more extreme forms in the thought of (for example) Scriabin and Cyril Scott, or the Rosicrucianism of Satie and Debussy, or even the fervent Catholic mysticism of Messiaen, without unduly hindering a lively appreciation of those composers' music. Clearly, Foulds's spiritual direction was greatly affected by Maud MacCarthy, and she was a direct influence on the conception of the *World Requiem* and on his decision to travel to India. Some have opined to me that this influence was unfortunate: that she involved Foulds in areas which, left to himself, he would probably have avoided.

Perhaps. But on the available evidence I think it premature to arrive at such a conclusion. We cannot ignore the numerous indications that Foulds was involved in the occult before he and Maud ever met; and that he remained perfectly capable of going his own way musically (as in the *Mantras*, which she greatly disliked but he clearly—and justifiably—felt to be one of his most important works). It was her unique first-hand experience of Indian music that opened up new musical perspectives for him; and in providing tuneful, "light" music for the widest possible tastes, he was responding to an idea of music's social usefulness that both of them shared. Maud was by all accounts a dominating personality, but there is no need to represent Foulds as the hapless servant of her will. The evidence may suggest that they both periodically needed their independence—but also that they were both able to secure it.

Maud once wrote that her husband composed "only a few" works for posterity. Her verdict seems unduly strict. Granted that a third or more of his output was ephemeral, that still leaves a formidable body of music; and even some of the "ephemera" prove on closer acquaintance to be not so ephemeral, but rather to contain craftsmanly qualities of elegance, tunefulness, and atmosphere which may well ensure their long-term survival. A repertoire that can find

---

53 Whether Foulds would at any period in his life have described himself as a Theosophist pure and simple, I am unable to say. In *Music To-day*, in the course of his discussion of Scriabin, he avers that "I am no theosopher" (p.300)—while maintaining that no examination of this composer can be worthwhile if it is not illuminated by personal acquaintance with occult theory and practice. Certainly his pre-1915 orientation was in the direction of Theosophy; he was friendly with several people who were practising Theosophists; and Maud MacCarthy came into his life after several years in close contact with leading personalities in the Theosophical movement—though it is clear that she subsequently developed independently as a result of her own experience of mediumship. It is possible that both of them recoiled from mainstream Theosophy in the immediate post-war years when the leaders of the movement accepted the boy Krishnamurti as the new "world teacher" (a role which Krishnamurti himself eventually rejected); it is also possible that Foulds's *Avatar* opera had a specific bearing on this question.

the occasional niche for Elgar's *Chanson du Matin* or *Salut d'amour*, for Sibelius's *Valse Triste* and *Suite Champêtre*, or Frank Bridge's *Cherry Ripe*, has no reason to look askance at Foulds's *Keltic Suite*, or *Basque Serenade*, or *La Belle Pierrette*.

As for his more serious works, it is not yet time to attempt any final "rating" of them against those of his contemporaries. It seems to me, however, that a single composer who can appear to different listeners (such as the critics cited above) to have written one of the greatest British string quartets (*Quartetto Intimo*), one of the greatest British piano solo works (*Essays in the Modes*), one of the greatest British cello sonatas, one of the greatest British piano concertos (*Dynamic Triptych*) — and, I would claim, one of the greatest British scores for full orchestra in the *Three Mantras*; this one composer, judged purely as a creative artist, is likely to have been one of the most important British composers of his time.

Perhaps, too, he composed one of the greatest British choral works; until a good modern performance of *A World Requiem* has been mounted, it will be impossible to be sure. Most of Foulds's works look good in score, and sound better than they look; the *Requiem* looks strangely quiescent, and clearly much of its effect will depend on the perfection of sonority and specific gravity of a real performance. There is a Foulds family tradition that Sir Donald Tovey called it the greatest choral work since Handel. As we can see from the letter quoted in Chapter 5, that was not quite what Tovey said; but what he did say remains a powerful recommendation that the piece should be heard again. Given the current interest in Foulds, doubtless its time will come. Mounting a production of Foulds's other, earlier, and never-performed choral epic would be considerably more difficult and costly, and apparently for smaller artistic returns. But I wish to record here my conviction that *The Vision of Dante* may well contain — although couched in largely 19th-century idioms — the finest and most visionary music of the composer's early years.

Whatever may be history's eventual verdict on John Foulds's creative achievement, it is clear that — in view of its exploratory and all-encompassing nature — this is an achievement rather unlike those of his better-known contemporaries. It is also clear, once one has heard more than a few of his works, that Foulds is an individual and distinctive voice in the British music of his lifetime. He rivals — and occasion-ally surpasses — those contemporaries in sheer command of technique; but he offers a different musical outlook, valuable precisely because of its difference. Although "impersonation" was one of his essential compositional ploys, in every role he remains the same rich and extremely likeable human being, who radiates a fundamentally positive, life-affirming spirit all too rare in 20th-century music. Whereas Elgar may be most typically characterized by the contrast of Edwardian opulence with what Havergal Brian called his "highly-strung and luminous" musical nature; Delius by his hedonistic languor; Holst by his aesthetic purity; Vaughan Williams by his pastoral mysticism; Brian himself by stoic heroism; Bax by his Celtic love of color and melancholy; Bridge by a haunted, shadowy chromaticism — Foulds, hedonist and mystic together, offers at his best an irrepressible *joie-de-vivre*. He can be an astonishingly invigorating composer; in his finest music there is a sheer generosity of melodic writing that seems to express an eminently sane optimism, a spirit in harmony with the best things life has to offer, and a sense that they should be enjoyed to the full.

Foulds's sudden death was of course a tragedy (for British music no less than his family), as was the consequent and almost total neglect of his work; and his professional career, though varied and distinguished, had been less than a brilliant success. But in his creative life I find *no* hint of tragedy: as Hugo Cole has observed, "Foulds does not write like a persecuted man." On the contrary, there is every reason to believe he enjoyed himself hugely. There is nothing shallow about his musical optimism: it emerges out of his entire attitude to existence. It is this sheer vitality, this zest for life in its many aspects, mystical and fleshly, tranquil and exciting, trivial and sublime, from the Celtic West to the Indo-Aryan East, that may be the most valuable thing his music has to contribute to our spiritually impoverished late-20th-century concert repertoire. Dying as he did in 1939, Foulds could hardly have envisaged the immeasurably more dangerous, and changelessly unjust, world in which we have had to live. But that simply makes his optimism more valuable. This most companionable of British composers has emerged out of a well-nigh buried past; but his music, in its clear-eyed, unsentimental way, inspires hope in a future of world-wide fellowship and infinite possibility.

"MR. JOHN FOULDS. *From a drawing by E. X. Kapp.* The Prince of Wales and Prince George were present at the Royal Albert Hall on Armistice Night, November 11, when a special commemoration concert was given in aid of the British Legion. Mr. John Foulds, who is not likely to remain a more or less unknown composer, provided a work for the occasion which has made an appeal to the hundreds of thousands of people in these islands who mourn those who gave their lives for their country. Mr. Foulds has written *A World Requiem* to an English text based upon the authorised version, and conveying 'A tribute to the memory of the Dead — a message of consolation to the bereaved of all countries.' This was its first performance. The composer conducted, and the singers (from fifteen choral societies of London) and players numbered over a thousand."
— Published in *The Tatler* for 21 November 1923. (Author's Collection)

APPENDIX: A BRIEF SELECTION OF
JOHN FOULDS'S WRITINGS

During the latter half of his life Foulds was a prolific writer. His one published book, *Music Today*, is known to have been preceded by two unpublished ones which are now lost, *Spirituality in Music* and *Consilium Angelicum* — both of which may be supposed to have dealt with the more occult aspects of the art. He also lectured on music at London University, gave talks about it on All-India Radio, and wrote many articles in a wide variety of British (and latterly Indian) publications, on topics ranging from the most abstruse regions of aesthetic theory to humorous musical anecdotes and reminiscences. Between 1929 and 1932 he contributed nearly a hundred brief columns under the title "Challenges" to *The Musical Mirror*, at first using the pen-name "Deva" but later abandoning this pseudonym.

The following brief selection is by no means representative of his full range of interests, but has been chosen partly to amplify various matters I have touched upon in the main body of the book: especially as regards modal composition, musical taste, microtones, and Indian music. Some of the material has never appeared before in any form, and is printed here from Foulds's manuscripts or typescripts.

1. *A CHAT ON ANCIENT GREEK MUSIC WITH SOME MUSICAL ILLUSTRATIONS* (1916)

[This article was published in the 11 March 1916 issue of *The Herald of the Star*, a magazine of the Theosophical movement, pp.126-33 inclusive. Its content, however, might be described as musical and speculative rather than strictly occult. The five musical examples given at the end (which appeared, as here, in Foulds's own hand) formed the basis of the *Five Recollections of Ancient Greek Music* he composed for piano in 1915. The example he mentions as "dating from 1910" is evidently Example 1, whose main theme is previously found in the orchestral suite *Music-Pictures Group III*, composed in 1912, as part of the third movement, "Old Greek Legend".]

THE ART of music as we know it in the twentieth century is generally held to owe very little to the Greeks, whose generous legacy to the arts of sculpture, architecture, and epic poetry has been, and is even down to the present day of such incalculable value. Only a few fragments of ancient Greek music — and these apparently of the decadent Roman period — were known to be in existence until the excavations at Delphi in 1893 and later, when others were unearthed, notably a hymn recording the prowess of Apollo (dating from the third century B.C.), and none of these fragments can be considered as representing Greek music at its highest excellence.

Nevertheless, there are at the present day a few musicians in the very van of progress in their art, men belonging to the pioneers of the coming race, who, aspiring toward the Unknown in the illimitable sphere of music, and obeying the irresistible urge of evolution, yet pause a moment to glance backward over the history of their art, and, realising that progress is cyclic, endeavour to trace the links and correspondences between the music of the present and the future, and that of the mighty civilisations of the past.

From this point of view, then, the somewhat meagre records we do possess of the music of the Egyptians, Hebrews, Assyrians, Greeks and Romans are extremely suggestive. More so still in the case of India perhaps, for nowhere has the ancient tradition been more carefully preserved and kept alive than in that country, the seat and root of so many of our modern western art tendencies. We are concerned here, however, with the Greeks, the founders in the West of the theory of the gamut and the modes, with whom it is customary, and very natural, to commence our histories of music. But this is evidently incomplete and short-sighted. Too long have the Greeks, intelligent and artistic as they were, prevented us from seeing humanity as a whole. Before their time there existed the whole of the East, and there is much evidence in support of the view that although they were indeed the founders of music in the West, they did not originate or discover, but merely elaborated and handed on to us as it were, part of the traditions of India and Egypt. Be this as it may, the creative artists of Greece added no doubt their quota of personal invention to what they imitated from abroad, and from this period music becomes the object of increasingly clear classifications, all having for foundation the "ethos" of the different social groups in which art took rebirth and received its characteristic stamp. We shall return to this question later during a consideration of the ethnical denominations of the modes, but for the moment let us seek for any traces of Greek influence upon modern composers.

Now the example of Greek tragedy, with the report of its all-pervading music (in many cases, as in that of Æschylus, composed by the dramatist himself) could not fail to fire the imagination of men like Monteverdi, Gluck, and Wagner, who convinced themselves that their work was amongst other things a revival of Greek tragedy. It has been said that "the Greeks made of music, philosophy." Nothing great was expected of men who were ignorant of music; women practised it assiduously—even playing the flute as did Lamia; children began their education with it, and we must not, therefore, be amazed that, in one of his comedies (*The Clouds*) Aristophanes distinguishes the scholars of different generations by the choruses they have learned at school. The authors, Aristoxenus, Euclid, Homer, Plutarch and Xenophon tell us how this classic race reverence music—not only as a personal accomplishment, but as a duty towards themselves and their country; and we should certainly not forget—though we are acquainted with them by name only—the popular songs. The Greeks sang while harvesting, while grinding the barley, when crushing the corn with the hand-cylinder, when pressing the bunches of grapes, when spinning and weaving—all work founded on collective action and on the spirit of co-operation. They had among them the airs of the shoemaker, the dyer, the water-carrier, the shepherd, etc.

But the single outstanding figure in the evolution of music in Greece at this period is that of Pythagoras (*circa* B.C. 600). He is often credited with the discovery of the extremely simple mathematical proportions of the intervals of the diatonic scale, but he more probably learned them either in Egypt or India, where he is said to have sojourned many years, before he returned to Greece and gathered around him the band of pupils and followers who accepted his teachings, and lived the life he taught. He utilised some of this knowledge gathered in India or Egypt,[54] to organise the Greek musical system, and was aided in the work by such theorists as Lasos and Terpander. The mathematical precision of harmonies or sound pulsations seems mostly to have occupied these great minds, but it is not to be believed that a nation which produced such practical musicians as Olympus the Phrygian, who introduced the art of flute playing, and the soldier-musician Tyrtaeus, was not keenly alive to the æsthetic value of the art. In Book VII of his *Republic*, Plato laughs at those musicians who limit themselves for the explanation of their art to arithmetic added to physics, and trouble not as to what is above this. To him the relationship of numbers, to which the grammar of music may be reduced, appears to be but the first stage of dialetics, that is to say, of a concatenation of ideas, ascending ever higher and higher, the last of which is that of the Good. According to him it is this idea of the Good which radiates through all the domains of life and makes its unity.

This is not the place for a dissertation upon the musical system of the Greeks, such as may be found in any book upon the subject; it will perhaps be more helpful to the reader in his understanding and enjoyment of the musical illustrations which follow, if we give a very brief glance at:

(a) The Greek modes and their ethnical designations.
(b) The three genera.
(c) Harmony in Greek Music.

---

54 Pythagoras's dates are c.570-c.500 B.C. Modern historians of philosophy cautiously accept that he may have studied in Egypt and Babylon, but not India. –MM.

(a) THE GREEK MODES AND THEIR ETHNI-CAL DESIGNATIONS

In the first place it is necessary to remember that in the West at the present day almost all our music is built upon two modes, and we give them abstract names no longer recalling the idea of a living reality; they are the modes *minus* (minor) and the mode *plus* (major). But the process of abstraction and drastic simplification which has brought us to this poverty stricken state and to this dry-as-dust mathematicians' language, should not make us forget either the richness or the significant nomenclature of the past. These two modes are the points in which end by concentration, the eight modes which the Middle Ages practised and which they derived from the Greeks; and probably in a return to and a freer use of many more than our present two modes lies part of the progress of music in the future. The writer is convinced that a "fertilisation" (to use Wagner's term) of Western by Eastern music will shortly take place, and among the technical devices worth borrowing from the East, the use of each and all of the modes according to the mood to be expressed, is perhaps the chief and the most valuable.

Now, among the Greeks the modes had ethnical designations which clearly recalled their origin: the Dorian, the Phrygian, the Lydian, the Æolian, the Ionian, and all their corresponding plagal modes; and, according to Combarieu, we should see by these appellatives that the modes had been constituted by two social groups; the Greeks of the Peloponnesus and the people of Asia Minor. To each of these modes there was attributed a particular "ethos"; that is to say, a special emotional state; and this musical ethos as it is designated in the Greek writers, principally in Plato (*Republic*) and Aristotle (*Politics*), agrees exactly for each mode with that of the nation whose name the mode bears. The Ionian and Lydian, for example, were considered as lascivious, suitable for banquets and dances; the Phrygian and Dorian were regarded as virile, energetic, and proper for the perfect citizen.

(b) THE THREE GENERA

The interval of a fourth (*e.g.*, C to G, downwards) is believed to be the earliest melodic relationship which the ear learnt to fix, and the Greeks divided this downward fourth into four notes, called a tetrachord. They also had three arrangements of the notes contained in the tetrachord, resulting in the three *genera* — enharmonic, chromatic, and diatonic. The enharmonic tetrachord was C, A flat, G*,[55] G; the chromatic: C, A, A flat, G; the diatonic: C, B flat, A flat, G. This last has become the foundation of modern music, and the Greeks soon preferred it to the other genera and found a scientific basis for it. Its notes could be connected by a series of those intervals which they recognised as concordant: the fourth, its converse the fifth, and the octave. And for more than ten centuries the theory of music has been dominated, and even rather tyrannised over, by the part attributed to these two intervals.

(c) HARMONY IN GREEK MUSIC

Whether the Greeks were acquainted with harmony — in the modern sense of the word — is a question that has been much discussed, and may now be regarded as settled. It is clear that they were acquainted with the phenomena on which harmony depends, viz., the effect produced by sounding certain notes together. It appears also that they made some use of harmony — and of dissonant as well as consonant intervals — in instrumental music. Their preference for the diatonic scale, as mentioned above, indicates a latent harmonic sense, and also that temperance, which is at the foundation of the general Greek sense of beauty. Nonharmonic music is a world of two dimensions — rhythm and melody — and the Greeks certainly came to rise from this "flatland" to the solid world of sound — rhythm, melody, and harmony. The first two are obviously as ancient as human consciousness itself, but with harmony, music assumes the existence of a kind of space in three dimensions, none of which can subsist without at least implying the others, and this is the world in which Palestrina, Bach, Beethoven and Wagner live.

* * *

The examples which follow were not composed so as to conform slavishly with what we know of the rules followed in those ancient days. This would result in a more academic exercise, an archaic ex-

---

55   Here Foulds applies his special symbol to indicate that the succeeding note is to be sharpened by a quarter of a tone — see pages 6, above, and 116, below. –MM.

humation more likely to lead to the closing of doors than the opening of them. The composer has preferred to trust his intuition—has "dreamed into the mood"—of Ancient Greece, and these are quota- tions from some of the results of such dreams; one dating from 1910, the remainder written at one sitting during the summer of 1915.[56]

EXAMPLE I.—In the Dorian Mode, might be a Dirge for some Hero in a Greek Tragedy.
(Played upon Harps, Flutes and Cymbals.)

SOLEMN MARCH TEMPO.

---

56 The examples, in the order in which they appear here, are the basis for the following movements in *Five Recollections of Ancient Greek Music*: Ex.1, "Dirge for a Hero"; Ex.2, "Processional"; Ex.3, "Solemn Temple Dance"; Ex.4, "Temple Chant"; Ex.5, "Song of Argive Helen". These movements later became part of Foulds's *Hellas* Suite. –MM.

EXAMPLE II.—In the Lydian Mode, is a Processional.
(Played upon Low Stringed Instruments with Drums and Gong.)

NOT TOO SLOWLY.

EXAMPLE III.—In the Hypo-Lydian Mode, is a Solemn Dance.
(*Played upon Low Stringed Instruments with Harp.*)

EXAMPLE IV.—In the Phrygian Mode, is a Temple Chant.
(*Men's Chorus.*)

NOT VERY SLOWLY.

EXAMPLE V.—In the Mixo-Lydian Mode, I call the Song of Argive Helen.
(*Sung by a Female Voice.*)

2. *DOES THE PUBLIC LIKE GOOD MUSIC?* (1925)

[This article, a good example of Foulds's more popular writings, appeared on p.167 of Volume V of *Music Masterpieces* edited by Percy Pitt, a monthly part-work published by the Educational Book Company Ltd., London in 1925. A very similar one—the wording is almost identical in several places—entitled "People Who Are Musically Starved" was issued on 19 May 1925 in Part 14 of a fortnightly part-work, *Harmsworth's Children's Music Portfolio* (London: Amalgamated Press, p.212). Both were ascribed to "J.H. Foulds, the Well-Known Composer".]

A GOOD deal of discussion goes on from time to time regarding the respective merits of "highbrow" and "lowbrow" music, and there is often a tendency to draw a definite line of demarcation in a way that, in my view, is not justified.

I regard this as a pity, because I do not think we shall serve the cause of music well by giving the average person, who lays no claim to a deep knowledge of the art, an impression that if he dares to derive pleasure from anything other than the heavy classics he will be musically damned.

The usual method in debates on the subject is to lay it down as incontrovertible that oratorios, symphonies, concertos, and grand operas are classical music, in a word, "highbrow"; while light operas, musical comedy music, jazz, and so on, are "lowbrow" and musically bad.

I do not agree with this arbitrary division in the least. There is good and bad music in every class, and there are bad symphonies just as there is bad jazz. I would rather hear a good light opera than a bad grand opera, and I should not consider that to express such views was to admit that my taste was decadent.

Of course, no one would pretend that all art is on the same plane, and that jazz and other light music is to be compared with the genius displayed in the works of Beethoven or Bach, but that does not prevent one from admiring appropriate art of whatever grade.

There are "highbrows" who sneer at restaurant and cinema music, and assume that it must necessarily be bad. Frankly, the music heard in these places is, sometimes, very depressing, but on the other hand it is sometimes excellent of its kind, and would be better still if the proprietors realised that the taste of the public in these matters is higher than they imagine it to be.

It is, perhaps, a strange coincidence that the largest numbers of people should generally be found in the cafés in which good music is played.

The same applies to the cinemas. The standard in some of them is very high. Indeed, music contributes to quite a considerable extent to the success of the entertainment. Incidentally, this is rather significant, for as no programme of the music is supplied the audience are often totally unaware that they are listening to an extract from a great classic, the mere name of which, if known beforehand, might have conjured up visions of a boring evening.

There is no doubt whatever that the British public likes good music. I have heard boys whistling melodies from classics played in the cinemas. They have not the least notion of whether the music is "highbrow" or "lowbrow", and probably care less; its beauty has just gripped them and remained in their memory.

I think the restaurants, cinemas, gramophones, and the wireless are doing wonderful propaganda work for music. Perhaps it is not all of the highest class, but a good deal of it is well worth listening to and distinctly educative in its effect.

The famous R.L. Stevenson was once asked by a friend to give his advice on what literature a boy ought to read. "I don't think it matters a great deal at the beginning," Stevenson said in effect. "The principal thing is that he should be reading at all. He'll gradually find the best."

That is very true of music. There has never been so much musical activity in this country as there is today. We find it everywhere we go—in café, restaurant, cinema, theatre, music-hall, concert-room, and dancing-hall, not to mention the wireless and the various mechanical instruments. The amount of music is colossal when one comes to think of it.

What a difference compared with a mere twenty-five years ago! We not only hear more music but more of it is of a better class.

The standard of public taste is constantly improving and the more music is heard the better will taste become. The late Dr. Richter, my master, once told me that Brahms had remarked to him that the future of music lay in England, giving as one reason the fact that this country was in a better position than any other in Europe to survey Russian, German, French, Italian, and other characteristic music, and distil therefrom, as it were, the next forward urge in the art.

I believe Brahms' prophecy is quite a possibility. Do not let us forget that England, in the Elizabethan period, and for many years, led the Western world in music. It contained the greatest composers and executants, and its musicians carried their knowledge to countries less advanced in this respect.

Then came the age of commerce, and we devoted our time and energies to increasing our trade. Music was neglected in the pursuit of commercial prosperity. But now the people are turning once more to the art which their forefathers loved so much, and I am confident that the future will witness great developments among the English-speaking peoples, comparable with that splendid period of the recent past in Germany.

3. DYNAMIC TRIPTYCH: *PROGRAM NOTE* (1929)

[This note appears in handwritten form in the manuscript full score of Foulds's *Dynamic Triptych*. It was printed in full in the program of the First Concert of the Sixteenth Season of the Reid Symphony Orchestra, for the world première of the work by Frank Merrick with the Reid Orchestra conducted by Professor Donald F. Tovey at the Usher Hall, Edinburgh, on 15 October 1931. I give below the note as it appeared on that occasion, with one introductory paragraph and one footnote by Professor Tovey.]

DYNAMIC TRIPTYCH for Pianoforte and Orchestra,
Op. 88   -   -   -   -   -   -   *John Foulds*

Pianoforte—FRANK MERRICK.

    I. Dynamic Mode.
    II. Dynamic Timbre.
    III. Dynamic Rhythm

(First Performance ; in the presence of the Composer.)

IT HAD BEEN the intention of the Reid Orchestra to produce this work in February; but the indisposition of Madame Suggia, who was to have played at the First Concert of this seaon, necessitated an interchange of programmes. Madame Suggia will play on February 11th, 1932, the programme originally intended for to-day; and, with extraordinary readiness and generosity, Mr. Frank Merrick has consented to transfer his engagement of February so that we may open our season with this important novelty.

In the special circumstances I have had no time to write an essay on Mr Foulds's work. The essay can wait for another occasion, which is certain to occur, for the work is not one to be neglected. Meantime, here is Mr Foulds's own programme-note, which conveys all the information needed by the listener, though it abstains from anything that another analyst might wish to say of the work and its author.

Composed in 1929, the three movements of which this "Triptych" consists are: 1. Dynamic Mode; 2. Dynamic Timbre; 3. Dynamic Rhythm.

1. *Dynamic Mode.* — The composer had already published (Maurice Senart: Paris) a "1st Volume" of "Essays in the Modes", wherein he gives a list of no fewer than 90 modes,[57] all of which, he asserts, are as interesting in their different ways as the two — major and minor — upon which the great bulk of our music of the past 300 years has been constructed. The present number uses no notes but those belonging to mode No. 6M of his table (here used on D), viz.: D, E sharp, F sharp, G, A, B sharp, C sharp, D. The character is extremely vivacious throughout; the first subject proper being marked *con bravura*, the second *con amore*. And although, after an orchestral *tutti*, there is a short passage marked *con tenerezza*, the ensuing coda is based on the first subject and the introductory modal flourish, in *fortissimo*.

2. *Dynamic Timbre. Lento molto.* — This movement opens with interchanging timbres of contrasting quality, in which also passages in quarter-tones (first introduced by this composer in 1911[58]) appear in the lower strings. The first theme now comes out in the solo instrument, and is immediately re-presented in the full orchestra. The last few notes are dying away in the first horn when the solo instrument dreams off into the second subject, the somewhat ritualistic character of the bass part of which is taken up by the percussion instruments. Ensues a further development of the timbre-variations of the first subject — a counterpoint of timbres, rather than of lines of melody as formerly — and a quarter-tonal

contrasted section leads to a kind of free meditation in the solo part, marked *romantico*. The third metamorphosis of the characteristic timbre of the first theme becomes more and more eloquent and reaches a climax of sustained tone. As this dies away in changing rainbow-hues the movement is brought to a close.

3. *Dynamic Rhythm.* — The basic rhythm upon which the whole of the movement rests, and which underlies it from first note to last, is a reiteration of 2/4, 3/4, 4/4.[59] It is first presented by the solo instrument and percussion. A characteristic theme marked *ben ritmico* is poised upon it, and yet another in the strings marked *ardente*. Now follows a rigid new theme in the pianoforte marked *alla marcia* (still accompanied by the unceasing though ever-changing original rhythmic figure). A slight development of all these factors leads to yet another theme marked *alla valse* (the tympani still tapping out the inescapable rhythmic pattern of the commencement). Brilliant figuration of truly pianistic type ensues, and the movement attains a climax in which the ear, though not the mind, perhaps loses contact with the basic rhythm. Now follows a peroration in which all the chief themes (the *ben ritmico* theme, the *ardente* melody, the *alla marcia* and the *alla valse*) are marshalled and combined simultaneously over the rhythmic figure which grows in insistence until the final iteration in *tempo largo molto.*

4. *ORCHESTRATING* DEATH AND THE MAIDEN (1930)

[Previously unpublished, this short manuscript is in fact untitled, and lacks both beginning and end. It has been written very rapidly in ink on the back of a letter from the publisher Ralph Hawkes, dated 10 December 1930, declining to publish Foulds's orchestration of Schubert's String Quartet in D minor, D.810, generally known as *Death and the Maiden* from its variation movement based upon the melody of Schubert's song of that name. "Whilst there is but little doubt that this is a great achievement on your behalf," writes Hawkes, "I am afraid that its commercial value

---

57   See page 58, above. –MM.

58   Foulds must mean "first introduced in the performance of an orchestral work". At least four chamber works written between 1896 and 1907 had employed them; they are also found in the orchestral tone-poem *Mirage*, composed in 1910, but not publicly performed in his lifetime. –MM.

59   Pronouce at a brisk uniform pace the words "*one* two *one* two three *one* two three four" again and again without pause, and with an accent on each "*one*", and you will feel the powerful swing of this rhythm. (D.F.T.)

is almost negligible.... I am accordingly returning the score to you herewith." The letter was found inside the score itself; its reverse side clearly furnished Foulds with scrap paper on which to draft part of an essay or program-note. Despite the obvious haste with which he was writing, and a number of cross-outs and corrections, almost every word is decipherable. The manuscript begins with a paragraph indentation.]

*H*AVING SAID which I am free to confess that I made this transcription with no such ideas in mind. The motive was purely personal and arose in this way. As a boy I was a 'cellist, and first played this quartet when about 13 or 14 years of age. The first contact with its power & beauty came upon me like a revelation & caused me two entire sleepless nights during which my mind continually regurgitated framents — melodic, harmonic, rhythmic — or whole movements of the work; but (and this is my point) *never in the similitude of a string quartet*. Always I would be hearing the trumpets and drums of his dramatic opening; the clarinets of his adorable second subject; the swirl and commotion of his semi-quaver figures among whole groups of violins, violas, cellos, what time he tosses titanic fragments of his chief themes from reeds to brass, from brass to woodwinds & back again; would feel the portentous tragedy of his coda, the despairing voices of an oboe, the answering clarinet — less agonised, more philosophical, equally hopeless — the weight of double basses in those last sad chords.

I would hear in my mind's eye his chorale-like *Tod*-motive in cold woodwind timbres, echoed by strings without nuances, would thrill to that lowest doublebass E in the second strain, and wait in a trembling ecstasy for a clarinet to lift up its lonely voice in that heavenly gloom-piercing major cadence. Followed his variations, every bar vital, no fustian, nothing mechanical — the third battering its way into my inmost consciousness with its dactyllic insistence, and the idyllic instrumental conversations in its all-too-brief major section. But most inescapable of all would I tremble to hear the drum taps of his fifth, those terrifying triplets growing growing increasing hammering at ones [indecipherable word] till it fell with one mighty cymbal-clash — one only. But from time to time the fateful triplets would tap out on the drums, a breath-taking reminder.

[The manuscript breaks off here, at the bottom of the page.]

5. *QUARTER TONES: AURAL POSSIBILITIES AND VAGARIES* (1934)

[This section comes from Foulds's book *Music To-day* (London: Ivor Nicholson & Watson, 1934). It is quite impossible to give any impression of the book itself by means of short extracts, so wide is its range — even the list of contents as advertised by the publishers (see their leaflet reproduced on page 79) omits many important headings. The present extract is edited from two sections of Part Two, Chapter Four (which carries the general title "Quarter-Tones"), pp.59-65.]

1. QUARTER-TONES

*I*N THE year 1898 I had tentatively experimented in a string quartet,[60] with smaller divisions than usual of the intervals of our scale, *i.e.* quarter-tones. Having proved in performance their practicability and their capability of expressing certain psychological states

in a manner incommunicable by any other means known to musicians, I definitely adopted them as an item in my composing technique....

It must be understood that the quarter-tone as here used has nothing whatever to do with those "microtones" with which Eastern musicians are wont to embellish their modal melodies. It is an indigenous

60   Programme of which bears this date. (J.F.) [The program referred to has since disappeared. The quartet performed must have been one of the two Foulds had composed in 1896, both of which are now missing. The earliest surviving quartet, the F minor of 1899, does not include quarter-tones. –MM.]

growth, natural offspring of the Bach equal-tempered scale, having no relation therefore to "natural tuning" of the scale, or "just intonation", to which we shall turn our attention in Chapter XVI. In our Western music a moment arrived when freedom of harmony and modulation could only be achieved by a mathematical division of the octave into twelve equal parts: Bach stabilized this, as everyone knows, in *Das Wohltemperirte Klavier*. Quarter-tones, as used in the above-mentioned and in other more recent works, are divisions of these twelve equally spaced semi-tones into equal parts—as nearly equal, that is to say, as the ear will ordinarily register—*i.e.* into quarter tones. In... *A Dictionary of Modern Music and Musicians* (1924), and in the *Encyclopedia Britannica* (1929), as well as in various fugitive articles, I am accused of using "third-tones": "tertia-tones". These are errors. The use of quarter-tones as above described is my only "offence" in this branch of music.

Smaller intervals than quarter-tones are certainly impracticable with our present instruments, and here is the test of which a practising artist will never lose sight. Now it has been ascertained by scientific measurement that any good violinist of our splendid orchestras of to-day tunes his instrument to the tenth of a tone before he is satisfied that it is what he would call "in tune". A practical composer needs no further proof of the practicability of this quarter-tonal device, so far as the power of the human ear is concerned. Of the instruments at our everyday disposal, only the strings and the voice can make use of this device, but its employment will surely extend in many other directions.

Facetious friends may assert roundly that they have heard quarter-tones all their lives, from the fiddle strings and larynxes of their musical friends, who produced them without any difficulty whatever... by accident! Very likely. Does this affect our argument? Columbus discovered America without in the least intending to, by a sort of accident; which does not prevent us of the twentieth century voyaging thither by design.

2. QUARTER-TONE SIGNS

This new device of the quarter-tone necessitated the invention of a new series of signs. The quarter-sharp sign, it was felt, would somehow resemble the ordinary sharp without confusion being possible between it and the sign for double-sharp. Similarly, the quarter-flat, while showing some affinity with the familiar flat, should be distinct from the double-flat sign. The following were adopted and have been used in many works:

The sign ⩲ sharpens the succeeding note one quarter of a tone.

The sign ꞵ flattens the succeeding note one quarter of a tone.

Here is a typical instance where the use of quarter-tones conveys a mood-picture which seemed to the composer, rightly or wrongly, not to be exactly communicable by any other means.[61]

---

61   The musical example which follows, in Foulds's own hand, as are all those in *Music To-day*, is a mystery. He does not identify it, and it does not appear in any work of his currently known to me, although the figure on woodwind and trombones is a form of a motif found as early as *Mirage*. It could well be from a score now missing—perhaps *Sappho*, which must have been contemporary with *Music To-day*. –MM.

I have recently made a close study of a work written throughout in quarter-tones; a string-quartet by Alois Hába, opus 7. Several points emerged from this scrutiny. In the first place there is scarcely a single bar in any of the four parts throughout the work in which this device is not employed. So far as my understanding can penetrate no new ideations are offered us in the work. The effect therefore is somewhat as if a poet should retell the old, old story of Cinderella in words every one of which should contain a "th". Or as if a *chef* should flavour every course from *hors d'oeuvre* to coffee with lobster.

Speaking generally, it certainly seems that a work of anything like extended scope and range of expression would need a far wider technical treatment. Were we to employ the whole of our technical resources in a work of any length, they would be inadequate to represent a tithe of the variety and glory that may be contacted in the inner realm of man's consciousness, and which it is the composer's privilege to transcribe in physical-plane terms for our edification and delight.

Upon the technical side a practical objection cannot fail to arise. For the signs adopted by this composer— +++ for quarter-sharp and +++ for quarter-flat—are unnecessarily confusing to the eye, even after prolonged acquaintance with them; the former having all the appearance of an ordinary flat sign whose stem had failed to print quite clearly along about one third of its length. At any rate the eye and the intelligence accept it at once as an ordinary flat sign and dire confusion results.

There are rumours also of a Mexican composer[62] and others elsewhere who are said to be using this device and, in my view, for the reasons already given, the time will certainly come when its acceptance as a "legitimate" means of musical expression and its adoption into our all-too-small musical vocabulary will be a *fait accompli*.

Again it seems necessary to repeat that, as we saw when discussing Modes, any demi-semi composer might seize upon this device of quarter-tones and exploit it for the sake of any cheap notoriety he might obtain because of its superficial newness. No real artist would countance such a procedure. But it would be a deadening philosophy indeed that should proscribe a valuable device because it is possible of abuse. Besides, no artist of discernment could be deceived into believing that the newness had been forced upon such a composer by inner compulsion to express. To others of less experience or power of discernment certain remarks in a later section devoted to considerations of æsthetic may be of help.

3. AURAL POSSIBILITIES AND VAGARIES

We have instanced the power of the good orchestral violinist to perceive intervals a great deal smaller than the quarter-tone, but it must be admitted that the gift varies greatly in different individuals. So gifted a musician as Stokowski admits having to concentrate most carefully in order to co-relate these small intervals. And in the nature of things there will be many who will be totally unable to do so.

Indeed *I believe there is as much tone-deafness as colour-blindness in the world.*

But the ear will improve as has the eye. (Time was, we are told, when only three colours were perceptible in the rainbow.) And even as it stands to-day, the ear is usually far in advance of the musical intelligence.

Cases such as one I came across recently of a man hearing every musical sound too sharp—technically known as *hyperacusis*—or another, where a man heard at a different pitch the one ear from the other; these, thank heaven, are rare cases and perhaps of more interest to *medico* than *musico*. In this connection the case of Bruckner may be recalled. I was present at a rehearsal in Vienna where the full symphony orchestra included ten double-basses. Not one note of these, so he declared emphatically, could the composer hear, below the D just under the bass-clef stave. At the same time his sense of intonation was rarely developed and his appreciation of balance of *timbres* decidedly beyond the normal.[63] At the other end of the scale discrepancies are also frequently to be noticed. Not everyone can hear the extremely high note of the bat-squeak. Increasing numbers, I have noticed, are becoming able to hear upper partials, harmonics resulting from a struck or sustained low bass note. Fewer, however, far fewer it seems to me, are able to detect the resultant tones *below* a given

62 Presumably Julián Carrillo (1875-1965), who worked also with eighth- and sixteenth-tones, and devised instruments capable of producing them. –MM.

63 Bruckner attended his last concert, a performance of his *Te Deum*, on 12 January 1896. The occasion to which Foulds refers can be no later than this—and Foulds would have been only 15. –MM.

chord. These are so clearly apparent to some composers that there is a distinct danger of leaving out the lower parts of the harmony altogether and trusting to the discernment of the listener. I suppose not one listener in ten thousand would fail to "realize" the major third at the end of those Palestrina movements which finish with a bare fifth upon the tonic. But the realization of resultant basses from chords only the upper parts of which are given, demands a degree of apperception not at all common in this country or Germany or Italy, whatever may be the case in France where my friend George Migot[64] seems to be working somewhat along these lines.

All which considerations, however, are beside the question of the practicability or otherwise of quarter-tonal music, which I have proved, at least to my own satisfaction, to be a common-sensible technical forward-step, and one, moreover, which is readily discernible and assimilable by the average "musical" ear and intelligence of to-day.

6. ORIENTALITIES—IMPROVISATION (1934)

[A further extract from *Music To-day*—two sections from Part Five, Chapter Seventeen, entitled "Non-Technical" (pp.343-346).]

1. ORIENTALITIES

I ANTICIPATE that the influence of Sanskrit literature will not be less profound than the revival of Greek in the fourteenth century.[65] To the person even slightly aquainted with a few facets of that literature, the above dictum of Schopenhauer's demands not merely enthusiastic concurrence, but its extension into many other activities than literature. For the ancient Easterns have also something to teach us of the profoundest importance to music. The Indian musical system, for example—a completed and settled tradition centuries before our Western system began to evolve—can probably teach us as much as it can learn from us. Whereas in all our music we employ but one system of dividing the notes within the octave, namely, into equal half-tones, they employ several different tunings according to the type of ideation they desire to express. Rhythmic patterns attain a degree of subtlety undreamed of here; the most admired of our jazz rhythms, for example, being quite infantile by comparison. They can teach us something too about *timbre*; certain of their instruments, as vina and tambura, I have never heard equalled in evocative power and sensitivity. In its metaphysical aspects too and those allied to its magical uses, as well as in its natural correspondences to other arts in the manner spoken of in a previous section on Colour and Music, they possess priceless teachings a thorough study of which would fertilize the whole of Western musical thought.

There has been an enormous amount of imitation-oriental music written during the past twenty years or so. In former days, when the world was so much larger than it is now, Mozart and Beethoven were quite content, and quite justified too, in sprinkling their score liberally with triangle and cymbal and calling it "Turkish" music! This was a convention accepted by the West at that period as standing for oriental music (much as a Shakespearean "prop" would be accepted as representing a castle, though it resembled one not at all). None but the most ignorant would have accepted it as a faithful transcription of Eastern music written down for our instruments.

Nowaday, when abundant information is available regarding oriental musical systems, no musician need lack first-hand experience of Indian, Chinese, Japanese, Burmese, Javanese and other types of oriental music, and the pseudo-oriental pinch-beck so frequently foisted upon the public nowadays is indefensible. Few things in music can make the artist

---

64 George Migot (1891-1976), a highly prolific composer whose enthusiasms for the Orient and for ancient modes to some extent paralleled Foulds's. –MM.

65 Foulds is quoting from Schopenhauer's *Die Welt als Wille und Vorstellung* (1819). Schopenhauer had been influenced by Vedic thought through the philosopher and Sanskritist Friedrich Schlegel's *Über die Sprache und Weisheit der Indier* (1808); Wagner—influenced in his turn by Schopenhauer—planned a Vedic opera, *Der Sieger*, which sounds like a forerunner of Foulds's *Avatara* project. –MM.

quite so quickly quite so sickly as those inane "orientalities" of some of the composers who should know better. Your oriental suites, song-cycles (Persian, Chinese, Greek, etc.), love-lyrics ("Indian" and what not), settings of Omar Khayyám, instrumental *intermezzi*, Egyptian suites, Eastern ballets, etc., exist and become popular by other means than by being true to their titles. For they are no more truly Eastern in conception and execution than my piano is African because of its ivory keys. They employ drone fifths in the bass, tam-tam and other percussive effects, avoid to a certain extent the baldest of everyday occidental musical *clichés*, and attempt to conjure up visions of the languorous dreams or phrenetic dances of the Orient. It is surprising that a modern artist of the eminence of Rimsky-Korsakov should have perpetrated such an egregious example of this sort of thing as he has done.[66]

There do exist, however, a number of *bona fide* transcriptions of oriental music. I have had the inestimable advantage of a close acquaintance with a great deal of Indian music in this way, hence the claims I have made at the beginning of this section for a study of it, and the importance of the results which seem to be certain to follow.

2. IMPROVISATION

The Indian musician sets less value than we upon "ready-made" music. Just as he dislikes to eat foods which, having already been prepared and cooked, are now rehashed and served up again and again. Food must be freshly prepared and cooked especially for immediate consumption. Similarly, music must be new-created here and now for his delectation; and from this point of view all our artist performers are not "musicians" at all, properly speaking. He regards them as something like second-hand dealers in other persons' ideas.

It must not be supposed, however, that the Indian musician's improvisation is either the spineless sprawl so frequently offered by our Western improvisers, or a cut-and-dried affair of rigid obedience to inelastic rules. Within certain fixed limits both of Raga (roughly Mode) and Tala (roughly basic-rhythm) there is apparently illimitable scope for free emotional play, for mental-constructive skill, and pre-eminently for those efforts to bring both creator and participator into *rapport* with "higher" states of consciousness which so much of our Western music makes, and so small a proportion achieves.

Here—in Improvisation, individual and collective—is a fertile field for the creative musician of the West, in future years.

7. INDIAN SUITE: *PROGRAMME NOTE* (1935)

[This previously unpublished note—a fair copy in ink for which an earlier draft has also survived—is gummed inside the manuscript full score of Foulds's *Indian Suite* for orchestra. It is headed simply "Note"; and I give the text as it was first written in ink, noting a substantial pencil alteration to the final paragraph in a footnote. The date and place given at the end shows that the note was written after the music, which was complete before Foulds arrived in India. His occasional use of the plural (e.g. "the present writers" in the first paragraph) is intended to associate Maud MacCarthy with him as a co-begetter of the composition, which is based on her then (and still, in 1988) unpublished collection of Indian melodies.]

THIS INDIAN Suite is not to be confused with those numerous pieces which attempt to conjure up an "oriental" atmosphere by use of a drone-bass, tamtam, so-called "oriental" scales, and other "tricks-of-the-trade". Successful as many of these imitations have been with the general public, the present writers have no desire to add to their number. It is rather their aim to present several authentic melodies from the rich inheritance of India's past—an inheritance with which we are none too familiar con-

---

66 Foulds presumably means Rimsky-Korsakov's *Chant Hindou.* Throughout this paragraph there seem to be glancing references to Amy Woodforde-Finden's *Indian Love Lyrics,* Luigini's *Ballet Égyptienne,* and Granville Bantock's cantata *Omar Khayyam,* as well as that composer's copious output of Persian, Chinese and Greek songs. –MM.

sidering the length of our sojourn in the country and the very real value and beauty of the music itself; beauty which, admittedly, had to be perseveringly sought by the devoted artist-collector under a welter of irrelevances and accretions.

In transcribing these melodies from voice and oriental instruments to our modern orchestra compromises have, of course, been made. These, however, are not of the kind indicated above. It is not possible to copy accurately upon our Western instruments the "microtones" (as Maud MacCarthy named them years ago) and other extraordinarily subtle embellishments used by Indian musicians. Apart from these details however, the melodies are presented exactly as taken down from fine Indian artists.

As to their instrumental form: the transcriber has not *imitated* the Indian instrumental sounds or layout. We have no instruments so curiously pervasive as Tambura and Vina, so subtle as Saranghi and Tabla. His aim has been so to paraphrase them by means of our Western instruments and musical technique as to convey to the listener something of the *effect* which these beautiful and characteristic melodies have made upon him.

> Nos. 1 and 5 are Classical Hindu songs of the South.
> No. 2 is a theatrical song from Bombay Presidency.
> Nos. 3 and 4 are Hindu Folk-Songs.

The whole suite therefore reflects the happy, joyous gaiety and, at the same time, the severity of the Hindu art. What the Western world commonly supposes to be *the* "oriental" type—the languorous, the magical, the more erotic (due to Persian influence)—is not represented at all in this work. There are many beautiful examples however in the collection from which this suite is taken;[67] and the transcriber would wish to present them to Western music-lovers at no distant date.

J.F. (Kangra: Punjab. 1935)

8. *"AN INDO-EUROPEAN ORCHESTRA" FROM* ORPHEUS ABROAD (1937)

[Foulds gave a total of 23 broadcast talks on All-India Radio from the Delhi station, on a wide range of topics, including profiles of modern composers, autobiographical reminiscences, "Eastern Songs for Western Singers", and "Personal Recollections of George Bernard Shaw". By far his most important contribution, however, was the series of twelve talks entitled "Orpheus Abroad" which he gave between 6 March and 30 May 1937. While the scripts of the eleven other talks no longer appear to be extant, all but one of the scripts for this series have survived. They are in very various conditions, ranging from neat typescripts to hasty pencil jottings; a few of them have written-out musical examples attached, but in many there are only blank staves or blank spaces, and it is impossible to identify or reconstruct what was actually being played from the studio. Nevertheless the talks as a whole (briefly described on page 83) constitute Foulds's most comprehensive argument for his ideal of a union of the musics of East and West.

The entire scheme of the series was as follows: 1. Is the Gulf between Eastern and Western Music Unbridgeable? 2. What have Eastern and Western Music in Common? 3. (This, the missing script, was titled "Where do the Eastern and Western Systems of Music Diverge?", and was presumably in any case the least essential to Foulds's developing argument.) 4. Whither Indian Music? 5. What Indian Music can give the West. 6. What European Music can offer the East. 7. Indian Harmony.

---

67 A pencil mark indicates the text should be altered so that it runs on directly from "true Hindu art" to "There are many...", omitting the second sentence entirely. The final sentence has also been changed to read "There are many other beautiful examples in this collection...". The effect of this change is to suggest that "the transcriber" wishes to present more of the same kind of melodies at a later date, rather than the Persian-influenced ones. However Foulds's piano piece *Persian Love-Song* (which also dates from 1935, in the Punjab) may be a survival of his original intention. –MM.

8. Musical Notation. 9. Indian Instruments. 10. An Indo-European Orchestra. 11. The Indo-European Orchestra. 12. East Meets West.

Apart from the first talk, which appeared under the title "Orpheus Wanders Abroad" in *The Indian Listener* for 7 April 1937, none of these scripts has previously been published. I give here the tenth talk complete, following it with extracts from the eleventh. The tenth (broadcast on 14 May 1937) dealt with what was to become a reality in 1938, the ensemble of Indian instruments; the eleventh (on 22 May) with the orchestra that would combine these instruments with Western ones. (This may be the significance which Foulds attached to the indefinite and definite articles in the otherwise identical titles.) The eleventh talk necessarily required some repetition from the tenth, and is also itself the sketchiest of manuscripts. It will be noted that the literary style is markedly simpler than that of *Music To-day*, and clearly designed for speaking rather than reading.]

*E*QUALLY INTERESTED as I am in occidental and oriental music – having a very wide experience of Western orchestral music, and seeing what a strong urge there is among young music lovers in India to form Indian orchestras, it is natural that the idea should develop of creating what I have written of and spoken of as the *Indo-European Orchestra*.

First let us make up our minds what we mean by "Indian orchestra".

The first thing I heard that was called an Indian orchestra was a collection of Indian instruments all playing, as nearly as they could manage it, the same melody; and playing it in unison, as nearly as they could manage it, with a singer. Now the distinctive tone of *sitar, sarangi, dilruba* and so on was completely lost when they were all playing the same notes at the same time. It was impossible to distinguish in the mass of sound, the grave delicacy of *sarangi*, the sweetness of *dilruba*, or even much of the real character of *sitar*. And particularly when they were playing the same melody as the singer.

Take a comparison.

Suppose a painter fills his brush with vermillion and paints a beautifully modulated line – one line. That may be charming and give us some satisfaction; a complete picture he could hardly call it. Next he takes a brushful of yellow and goes over the same line, next blue and so on. He has muddied the clarity of his original colour, destroyed the definitiveness of his original line and he is no nearer achieving a picture.

Similarly, a *dilruba* plays a single line of melody, one line. That may be charming and give us some satisfaction. Add to it *sitar, sarangi, shanai*, going over the same line at the same time you muddy the tone colours and destroy the definitiveness of the melody and are no nearer achieving an orchestration.

The second so-called Indian orchestra I heard was mainly Goanese playing Western music upon Western instruments so that here the title "Indian orchestra" was clearly a misnomer.

Another "Indian" orchestra that I hear frequently includes a European violin, a European clarinet, a collection of European tin whistles and a harmonium that I am ashamed to say is European also.

Admittedly my experience is incomplete. India is a big country. I heard the other day of an Indian orchestra in Madras and enquired eagerly about *its* constitution. And it was something of a shock to hear that it included a banjo and suchlike anomalies.

And I have heard Indian instrumental music accompanying films, and also a few very excellent gramophone records composed by and recorded under the supervision of an Indian friend. All these show the direction in which young India is pushing along towards orchestral music. But, looking dispassionately at all these endeavours one is bound I think to reach the conclusion that the real Indian orchestra, properly so-called, does not as yet exist.

As I see it, it must be a gradual growth; and these are the steps: having first recognized that a mere collection of Indian instruments all playing the same tune in unison, is not properly speaking an orchestra, what is the next step? The next step is to separate out these instruments spatially so that their different tone-colours have a chance to make their due effect. You have, as I showed in my last talk, a wealth of indigenous instruments in India, and, spaced out in the way I have just indicated, you have the basic materials for your Indian orchestra.

But, step two, the moment you cease this habit of all the instruments playing the same tune in unison, which, musically speaking, is a babyish thing to do, the moment you separate them in order to retain their characteristics and to make a beautiful total effect, then you have some sort of harmony, as the word is understood in the West. I have already devoted one whole talk to the subject of Indian harmony arising from India's own melodic system, and I will only say now that in my view that is perfectly feasible.

Now step three: the moment you have groups of instruments all playing different parts to make up a harmonious and homogenous whole—that moment you have to abandon improvisation and also you have to adopt some system of notation which can be quickly read. For it would be very difficult indeed for each individual in an orchestra to remember every note of his part of the harmony: very much more difficult than to remember merely a melody. And I remember His Majesty the King[68] after making some comments on a choral performance in London, remarking to me that he had realized as a boy in the school choir, the difficulty of sticking to one's own part of the harmony whilst others were singing something different.

The same difficulty arises in orchestras, hence the necessity for some clear and concise notation.

This again is a subject to which I have already devoted a whole talk in this series, so the ground is cleared in three directions. We see the desirability of allowing the different tone-colours of the instruments to be heard: arising from that we see the growth of harmony; and as a corollary to that we see the need for a system of notation which shall be readily comprehensible to the eye.

Now all artists throughout the world, particularly creative artists, know what a dead weight of inertia there exists which automatically opposes itself to any forward movement. I suppose ninety-five percent of people would say, "Oh, the *old* tunes are good enough for me." And every artist will tell you how often he is asked by people, "Play us, or sing us, something we know." And it is no surprise to find that the ideas I have put before you this evening about the independence of the instruments, about harmony, and about the necessity for an adequate musical notations—it is no surprise to hear the opinion that it is impossible; that you will never get Indian musicians

to play independent musical parts; or get them to maintain what we would call vertical harmony; and least of all will they be able to master staff notation, which is, after all, a highly complicated and very intricate system. Nor will you get, I was warned, the kind of team spirit, the give-and-take, the *ensemble* as the French term it, which is the first essential. These have been some of the doubts expressed, not by Europeans but by Indian music-lovers. But there is really such an opulence of talent among the people of this country that it seemed worth while at least to make an attempt. And there were those who in the genuine spirit of real altruistic patrons of the art of music, have made possible certain tentative experiments. Listeners who are accustomed to finished performances will find it a change, at any rate, to hear these tentative attempts.

First, I wrote down in staff notation a tiny piece for *sitar* and *dilruba*. This is it:

> [Example 1. (Foulds noted at the end of the script: "Musical portion recorded May 13, '37." It is not known what music was played. –MM.)]

Then another little fragment for which I added *sarangi* to the *dilruba* and *sitar*:

> [Example 2. (See above.)]

Already you had, in one short week, the difficulties *beginning* to be surmounted. However gropingly, you had musicians reading this very strange musical script: you had them each maintaining his own part, resulting in harmony.

Next I added *tambura* and wrote an Indian *raga*—harmonizing the melody with notes of the same *raga* only:

> [Example 3. (See above.)]

Then, by way of variety of tone-colour and also by way of changing the key (another innovation which we have discussed in a previous talk) I put in a small interlude on the *vina* based on an ancient *raga*:

> [Example 4. (See above.)]]

---

68   King Edward VIII, who as Prince of Wales had attended the first performance of Foulds's *World Requiem*. —MM.

Thus you have listened (with the cooperation of these five artists) to a tiny demonstration of the inception of what could become the veritable Indian orchetra of the future. And what you have heard — the work of only two weeks — though it may not strike you as much of actual achievement, represents a leap of centuries on the part of these musicians. For to translate these strange signs into sounds, to maintain each his own part of the harmony, and to coalesce into the ensemble you have just heard, is something of a feat, and gives a glimpse of great possibilities for the future of Indian orchestral music. What has just been done by these five players is capable of extension. I should like to add *saranda, sarod*, another *vina*, bamboo flute, *shanai, tabla*, another percussion instrument of the *jaltarang* type, and, if one could get hold of them, a couple of large bass *tamburas*. Of course all music has to be composed and written down for these instruments. The range of each instrument and its characteristics and possibilities understood; as also the capabilities of the players concerned. But I do want to point out that nothing in all this militates against the old Indian traditional system, against the *ragas*, against *harmony growing out of ragas*, or against the *Sa Ri Ga Ma Pa*,[69] or indeed against any of the beauties of Indian music as hitherto practiced, of which I am an ardent lover.

Next Saturday (tomorrow week) I shall carry forward this subject and put before listeners my conception of the Indo-European orchestra, an ideal I have long nursed, and many details of which I have already worked out in theory, if not yet in practice.

* * *

....Tonight I want to complete the idea as it has been present in my mind for some time and put before you a few ideas about the Indo-European Orchestra.

But first let me quote from an article written by the Controller of Broadcasting in India. In this article he said, "To a newcomer who admittedly knows little of India, it seems sometimes that Indian arts are in danger of becoming obscured by the veneer of Western influence, producing aesthetic hybrids which are characteristic of neither, and of doubtful value."

So far as music is concerned he is undoubtedly right. There is a distinct danger that Western gramophone records, film music, dance and other music broadcast from the West may produce (indeed, is producing) in India these aesthetic hybrids. So that, visualising this Indo-European Orchestra I want to make it quite clear that there is no intention of creating just another of these hybrids.

A hybrid is one thing.

A beautifully poised contrast between two different, but complimentary demonstrations of the same art, may be satisfying and congruous, and the result anything but a hybrid. The way in which it is *done* is the all important thing and involves a great many technical points which I don't propose to touch [upon] this evening.

The Indo-European Orchestra as I hear it in my mind's ear, will be capable of giving expression to many shades of emotion which have not hitherto been expressible in either hemisphere.

The tendency of Western orchestras is towards massive effects. You have in the ordinary symphony orchestra not fewer than 20 violins, 10 violas, 8 violoncellos, 4 doublebasses; and powerful instruments like trumpets, horns, trombones, and drums. And it is not at all unusual to hear performances like those I conducted in London some years ago where I had 55 violins and violas, 16 cellos, 10 doublebasses, 12 trumpets, 12 trombones, 9 drummers, a grand organ, and a chorus of over 1,000 voices. Of course the effect of this great body of musicians inside a large concert hall was exceedingly impressive, and although they were not all singing and playing together *all* the time, there were moments when the composer had arranged for the whole body to be in action, when the words called for some muted outburst of praise, or of supplication or of supra-national [affirmation].[70]

At such moments the mighty sonority of such a chorus and orchestra was very impressive indeed and the effect was massive, in the way that some ancient Gothic cathedral pile is massive, dignified and weighty.

Now this quality is absent from Indian *music and instruments* and in my view no attempt should be made to give a massive effect to Indian orchestras but they should be kept in their own natural linear

69 The traditional Indian equivalent to the Tonic Sol-Fa system. –MM.

70 Foulds is referring to the performances of *A World Requiem* given in 1923-26. –MM.

character—all their delicate, gossamer, subtle, sweet and magical qualities should be guarded carefully. So that, compared with the massive Gothic cathedral style of Western type you enjoy the delicate pierced complexity, and the ethereal tracery of a Taj Mahal type.

But there is one thing that will have to be attended to very carefully before the Indian orchestra can really become a satisfactory body and it is this. The neglect here of instruments here is awful. Just as in the case of so many singers here even those who have great control of technique, there is a sad lack of attention to quality of tone. There seems to be an impression that if flexibility of voice is attained the actual sound of the voice, its sweetness and so on is unimportant.

Similarly with instruments. The players are on the whole extraordinarily careless of their condition, and allow them to get into the most awful [state] of disrepair without apparently noticing how terribly the quality of the tone suffers. I must say, too, that the actual makers of instruments are fearfully casual in their work in general. The all important choice of materials and fittings are matters about which they appear to be comparatively unconcerned, and if it should be that some wealthy amateur or patron of music is prepared to spend lavishly on an instrument, all that happens is that extra and lavish decorations are applied to the instrument—that is all.

Now in these two matters—care in construction of instruments and care of the instrument by the player—progress will be necessary if the Indian Orchestra is to vie with the Western, or if the two branches of my proposed Indo-European Orchestra are to be really complementary the one to the other....

Now for a few practical details about this Indo-European Orchestra, which admittedly only exists in my mind up to the present.

Its constitution will be something like this. The Indian section will include as plucked instruments: *sitar*; *tamburas* of various sizes; *vina*; *sarod*. As bowed instruments: *sarangi*; *saranda*; *dilruba*. As wind instruments: the bamboo flute; the *shanai*; and perhaps one of those long trumpet-like brass instruments one of which—from Nepal I think—made a deep impression on me. Of percussion instruments—of course the *tabla* and *mrdanga* and other types of drum, and also the great drum which is sometimes heard in this country with such thrilling effect. Gongs of various kinds too, and other accessory percussion instruments such as *gamelang*, *jaltarang*, silver ankle-bells and so on.

The European section already exists, consisting of the violin family of strings, the flute, clarinet, oboe, bassoon, the horns, trumpet and trombone, the harp, and the drums, cymbals, and triangle.

* * *

Music will of course have to be specially written for this dual orchestra and the doing of this presents some interesting problems for the composer.

First as to tuning: all the Western instruments excepting strings, trumpet and trombone are in tempered tuning; that is, they are tuned with the octave divided into twelve equal semitones—like a piano [JF plays example]. But the Indian instruments are mostly in *natural* tuning: that is, the intervals between the various degrees of the scale within the octave are anything *but* equal, though they correspond with each other.

The natural inference would be, "Oh, very well then—there you are—it is impossible for the occidental and oriental instruments to play in tune together." But this is not so in practice and I have already worked out a list of chords which are common to *both* systems of tuning (there are quite a number of them) and there is more in common than you *dis*paratists would have us think.

But, further, most of the Indian instruments are far inferior in carrying power to the Western ones. They more than compensate for this, in my opinion, by greater subtlety, by extraordinary sweetness, and by their magical capacity for carrying the listener on the wings of sound, far away from mundane considerations, and mechanical, materialistic affairs. Still, there it is, great care will be needed in balance of tone as well as in the matter of intonation, tuning which I spoke of before, if a satisfactory and beautiful result is to be obtained from this proposed blend of East and West.

And there are other, many other difficulties in practice, some of which I confess have suprised me. I may mention one amusing one. My Indian players here, by no means illiterate people, are so accustomed to reading from right to left, that they have great difficulty in realising that an accidental flat or sharp applies to the note on the right of the sign and not to that on the left of it.

But all difficulties of what kind soever vanish in the generous warmth of the imagination when one considers the potentialities of this Indo-European Orchestra.

Such an orchestra, properly constituted, written for with sympathy and understanding, and adequately handled for performance (for some sort of conductor is essential in "team-work" of this scale) might well outrival any in Europe or America because of its greatly extended variety and scope. I am certain that such an orchestra would focus the attention of the whole musical world, and not only vie with but

go beyond what has been done as yet in the West; and as surely as day follows night would send such a glow of light into the future of music in India as would not be unworthy of her glorious achievements in the past; as well as this it could carry the torch of her splendid musical inheritance into the Western world where her achievements in other arts and particularly her magnificently inspiring philosophical and spiritual legacy are held in such warm admiration.[71]

9. *NOTES FOR THE INDO-EUROPEAN ORCHESTRA* (1938)

[Among the materials relating to Foulds's Indian instrumental ensemble or "Indo-European Orchestra" are a number of short program-notes, most of them obviously intended to be read over the microphone during its recitals on A.I.R., and I include here a small miscellany of these previously unpublished items. The first is a neat typescript (with a couple of ink corrections which I take up silently into the text), headed "Tuesday 6th September 1938. 9-45 p.m. Indo-European Orchestra. (Under the direction of John Foulds)." This was the ensemble's very first broadcast.]

*T*HROUGHOUT MUSICAL circles in India there is a demand for harmonised music and for an orchestra of Indian instruments. The Delhi Station of A.I.R. offers listeners an experiment along these lines which has already received a measure of approbation from Indians and Europeans alike. The orchestra consists of Indian instruments *only*. The harmonies employ only notes belonging to the Ragas in which the various melodies are cast. Thus, purity of instrumentation and of harmonization are maintained....

I. *A Pahari (Hill) tune.*

Played upon bamboo flute to the accompaniment of Esraj, Saranda, Sarod, Tambura and Tabla.

II. *A Punjab Dance Tune (Joghir).*

The Sarangi plays this highly characteristic melody supported by Sarods, Tambura and Tabla. A contrasted section (in another raga) is played on the bamboo flute, and a recapitulation of the first part rounds off the piece. It is a classical melody in a Raga associated with early morning.

III. *Mera Salaam Leja.* (A popular [Bengali deleted] melody)

This is an orchestration of a popular tune of the moment arranged with a second part (played on Esraj and Tabla) by way of relief. The jaltarang adds its special tone-colour to the ensemble.

[I follow this with undated notes on five pieces. Numbers 1-3 are roughly written in pencil, while 4-5 are more neatly written in ink on a different sheet; so that, though the numbering appears continuous, it is by no means certain that the two groups of pieces were being presented in the same program. Item 3 is obviously the same as III above — pieces were often repeated from program to program — and Item 5 cor-

---

71 This final paragraph is a verbatim quotation from an article entitled "Orchestration" which Foulds had published in Vol. 2, No. 3 (January 1937) of *The Music Magazine*, a bi-monthly magazine published in Bombay under the patronage of the Maharana of Dharanpur. This was the third of a series of five articles written for that journal (only four of which were published), under the general title "The Present and the Future of Music in India". –MM.

responds to II above. Item 2 is probably a piece called *Bahaar* in Foulds's own lists;
Item 4 is one he called *Afghan Dance Tune*.]

1. Here is a little Punjabi Dance. Western listeners will be intrigued with the quick change between the major and minor 3rd of the key.

2. Now we give you a pensive little melody—a classical Hindustani melody—just an outline of it. I suppose all Western listeners from Day and Fox Strangways to Aldous Huxley in our day have noticed that what seems to us rather sad, or at least contemplative music, is accepted in India as joyous. This melody is a joyous song in the view of Indian musicians.

3. Mera Sala[a]m Leja. A popular Bengali song of the mo[ment].

4. Here is a record of another experiment in presenting an Indian melody in a manner more easily comprehensible to the Western world. That is to say it is harmonised (though only with notes which belong to its own Raga) and instrumented with some regard for the distinctive qualities of the Saranda, Esraj, Sarod, Tambura, Bamboo Flute, Tabla and jalterang. It is an Afghanistan tune.

5. This is a classical melody in a Raga associated with early morning—called Joghia.[72] A contrasted section in a different tempo is frankly a concession to European tastes for the first criticism usually brought against Indian music by listeners of 4 continents is—monotony. As the records are called Indo-European records the purists really have no grounds for objection.[73]

[Finally, a roughly-pencilled sheet dated "Ap.11.10.15pm" is clearly the announcer's preamble to one of Foulds's last concerts with his ensemble.]

Now we hear the Indo-European Orchestra broadcasting a number of items selected from their repertoire.

These are Indian melodies, which have been orchestrated and harmonised with a two-fold purpose. Treated thus they are more intelligible to our Western listeners; and also they show those Indian music-lovers who want harmonisation & orchestras, how these melodies can be harmonised without using Western harmonic methods, and orchestrated without using Western instruments.

The harmonies used are those of the Ragas (the melodies) themselves and none other.

The instruments used are Indian instruments and none other.

And also, the players, who are reading from a musical script are all Indian musicians; Saranghi, Sarinda,Esraj, Sarod, Sitar, Tambura, Bamboo Flute, and Tabla (drums).

---

72 Spelled thus in the manuscript. All other references to this melody I have traced call it *Joghir*. —MM.

73 The reference here to "records" is puzzling, though Foulds probably means "records of an experiment". His correspondence file shows that there were many requests for the ensemble's work to be released in commercial recordings, but this did not happen. —MM.

CATALOG OF WORKS

Note: See also Supplement — List of Works by Opus Number

VOCAL MUSIC

● **CHORUS** (SATB unaccompanied unless otherwise specified)

3 Choruses in the Hippolytus of Euripides (*t.* transl. Gilbert Murray) for female chorus with mezzo-soprano solo & piano, op 84b (1928)(16m)(see also incidental music to *Hippolytus*, op 84 (orchestral works))
1) *There riseth a rockbourn river*
2) *Refuge*
3) *Aphrodite triumphant*

Echo's Song for 2-part female chorus)(1898)(lost)

2 English Madrigals (publ. 1933)(8m)
1) *A May Burden* (*t.* Francis Thompson)
2) *Old Wine, Old Books* (*t.* Robert H. Messinger) for male chorus (TTBB)

Fantasie of Negro Spirituals for chorus *ad lib.* & orchestra (publ. 1932)(13m)

The Fires Divine: see incidental music (Orchestral)

Hymn of the Redeemed: see *A World Requiem,* op 60.13

Keltic Lament (*t.* from the Ancient Erse) for chorus & piano (or harp)(publ. 1933)(arr. of *Keltic Suite* for orchestra, op 29.2; orig. as *Keltic Melodies* for string orchestra & harp [.2]; also for male chorus, for violin [or cello] & piano, and as *A Prayer for Freedom* for solo voice, piano & organ *ad lib.*)

Mantra of Bliss: see opera *Avatara*

3 Marching Songs (*t.* adapted from Bulwer Lytton novel *Rienzi*) for chorus & orchestra (or piano), op 5 (publ. 1929)(10m)(also for male chorus, op 5a)
1) *Santo Spirito*
2) *Lances of the Free*
3) *The Grand Compagnie*

The New Noel (carol)(*t.* H.K. Ainsworth)(1920)

5 Scottish-Keltic Songs, op 70 (publ. 1925)(20m)
1) *West Highland Boat Song* (*t.* anon)

[CHORUS (continued)]
2) *Cro' Chaillean (Colin's Cattle)*(*t.* anon)
3) *Quidry Bay (A Song at Sundown)*(*t.* H.K. Ainsworth)(also arr. for male voices)
4) *Oimè* (*t.* George MacDonald)
5) *John Heilandman* (*t.* Robert Burns)(also for chorus & orchestra)

Veils: see incidental music (Orchestral)

● **DRAMATIC WORKS**

Film music: see Orchestral music

Henry VIII: see incidental music (Orchestral)

Incidental music (for plays, etc.): see Orchestral music

MELODRAMAS

The Gay Gordons (*t.* Henry Newbolt) for speaker & orchestra (*c.*1932)(lost)

The Song of Honour (*t.* Ralph Hodgson) for speaker, female chorus *ad lib.* & chamber orchestra (2 flutes [or piccolo, flute] clarinet [or bass clarinet], horn, piano, triangle, side drum & string quintet), op 54 (1918)(14m)

The Tell-Tale Heart (dramatic monologue)(*t.* after Edgar Allan Poe story) for speaker & orchestra (or piano), op 36 (1910)(15m)

OPERAS

Avatara (3 acts), op 61 (1919-32)(Act III not finished, score prob. destroyed except for *3 Mantras*)

¶*3 Mantras* for female voices *ad lib.* & orchestra, op 61b (1919-30)(22m)
1) *Mantra 1 (Of Action)*(Impetuoso)(orig. Act I Prelude)
2) *Mantra 2 (Of Bliss)*(Beatamente)(orig. Act II Prelude, with female chorus *ad lib.*)
3) *Mantra 3 (Of Will)*(Inesorabile)(orig. Act III Prelude)

Cleopatra (miniature opera), op 27 (*c.*1911)(lost)

[DRAMATIC WORKS (OPERAS) (continued)]

Marmion (*c.*1900)(fragments only for operatic project)

Solomon, op 26 (*c.*1911)(unfinished, lost except for excerpt)

¶*An Eastern Lover*(scena)(*t.* from the Song of Songs) for voice & orchestra (or piano), op 26a (perf. 1911)(6m)

Undine (*c.*1900)(fragments only for operatic project)

The Vision of Dante (concert-opera)(*t.* composer, after Dante Alighieri's *Divina commedia*) for soprano, contralto, tenor, baritone, bass, semi-chorus, chorus & orchestra, op 7 (*c.*1905-08)(2 hrs)(some music prob. also arr. as *12 Pièces d'occasion* for chamber orchestra, op 57.8-.12)

Part 1: *Hell*
   Prologue (orchestral)
   Scene 1: Ante Hell (Dante, Virgil)
   Scene 2: The Gates of Hell (Virgil, Charon, Lost Souls)
   Scene 3: Upper Hell (Dante, Virgil, Francesca)
   Scene 4: Lower Hell (Virgil, Plutus)
   Scene 5: The Styx (Virgil, Dante, Phlegias)
   Scene 6: The City of Dis (Dante, Virgil)
   Scene 7: Phlegethon (Dante, Virgil)
   Scene 8: Malebolge (Dante, Virgil, Demons)
   Scene 9: The Lake of Ice (Dante, Virgil)

Part 2: *Purgatory*
   Scene 1: Ante Purgatory (Dante, Virgil, Chorus of Ransomed Souls)
   Scene 2: The Mountain of Purgation: First Circle (Virgil, Dante, Angel, Celestial Voices)
   Scene 3: The Mountain of Purgation: Second Circle (Virgil, Dante, Angel, Celestial Voices)
   Scene 4: The Mountain of Purgation: Third Circle (Virgil, Dante, Angel, Souls in Purgatory, Celestial Voices)
   Scene 5: The Mountain of Purgation: Fourth Circle (Virgil, Dante, Angel, Souls in Purgatory)

[DRAMATIC WORKS (OPERAS) (continued)]

   Scene 6: The Mountain of Purgation: Fifth Circle (Dante, Souls in Purgatory)
   Scene 7: The Mountain of Purgation: Sixth Circle (Angel of Glory, Virgil)
   Scene 8: The Earthly Paradise (Dante, Virgil, Spirits in Paradise)

Part 3: *Paradise*
   Scene 1: The Heaven of the Moon (Beatrice, Dante)
   Scene 2: The Heaven of Mercury (Spirits in Paradise)
   Scene 3: The Heaven of the Sun (Dante, Beatrice)
   Scene 4: The Heaven of Mars (Dante, Beatrice)
   Scene 5: The Heaven of Jupiter (Souls of the Faithful and Just Rulers)
   Scene 6: The Heaven of Saturn (Dante, Beatrice)
   Scene 7: The Stellar Heaven (Beatrice)
   Scene 8: The Crystalline Heaven (Beatrice, Chorus)
   Scene 9: The Spaceless Empyrean (Dante, Beatrice, Celestial Voices)

¶*2 Excerpts from "The Vision of Dante"* arr. for string quintet, op 41 (1915)(lost)[†]

● **VOICE & INSTRUMENT(S)** (piano unless otherwise specified)

Beatrice's Song: see *The Cenci* (Orchestral: incidental music)

Charm Me Asleep (*t.* Robert Herrick)(1925)

Come back beloved (perf. 1938)(lost)

An Eastern Lover: see opera *Solomon*

Garland of Youth (song-cycle), op 86 (1925)(12m)
   1) *Life and Love* (*t.* Henry Wadsworth Longfellow)
   2) *A cradle-croon* (*t.* anon)(rev. vers. as *Mavourneen my darling*)
   3) *My garden* (*t.* T.E. Brown)
   4) *The Fairies* (*t.* William Allingham)

The Gay Gordons: see melodramas, above

Lyra celtica (concerto) for wordless solo voice & orchestra, op 50 (mid-1920s)(c.20m)
   1) Lento–Allegro comodo
   2) Largo–Quasi allegretto piacevole

[†]   A brief manuscript diary record of 1915 mentions working on a *third* "Dante" Excerpt, but Foulds's catalogues only list two.

[VOICE & INSTRUMENT(S) (continued)]

3) Brioso, tempo giusto (unfinished)

Melody Divine for tenor (c.1910)

Mood Pictures (song cycle)(*t.* Fiona McLeod
[pseud. for William Sharp])

Set 1: Op 51 (1917)(15m)

1) *The Shadowy Woodlands*

2) *Evoë!*

3) *The Reed Player*

4) *Orchil* (see also *A World Requiem* for
voices & orchestra, op 60.16)

5) *Lances of Gold*

Set 2: Op 52 (unfinished)

Oriental Vocalise for unaccompanied mezzo-
soprano (1936)

Orpheus with his Lute: see *Henry VIII* (orchestral
works — incidental music)

Pagan Hymn (*t.* unknown) for mezzo-soprano
(or tenor) (c.1925)

Parting and Meeting (*t.* Marten Cumber-
land)(publ. 1931)

A Prayer for Freedom (*t.* William Akerman) for
voice, piano & organ *ad lib.* (publ. 1918)(arr.
of *Keltic Suite* for orchestra, op 29.2; also
arr. as *Keltic Lament* for chorus & piano (or
harp); orig. as *Keltic Melodies* for string orchestra & harp (.2))

Roses and Rue: see *The Whispering Well* (Orchestral: incidental music)

A Roundelay for soprano (c.1914)

4 Rumanian Gypsy Songs (1932)(unfinished)(lost)

The Seven Ages (monologue)(*t.* Shakespeare,
from *As You Like It*) for baritone & orchestra
(or piano)(1932)(7m)

Singing Lessons by means of the "Inner Voice"
for unaccompanied voice (1915)

The Song of Honour: see melodramas, above

The Song of the Blest: see *A World Requiem*, op
60.13

2 Songs for baritone, op 2 (c.1898)(lost)

1) *Du bist wie eine Blume [Thou art like a
flower]* (*t.* Heinrich Heine)

2) *The Vagabond* (*t.* Robert Louis Stevenson)

2 Songs (*t.* Charles d'Orleans) for tenor, op 15
(c.1908) (lost except for sketch drafts)

1) *Rejected Love*

2) *Renouveau*

3 Songs, op 69 (c.1922)

1) *Allah* (*t.* Henry Wadsworth Longfellow)

2) *Eleen Aroon* (*t.* Gerald Griffin)

[VOICE & INSTRUMENT(S) (continued)]

3) *Spring Joy* (*t.* Henry Wadsworth Longfellow)

2 Songs in "Sacrifice": see incidental music (Orchestral)

6 Songs in Indian Style (*t.* Kabir) for mezzo-
soprano (unaccompanied), op 43
(c.1915)(unfinished)(lost)

3 Songs of Beauty, op 11 (1925-38)

1) *There be none of Beauty's daughters* (*t.*
Byron)

2) *Helen* (*t.* Edgar Allan Poe)

3) *To One in Paradise* (*t.* Edgar Allan Poe)

Sweet Babe (*t.* Charles d'Orleans, transl. Longfellow) for contralto (c.1910)

4 Tagore Songs for voice & harp (lost)

The Tell-Tale Heart: see melodramas, above

Weaver of Songs (*t.* unknown) for mezzo-
soprano (c.1925)

A World Requiem (*t.* from the Bible, Requiem Mass,
Benedicite, John Bunyan, the Hindu poet Kabir,
with additional words by Maud MacCarthy) for
soprano, contralto, tenor, baritone (or bass),
small chorus of boys & youths, full chorus,
organ & orchestra (incl. extra brass & percussion at corners of the hall, distant ensemble of 2
harps, celesta, sistrum & 4 solo violins), op 60
(1919-21; partly rev. post-1923)(2 hrs 5m)

Part 1

1) *Requiem* (incl. theme from *Music-Poem 5*
for orchestra, op 20)

2) *Pronuntatio* (incl. ground-bass from
Gandharva-Music for piano)

3) *Confessio*

4) *Benedictio*

5) *Audite*

6) *Pax* (see also *Peace and War* for orchestra)

7) *Consolatio*

8) *Refutatio*

9) *Lux veritatis*

10) *Requiem*

Part 2

11) *Laudamus*

12) *Elysium*

13) *In pace* (incl. *Hymn of the Redeemed* for
unaccompanied chorus; alternate vers.
incl. soprano aria *The Song of the Blest*)

¶*The Song of the Blest* (*t.* from the Book of
Revelations) arr. for voice, piano &
violin *obbligato*(c.1922)(5m)

14) *Angeli*

15) *Vox Dei*

16) *Adventus* (based on music from *Mood-Pictures* for voice & piano, op 51.4)

17) *Vigilate*

18) *Promissio et invocatio*

19) *Benedictio*

20) *Consummatus*

CHAMBER MUSIC

Caprices

3 Caprice-Etuden for 2 cellos (1895)(lost)

Caprice Pompadour: see 3 Pieces for violin & piano, op 42.2

Cello & piano

Evening in the Odenwald for cello & piano (1938)(4m)(arr. of *Holiday Sketches*, op 16.3)

2 Pieces, op 25 (publ. 1914)(8m)

    1) *Canadian Boat Song*

    2) *Old French Gigue*

Polonaise brilliant (1895)(lost)

3 Small Pieces (1895)(lost)

Sonata, op 6 (1905; rev. 1927)(26m)

    1) Moderato quasi allegretto

    2) Lento

    3) Brioso ed amabile (main theme also used in *Concerto 1* for cello & orchestra, op 17.1)

4 Stücke [4 Pieces] (1895-96)(lost)

Suite in b (1896)(lost)

Duetto in G for violin & cello (1889)(lost)

2 Excerpts from "The Vision of Dante": see operas (Vocal)

Fantasie nach Heine: see 3 Pieces for violin & piano, op 42.2

Greek Processional for string quintet (1915)(4m)(arr. & conflation of *5 Recollections of Ancient Greek Music* for piano, op 45.2 & .4)

Impromptus on a Theme of Beethoven for 4 cellos, op 9 (1905)(6m)

● **INDO-EUROPEAN MUSIC** for combinations of traditional Indian instruments (bamboo flute, dilruba, esraj, ghungharu, saranda, sarangi, sarod, sitar, tabla, tambura, vina)(1938-39)(scores largely fragmentary; each 3-5m)

Brindaban (A Little Indian Music-Picture)

Golconda

Indo-European Idylls (3)

Kashmiri Wedding Procession (orig. for small orchestra)

[INDO-EUROPEAN MUSIC (continued)]

Orientale (orig. for piano solo)

Poem

Sonorities (A Study for Indian Instruments)

Vision of the Orient

Transcriptions & arrangements (Indian folk sources unless otherwise specified):

    Afghan Dance Tune

    Bahaar (classical Hindustani melody)

    Bengali Melodies

    Bharair (dance tune)

    Bhopali and Durbari

    Chant Hindu (Rimsky-Korsakov)

    Deshkar (Hindu melody)

    Joghir

    Kabuli Dance

    Mera Salam Leja (popular Bengali tune)

    Nautch Dance

    A Pahari [Hill] Tune

    Peraj

    Peshwari Dance Tune

    Punjabi Dance Tune

    Punjabi Village Love-Song (Mahîa)

    Punjabi Village Tune

Interludes for organ (1915)(lost)

Music-Pictures

Group 1: for violin, cello & piano, op 30 (perf. 1921)(lost)

    1) *Refugium* (after Paul Leroy)

    2) *In Provence* (after La Thangue)(see also Group 2, op 32.1)

    3) *Aeolian Harps* (after Rossi)

    4) *Gargoyles* (after Michelangelo)

Group 2: *Aquarelles* for string quartet, op 32 (1905-?; perf. 1926)(12m)

    1) *In Provence (Refrain Rococco)*(after La Thangue; prob. arr. of Group 1, op 30.2; for early vers. of main theme see *Quartet 8* for strings, op 23.2; distorted variant in *Miniature Suite* for orchestra, op 38.4;

[*Music-Pictures* Group 2 **(continued)**)]
    movement also arr. & adapted as *Sin-fonietta* for orchestra, op 37.3)
  2) *The Waters of Babylon* (after Blake)
  3) *Arden Glade (English Tune with Burden)*(after Crome)(rev. of *English Tune with Burden* for piano solo)
Group 3: see orchestral works
Group 4: see orchestral works
Group 5: for flute, clarinet, violin & cello, op 73 (1922)
  1) *Ossian Sings* (Gaelic Melody)
  2) *Wendaway* (English Tune with Burden)(after Morland)(lost)
  3) *Orientale* (after Bose)(lost; possibly arr. of *Orientale* for piano solo)
  4) *Gypsies* (after Goya)(lost)
Group 6: see orchestral works (also for piano solo)
Group 7: see piano solo
Group 8: see piano solo
Group 9: see orchestral works
Brindaban (A Little Indian Music-Picture): see Indo-European music for combinations of traditional Indian instruments, above
Eddies (A Little Music-Picture): see piano solo
Pasquinades
  Pasquinade: see *Quartet 9* for strings, op 89.3
  Pasquinade: see *Quartet 10* for strings, op 97.2
  Pasquinade for flute, oboe, clarinet & bassoon (c.1936)(sketch only)
  Pasquinades for 2 pianos, op 93 (c.1935)
    1) *Symphonie (Classical)*(Allegro, non troppo presto)(incl. theme from *Quartet 9* for strings, op 89.5; arr. & expanded as *Pasquinades symphoniques* for orchestra, op 98.1)(partly lost)
    2) *Parallels (Romantic)*(Lento quieto molto)(incl. main theme of *Music-Pictures* (Group 7) for piano solo, op 13.1)(partly lost)
    3) *Military (Futuristic)* (lost)
  Pasquinades symphoniques: see symphonies (Orchestral)
  Sinfonietta (orig. *3 Pasquinades*): see orchestral works

● **PIANO SOLO**
Andante affetuoso in E^b (1896)(2m)
Canon in F (1896)(2m)
Chromatic Valse (c.1937)(5m)

[**PIANO SOLO (continued)**)]
Dichterliebe [Poet's Love] (1897-98)(25m)
  1) *Prolog [Prologue]*
    Waldwanderung [Forest wandering] (Sempre molle e muovendo–*Intermezzo*–Tempo im vorigen Stück
  2) Lento molto e triste
  3) *Impromptus über ein Thema von Ideala*
    i) in e^b (Morvido, calmo ma mosso)
    i) in E^b (Un poco piu mosso)
    iii) in g$^{\#}$ (Feroce e spaventoso)
    iv) *Zum Beschluss* (Presto focoso ed incalzando) in E
  4) *Rhapsodie über motiven von Richard Wagner*
  5) *Einleitung [Introduction]*–Lento–Molto largo–*Forsetztung und Schluss [Continuation and Conclusion]*–Come prima
  6) Lentamente e festivo
  7) *Der Liebe Tod [The Love-Death]* (unfinished)
    Prolog (Largo con digità)–Beginning of fugal movement
Eddies: see *Music-Pictures* for piano, below
English Tune with Burden (c.1914)(5m)(also rev. as *Music-Pictures* (Group 2) for string quartet, op 32.3)
Essays in the Modes, op 78 (1920-27)
  Volume 1
    1) *Exotic* (Quasi lento)
    2) *Ingenuous* (1/8th = 72)
    3) *Introversive* (Semplice con rassegnazione)
    4) *Military* (Burlesco ma ben ritmico)
    5) *Strophic* (Come una memoria)
    6) *Prismic* (Con alcuna licenza)
  Volume 2 (sketches)
    ¶*Egoistic*(1927)(4m)(only completed piece of Volume 2; may be performed between .5 and .6 of Volume 1)
    ¶*Piece in Mode IA* (2m)(realization by Malcolm MacDonald from sketches)
The Florida Spiritual (also as 2 Pieces for orchestra, op 71.1)
Gandharva-Music, op 49 (1915-26)(3m)(groundbass also used in *A World Requiem* for solo voices, chorus & orchestra, op 60.2)
Holiday Sketches (also for orchestra)
Humoreske in D^b/c$^{\#}$ (1897)(5m)

[PIANO SOLO (continued)]

Impressions of Time and Place, op 48
    1) *April–England* (1926)(7m)(partly based on
        motive from incidental music to *Saint
        Joan* and central section of melodrama
        The Song of Honour; also arr. for or-
        chestra, op 48.1)
    2) see orchestral works
    3) *Sea-Moods* (c.1925)(unfinished; incl.
        theme used in *Peace and War* for or-
        chestra)
Indian Garland, op 96 (c.1937)(lost)
Indian Melodies, op 102 (1938-39)(unfinished?
    only .3 definitely complete, though rough
    draft of .1 extant in version for small or-
    chestra)
    1) *Village Tunes*
    2) *Love Song* (Bhajan)
    3) *Dance Tunes from Punjab* (one tune also
        used in *Grand Durbar March*)
    4) *Pahari Tune* (from the Hills)
2 Little Râgâ Studies (1937)(2m)
    1) *Kanara*
    2) *Todi*
Menuetto in G (1890)(lost)
Mississippi Savannahs (Negro spiritual)(also as
    2 Pieces for orchestra, op 71.2)
Music-Pictures (see also above)
    Group 6: *Gaelic Melodies* (also for orchestra)
    Group 7: *2 Landscapes,* op 13 (c.1927)(7m)
        1) *Moonrise–Sorrento* (principal theme
            also used in *Pasquinades* for 2 pianos,
            op 93.2; theme also used for *Sinfoniet-
            ta* for orchestra, op 37.2)
        2) *Nightfall–Luxor*
    Group 8: *For the Young,* op 21 (publ.
        1927)(8m)
        1) *The New Spinet (Minuet)* (after Lucas)
        2) *Dignity and Impudence (Polka bur-
            lesque)*(after Landseer)
        3) *The Rainbow* (tone poem)(after
            Kirkpatrick)(also arr. for small or-
            chestra)
    Eddies (A Little Music Picture)(publ.
        1924)(4m)
Music-Poems (see also orchestral works)
    1) *Lyrics,* op 1 (1900)(3m)
    3) *The Wanderer,* op 14 (c.1907)(lost)
Orientale (c.1927)(3m)(also for traditional Indian
    instruments; see Indo-European music,
    above)

[PIANO SOLO (continued)]

Persian Love Song (1935)(4m)
5 Recollections of Ancient Greek Music, op 45
    (1915)(15m) (also arr. as *Hellas (A Suite of
    Ancient Greece),* op 45.1-.5; .2 & .4 also arr.
    as *Greek Processional* for string quintet)
    1) *Solemn Temple Dance* (in the Lydian
        mode)(Remoto e senza passione)(also
        for harp, gong & strings)
    2) *Processional* (in the Ionian mode)(1/2 =
        88 senza deviazione)
    3) *Song of Argive Helen* (in the Dorian
        mode)(1/8th = 84)(also for 3 flutes, oboe,
        cor anglais, 2 clarinets, horn, harp &
        strings; theme also used in incidental
        music for *Hippolytus* (prelude), op 84)
    4) *Temple Chant* (in the Dorian mode)(whole
        note = 58)(also for 20 wind instruments)
    5) *Dirge for a Hero* (in the Phrygian mode)(1/4
        = 69-92)(combiamente di tempi sempre
        insensibilimente)(uses theme from *Music-
        Pictures* (Group 3) for orchestra, op 33.3)
Rondo in G (1893)(lost)
Scherzos
    in a (1895)(lost)
    Scherzo chromatique (c.1927)(lost)
Sicilian Aubade (1927)(6m)(also arr. for or-
    chestra)
Sonata (A Study in Structure) in F# (1897)(un-
    finished)
Strophes from an Antique Song
    (c.1927)(3m)(also arr. for small orchestra)
Suites
    Henry VIII Suite (orig. for orchestra)
    Keltic Suite (orig. for orchestra)
    Saint Joan Suite (orig. for orchestra)
    Suite fantastique (arr. from incidental music
        for *Deburau*; also for orchestra)
*Variazioni ed improvvisati su una thema
    originale,* op 4 (publ. 1905)(14m)
Pianos (2)
    Grand Durbar March (1937)(c.6m)(this vers. lost;
        also arr. for European symphony orchestra
        & ensemble of Indian instruments)
    Pasquinades, op 93: see above
Quartets for strings (2 violins, viola, cello)
    1) in d (1896)(lost)
    2) in a (1896)(lost)
    3) *Quartett romantische* (1899)(lost)
    4) in f (1899)(22m)
        1) Lento lugubre–Allegro molto vivace

[*Quartets* for strings (**continued**)]
> 2) All' arabesco (Presto comodo assai)
> 3) Quasi impromptus (Andante assai lento)
> 5) *Quartetto in Semplicitá* in c# (1900)(lost)
> 6) *Quartetto romantico* (1903)(24m)
>> 1) Allegro
>> 2) Largo, quasi una tragedia (main theme also used in *Concerto 1* for cello & orchestra, op 17.2)
>> 3) Presto, molto passionato
> 7) in E (c.1907)(lost)
> 8) in d, op 23 (1907-10)(15m)
>> 1) Andante lento
>> 2) Allegro, non strepitoso (incl. early vers. of main theme of *Music-Pictures* (Group 2) for string quartet, op 32.1)
> 9) *Quartetto intimo*, op 89 (1931-32)(34m)
>> 1) Poco trattenuto–Impetuoso
>> 2) Lento introspettivo
>> 3) Pasquinade (Con umore)
>> 4) Colloquy (Serioso)
>> 5) Energico passionato, non stretto (theme also used in *Pasquinades* for 2 pianos, op 93.1)
> 10) *Quartetto geniale,* op 97 (c.1935)
>> 1) Animato assai (partly lost)
>> 2) Pasquinade (Allegro)(lost)
>> 3) Lento quieto
>> 4) Colloquy (Moderato)(lost)
>> 5) Finale gai (lost)

Recitative and Adagio for bassoon & piano (1895)(lost)

Sonatas
> for cello & piano: see cello & piano works, above
> in d for 2 cellos (1895)(lost)
> *Sonata in Ancient Style* for solo cello (pre-1914)(lost)

Trios
> in a for violin, cello & piano (1896)(lost)
> in F for violin, viola & cello, op 24 (1911)
>> 1) Poco allegro (unfinished)
>> 2) Ritornello con variazione (Allegretto comodo e piacevole)(early vers. of theme also used in *Fiddler's Jig* for violin & piano (op 42.3) and for string orchestra (op 55.3))
> *Darby and Joan*, op 42.1 (vers. with piano of work for violin, clelo & string orchestra)
> *Music-Pictures* Group 4, op 55, arr. for violin, cello & piano (orig. for string orchestra: see orchestral works)

[*Trios* (**continued**)]
> *Oriental Nocturne* for violin, cello & piano (arr. of *An Arabian Night* for small orchestra)
> *Variations on "The Ash Grove"* for solo violin (1890)(lost)

● **VIOLIN & PIANO**
> *Keltic Lament* for violin & piano (1915)(4m)(arr. of *Keltic Suite* for orchestra, op 29.2; also for cello & piano)
> *Keltic Melody* for violin & piano (publ. 1932)(transcr. of *Keltic Overture* for orchestra, op 28)
> *Marche* in D for violin & piano (1888)(lost)
> Piece (*c.*1898)(unfinished)
> *3 Pieces*, op 42 (1916)
>> 1) see orchestral works
>> 2) *Caprice Pompadour* (7m)(rev. of 1897 *Fantasie nach Heine*; theme also used in *Suite fanastique*, op 72b.1 (see incidental music for *Deburau*))
>> 3) *Fiddler's Jig* (also arr. as *Music-Pictures* (Group 4) for string orchestra, op 55.3)
> *4 Pieces*, op 40 (c.1909)
>> 1) *Ballade and Refrain Rococco*
>> 2) *Westwind (An Encore Study)*(lost)
>> 3) *Toccata Baroque (Etude diabolique)*(lost)
>> 4) *La Joyeuse (Valse nobile)*(lost)
> *Sonia* (character study) (publ. 1925)(5m)(arr. of incidental music for *Masse-Mensche*, op 83.13)
> *Zephyr (Un petite idyll)* for violin & cello (c.1929)(lost)

● **TRANSCRIPTIONS & ARRANGEMENTS:**
> BRIDGE (FRANK)/FOULDS
>> *An Easter Hymn* arr. for flute, string quartet, organ & bells (c.1918)
> GOUNOD/FOULDS
>> *Judex (*from *Mors et Vita)* arr. for flute, piano & string quartet (c.1918)
> SCHUMANN (R)/FOULDS
>> *Traümerei* (from *Kinderszenen*) arr. for cello & piano (c.1908)
> WAGNER/FOULDS
>> *3 Excerpts from Das Rheingold* arr. for flute, piano & string quartet (c.1918)
>> *Parsifal-Music* arr. for flute, trumpet, tuba, organ, piano & string quartet (c.1918)

● **WORKS FOR UNKNOWN FORCES:**
> *The Glaston Chant in 4 Aspects* (before 1926)(sketches only)

[WORKS FOR UNKNOWN FORCES [continued)]
Poetical Reveries, op 99(c.1937)(lost)
   1) *The Lost Traveller's Dream under the Hill*

[WORKS FOR UNKNOWN FORCES [continued)]
   2) *The Land of Beaulah beyond the Delectable Mountains*
   3) *Beneath the Tent-tree by the Wayside Well*

ORCHESTRAL MUSIC

An Arabian Night (Oriental nocturne) for small orchestra (flute, oboe, clarinet, bassoon, 2 horns, percussion & strings)(also for piano trio)(c.1936)(6m)(incl. material adapted from *Nature-Notes 3* for small orchestra)
Badinage for flute, clarinet, celesta, triangle & strings (c.1937)(4m)
Basque Serenade (Serenata espagnole) for 2 flutes, 2 clarinets, 2 horns, castanets, triangle & strings (c.1938)(7m)
La Belle Pierrette (Intermezzo Impromptu) for orchestra (publ. 1922)(5m)
Carnival for orchestra (1934)(5m)(theme also used in *A Puppet Ballet Suite* (.1) for orchestra)
Chinese Boat Song for small orchestra (c.1937)(sketches only)
Concertos
  for cello & orchestra
    1) in G, op 17 (1908-09)(30m)
      1) Allegretto piacevole (incl. main theme of *Sonata* for cello & piano, op 6.3)
      2) Adagio molto (incl. main theme of *Quartet 6* (.2) for strings)
      3) Impetuoso
    2) in d for cello & small orchestra, op 19 (c.1910)(free arr. of a *Concerto grosso* by Corelli)(lost)
    Lento e scherzetto, op 12 (c.1906)(15m)(movement .2 of an early abandoned *Concerto*)
    Lyra Celtica: see voice & instrument(s)(Vocal)
  for piano & orchestra
    Dynamic Triptych: see below
12 Dedicated Works for chamber orchestra (lost apart from fragments)
  Set 1: op 44 (1915)(12 pieces)
  Set 2: op 47 (c.1926)(12 pieces)
Deva-Music (Symphonic Pieces) for orchestra, op

94 (1935-36)(25m)(score lost; many sketches & drafts for .2)
  1) *Of Gandharvas*
  2) *Of Apsaras*
Dynamic Triptch for piano & orchestra, op 88 (1929)(27m)
  1) *Dynamic Mode*
  2) *Dynamic Timbre*
  3) *Dynamic Rhythm*
Fantasies
  Fantasie classique for small orchestra (lost)
  Fantasie of Negro Spirituals: see vocal works (choral)
  Fantasie russe for orchestra (1932)(12m)(on themes by Tchaikovsky)
● **FILM SCORES** (all short films)(no separate scores extant)
  Belgian Curiosity
  Clef de Bronze
  Four Barriers (1937)(comp. with Benjamin Britten)
  Hullo Everybody
  Locomotives (1935)
  Many a Pickle (1938)(credited as jointly composed with Benjamin Britten and Victor Yates)
  Scotland Yard
  So This Is London (1933)
  Spring Comes to England (1934)
  Superman
  Ten-Minute Alibi
  Ulster
Grand Durbar March for European symphony orchestra & ensemble of Indian instruments (1938)(6m)(orig. for 2 pianos)
Hebrew Rhapsody for orchestra (publ. 1936)(15m)
Holiday Sketches for orchestra, op 16 (publ. 1909)(20m)(also for piano solo)

[*Holiday Sketches*, op 16 **(continued)**]
1) *Festival in Nuremburg* (Allegro giocoso)
2) *Romany from Bohemia* (Quasi presto e focoso)
3) *Evening in Odenwald* (Lento calmo assai)(also arr. for cello & piano)
4) *Bells at Coblenz* (Moderato pesante–Allegro)

Impressions of Time and Place, op 48
1) *April–England* (1932)(8m)(arr. & exp. of piece for piano solo)
2) *Isles of Greece* for small orchestra (2 flutes, oboe (or cor anglais), 2 clarinets, 2 horns, timpani, celesta, organ & strings)(1927)(5m)(also earlier vers. for 2 flutes, oboe, clarinet, trumpet, harp & strings)
3) see piano solo

● **INCIDENTAL MUSIC** for plays (*lost)
At the Hawk's Well (W.B. Yeats) for 3 players (1917)(comp. with Maud McCarthy)
Baldur the Beautiful (Violet Rawnsley) for small orchestra (at least 12 players), op 79 (*c.*1923)
The Cenci (Percy Bysshe Shelley), op 77 (1923)
1) *Interlude* for instruments (lost)
2) *Beatrice's Song* for voice & piano
Cymbeline (Shakespeare), op 80 (1923)
The Dance of Life (Hermon Ould), op 85 (1925)
Dear Brutus (11 numbers for J.M. Barrie play) for small orchestra (flute, oboe, horn, piano, timpani, 3 violins, viola, 2 cellos, bass)(1934)(sketches only)
Deburau (Sacha Guitry), op 72 (1921)
¶*Le Cabaret (Overture to a French Comedy)* for orchestra, op 72a (publ. 1925)(4m)(arr. from incidental music; also for piano solo)
¶*Suite fantastique* for orchestra, op 72b (publ. 1924)(15m)(arr. from incidental music; also for piano solo)
1) *Pierrette and Pierrot* (incl. theme from 3 Pieces for violin & piano, op 42.2)
2) *Chanson plaintive*
3) *The Wayside Cross*
4) *Carnival Procession*
The Fires Divine (Rosaline Valmer) for boys' chorus & instrumental ensemble, op 76 (1922)
The Goddess (Nirjal Pal), op 75 (1922)
1) Overture
2) Entr'actes
3) Incidental Music

[**INCIDENTAL MUSIC** for plays **(continued)**]
Henry VIII (overture & 29 numbers for the Shakespeare play) for voices & small orchestra (flute, oboe, clarinet, horn, 2 trumpets, tuba, timpani, organ, celesta, lute, cymbals, side drum, bass drum & strings), op 87 (1925)
¶*Henry VIII Suite (Suite in the Olden Style*, op 87b (publ. 1926)(13m)(arr. from incidental music; also for piano solo)
1) *The King's Pavan* (Allegretto pesante)
2) *Ayre* (for Buckingham)(Poco lento e nobile)
3) *Passamezzo* (for Anne Boleyn)(Allegro giocoso)
4) *Queen Katharine's Vision* (Andante patetico)
5) *Baptism Procession* (Marcia moderato con dignita)
¶*Henry VIII Overture* for small orchestra (incl. material from the *Ayre* for Buckingham, op 87b.2)
¶*Orpheus with his Lute* (song) for voice, lute & strings (also for voice & string quartet, and for voice & piano)
¶*3 Pieces* for organ (arr. by Peter Williams from op 87b.2,.3,.5)
Hippolytus (prelude & 12 numbers for Euripides play as transl. by Gilbert Murray) for small orchestra (oboe, timpani, harp & strings), op 84 (1925)(prelude incl. theme from *5 Recollections of Ancient Greek Music* for piano solo, op 45.3; see also *3 Choruses in the Hippolytus of Euripides* (vocal works/choral))
¶*Huntsmen's Chorus* for tenor, male chorus & harp
The Idol of Thade (Joseph Fraser)(1933)
Julius Caesar (Shakespeare), op 39 (1913)(fanfares & unaccompanied song)(lost)
The Lonely House (T.S. Troubridge?)(1924)
The Man in the Mount (Maud McCarthy mystery play for puppets) (unfinished; incl. sketch for prelude)
Le Masque de fer (Maurice Rostand)(1930-31)
Masse-Mensch [Masses and Man](14 numbers for Ernest Toller play in Vera Mendel transl.) for small orchestra, op 83 (1924)(lost except for .13, arr. as *Sonia* for violin & piano)
The Merry Wives of Windsor (Shakespeare)(1932)
The Pearl Tree (R.C.Trevelyan)

[INCIDENTAL MUSIC for plays (continued)]

Sacrifice (Rabindranath Tagore), op 66 (1919)

¶*2 Songs in "Sacrifice"* for voice & string quintet (violins & tambura)(4m)
1) *I am going alone in this world*
2) *Ye dweller in the house*

Saint Joan (overture & 14 numbers for George Bernard Shaw play) for orchestra, op 82 (1924)

¶*2 Interludes from "Saint Joan"* for flute, bassoon, 2 horns, 6 trumpets, 3 trombones, tuba, timpani, percussion & strings (1938)(7m)(arr. from incidental music)
1) Moderato solenne
2) *The Fairy Tree* (rev. from *Saint Joan Suite*, op 82b.2 below)

¶*Saint Joan Suite* for orchestra, op 82b (1925)(16m)(arr. from incidental music; also for piano solo)
1) *Donremy* (Rather slow, rhapsodical)(incl. theme from *Peace and War* for orchestra and motif from *Miniature Suite* for orchestra, op 38.3)
2) *The Fairy Tree* (Childlike, tempo quite deliberate)(rev. as *2 Interludes* (.2), above)
3) *The Maid* (In medieval style)
4) *Orleans* (Quick)
5) *The Martyr* (Not too slow but measured)(based on part of *Music-Pictures* (Group 3) for orchestra, op 33.1, and a theme from *Music Poem 5* for orchestra, op 20)
6) *Epilogue*

*Sakuntala (Kalidasa), op 64 (1918)

**Les trois légendes franciscaines [Legends of St. Francis]*(Stephanie la Baronne de Tanfani)(1929)

*The Trojan Women (Gilbert Murray transl. of Euripides play), op 65 (1919)

**The Unseemly Adventure* (Ralph Strauss)(c.1931-34)

Veils (Maud MacCarthy Imaginative Ritual) for voices & chamber ensemble (flute, oboe, clarinet, horn, organ, celesta, harp, gong & strings)(1926)(unfinished)

¶Realization of surviving materials
1) Introduction and scene (speaker, ensemble)
2) Ballet and song (tenor, chorus)
3) Fugue

[INCIDENTAL MUSIC for plays (continued)]
4) Hymn 1 (chorus, organ)
5) Hymn 2 (solo voices, chorus, organ, ensemble)

*The Velvet Mask (John Wyne?)(1930-31)

*The Voice (Lynd Nathan & Joseph Fraser)

The Whispering Well(–Frank H. Rose)(1913)

¶*Roses and Rue* (song) for voice & piano

Wonderful Grandmama and the Wand of Youth (overture & 37 numbers for Harold Chapin play), op 34 (1912)(lost, but see *Miniature Suite*, below)

¶*Miniature Suite* for orchestra, op 38 (1913)(16m)(arr. from incidental music)
1) *The Old Castle: Midnight* (Lento calmo)
2) *Robin Goodfellow* (Allegretto moderato)
3) *In the Forest: The Mocking Bird* (Allegretto)(motif also used in *Saint Joan Suite*, op 82b.1 (see incidental music, above))
4) *Scarabang and His Minions* (Andante burlesco)(incl. distorted variant of theme from *Music-Pictures* (Group 2) for string quartet, op 32.1)

Indian Ballet 1 for small orchestra (c.1936)(fragments only)

Kashmiri Boat Song for small orchestra (c.1937): see *Nature-Notes*

Kashmiri Idyll for small orchestra (c.1938)(lost)

Kashmiri Wedding Procession for small orchestra (2 flutes, oboe (or cor anglais), 2 clarinets, bassoon, 2 horns, 3 trumpets *ad lib*, timpani, harp *ad lib.*, celesta *ad lib.*, glockenspiel, bells & strings)(1936)(5m)(based on original Indian melodies; also arr. for ensemble of traditional Indian instruments (see chamber works: Indo-European music))

Keltic Melodies for harp & string orchestra (1911)(12m)
1) *The Clan* (also expanded & arr. as *Keltic Suite* for orchestra, op 29.1)
2) *A Lament* (also arr. as *Keltic Suite* for orchestra, op 29.2)
3) *The Country Fair* (rev. as *Music-Pictures* (Group 6) for orchestra, op 81.3)

The Lament of Tasso (poem) for orchestra (1899)(lost)

Lento e scherzetto: see *Concertos* for cello & orchestra

3 Mantras: see opera *Avatara* vocal: dramatic works)

Music-Pictures

Group 1: see chamber works

Group 2: see chamber works

Group 3: for orchestra, op 33 (1912)(22m)

  1) *The Ancient of Days* (Lento tragico) for winds, brass, harp & percussion (after Blake)(some material adapted for *Saint Joan Suite*, op 82b.5 (see incidental music, above)

  2) *Columbine* (study in full-tones, half-tones & quarter tones) (Allegretto senza deviazione) (after Brunet)

  3) *Old Greek Legend* (in the Phrygian mode)(Adagio misurato)(after Martin)(see also *5 Recollections of Ancient Greek Music* for piano, .5)

  4) *The Tocsin* (Allegro preciso)(after Boutigny)

Group 4: for string orchestra, op 55 (c.1917)(11m)(also for string sextet, for string quartet, and for piano trio)

  1) *At the Theatre* (after Degas)

  2) *Evening in the Forest* (after Farquharson)

  3) *Fiddler's Fancy* (a country dance)(after Morland)(arr. of 3 Pieces for violin & piano, op 42.3)

Group 5: see chamber works

Group 6: *Gaelic Melodies* for orchestra, op 81 (publ. 1924)(8m)(also for piano solo)

  1) *The Dream of Morven*

  2) *Deirdre Crooning*

  3) *Merry Macdoon* (rev. of *Keltic Melodies* (.3) for harp & string orchestra)

Group 7: see piano solo

Group 8: see piano solo

  ¶*The Rainbow* (.3) arr. for small orchestra (1937)

Group 9: *Indian Scenes* for orchestra, op 90 (c.1935)(lost, apart from sketches)

  1) *In the Village (Morning)*

  2) *Buffalo Dust (Sunset)*

  3) *In the Bazaar (Night)*

Music-Poems

  2) *Epithalamium* for orchestra, op 10 (1905-06)(15m)

  4) *Apotheosis (Elegy in Memory of Joseph Joachim)* for violin & orchestra, op 18 (1908-09)(10m)

  5) *Mirage* for large orchestra, op 20 (1910)(24m)(theme also adapted for *A World Requiem* for solo voices, chorus & or

[*Music-Poems* for orchestra **(continued)**]

chestra, op 60.1; theme also adapted for *Saint Joan Suite*, op 82b.5 (see incidental music, above; some material also adapted for *Peace and War* for orchestra)

Nature-Notes

  1) *Raindrops* for flute, oboe, clarinet, 2 horns, xylophone & strings (c.1936)(4m)

  2) *Kashmiri Boat Song* for small orchestra (2 flutes, oboe, 2 clarinets, bassoon, 2 horns, harp, percussion & strings)(c.1937)(5m)

  3) *Scene picaresque (Spanish Serenade)* for small orchestra (flute, oboe, 2 clarinets, bassoon, 2 horns, percussion & strings) (1936)(5m)

  4) *Shalimar (Indian Nocturne)* for small orchestra (c.1936) (sketches only; some material used in *An Arabian Night* for small orchestra)

  5) *Butterflies at Dusk* (sketches only)

• **OVERTURES**

Le cabaret (Overture to a French Comedy): see incidental music for *Deburau*

Keltic Overture for orchestra, op 28 (1930)(5m)(theme also transcr. as *Keltic Melody* for violin & piano)

Overture for small orchestra (1896)(unfinished)

Pasquinades (see also chamber works)

  Pasquinade for orchestra (c.1933)(orig. movement .4 of *Puppet Ballet Suite*, replaced by Passepied; full score lost, piano-conductor score extant.)

  3 Pasquinades: see *Sinfonietta*

  Pasquinades symphoniques: see symphonies

Peace and War (meditation) for orchestra (1919-20)(12m)(orig. part of *A World Requiem* for solo voices, chorus & orchestra, op 60.6; some material adapted from *Music-Poem 5* for orchestra, op 20; theme also used in 3 Pieces for piano solo, op 48.3)

Pieces

  3 Pieces, op 42

    1) *Darby and Joan (Old English Idyll)*(duet) for violin, cello & string orchestra (publ. 1916)(7m)

    2) see chamber works

    3) see chamber works

  2 Pieces *(Spirituals)* for orchestra, op 71 (c.1925)(also for piano solo)

    1) *The Florida Spiritual* (4m)

[Pieces for orchestra - 2 Pieces *(Spirituals)*, op 71 **(continued)**]

    2) *Mississippi Savannahs* (Negro Spiritual) for small orchestra (incl. ironic quotation from *A World Requiem* for solo voices, chorus & orchestra, op 60)

12 Pièces d'occasion for chamber orchestra, op 57 (c.1917- 18)(largely based on bell-chimes & carillons? .8-.12 prob. arr. from concert opera *The Vision of Dante*)(mainly lost)

5 Recollections of Ancient Greek Music: see *Hellas* suite, below

The Return of the Legions (marche militaire) for chamber orchestra, op 58 (c.1918)(on a theme of Saint-Saëns)(lost)

Sappho (symphonic ode) for orchestra, op 91 (c.1934)(lost)

Scena idillico for cello & orchestra (sketch only) Eclogue–Colloquy–Rout

Sicilian Aubade for orchestra (1927)(7m)(orig. for piano solo)

Sinfonietta for orchestra, op 37 (c.1935)(12m)(orig. titled *3 Pasquinades*, retitled by Malcolm Mac-Donald to distinguish from *Pasquinades symphoniques*)

    1) Ironic (Moderato molto pesante)(based on sketches for incomplete movement intended for *Puppet Ballet Suite*)

    2) Erotic (Lento calmo)(uses theme from *Music-Pictures* (Group 7) for piano solo, op 13.2; note: does not correspond to the *Pasquinades* for 2 pianos, op 93.2)

    3) Rustic (Allegretto piacevole)(incomplete; orig. as *Music-Pictures* (Group 2) for string quartet, op 32.1)

The Song of Ram Dass for small orchestra (flute, cor anglais, clarinet, bassoon, 2 horns, 2 trumpets, organ *ad lib.*, harp, bells & strings)(1935)(4m)

Strophes from an Antique Song for small orchestra (flute, oboe (or cor anglais), clarinet, bassoon, 2 horns, timpani, harp, harmonium, glockenspiel, triangle & strings)(publ. 1934)(c.3m)(orig. for piano solo)

• **SUITES** for orchestra

Chinese Suite, op 95 (1935)(17m)
    1) *In the Gardens of Bliss (Pei Hai)*
    2) *The perfume Pagoda (Fo Hsiang Ko)*
    3) *Procession to the Temple of Heaven*
    4) *The Ming Mandarin*

[**SUITES** for orchestra **(continued)**]

Hellas (A Suite of Ancient Greece) for double string orchestra, harp & percussion, op 45 (1932)(17m)(.1-.5 a rev. of 5 *Recollections of Ancient Greek Music* (1915), itself orig. for piano solo; .2 & .4 also as *Greek Processional* for string quintet)

    1) *Solemn Temple Dance* (in the Lydian mode)(also for harp, gong & strings)

    2) *Processional* (in the Ionian mode)

    3) *Dirge for a Hero* (in the Phrygian mode)

    4) *Song of the Argive Helen* (in the Æolian mode)(also for 3 flutes, oboe, cor anglais, 2 clarinets, horn, harp & strings)

    5) *Temple Chant* (in the Dorian mode)(3m)(also for 20 wind instruments)

    6) *Corybantes* (in the Mixolydian mode)

Henry VIII: see incidental music to *Henry VIII*

Indian Suite (1932-35)(16m)(based on authentic Indian melodies from the collection of Maud MacCarthy)

    1) *Bhavanutha (A Joyful Song to Shri Râma)*(Moderato goioso)

    2) *Da ta Sé (Prelude to a Play)*(Allegro misterioso)

    3) *Navali Lâdali (Love Song of Krishna and Radha)*(Lento)

    4) *Tândava nritya Keri (The Elephant-god is invited to perform Tandava)* (Allegretto quasi allegro)

    5) *Manasu Karagathemi (Hymn to Vishnu)*(Allegro brioso)

Keltic Suite, op 29 (1911)(12m)(also for small orchestra (1914), for military band (1915) and for piano (1923))

    1) *The Clans* (Allegro molto brioso)(developed from *Keltic Melodies* (.1) for harp & string orchestra)

    2) *A Lament* (Lento eroico)(orig. as *Keltic Melodies* (.2) for harp & string orchestra; also arr. as *Keltic Lament* for violin (or cello) & piano, as *Keltic Lament* for chorus & piano (or harp), as *Keltic Lament* for male chorus, and as *A Prayer for Freedom* for solo voice, piano & organ *ad lib.*)

    3) *The Call* (Allegro giocoso)

Miniature Suite: see incidental music for *Wonderful Grandmama*

[SUITES for orchestra (continued)]

A Puppet Ballet Suite (1934)(20m)

  1) Prelude–Ensemble (Allegro moderato)(incl. theme from *Carnival* for orchestra)

  2) Puppet love scene (Andante lento)

  3) *Passepied (Ancien Régime)*(Allegretto)

  4) *Dream-Valse* (incl. theme from *Quartet 9 (Quartetto intimo)* for strings, op 89.1)

  5) *March-Finale* (Marcia con bravura)

Saint Joan Suite: see incidental music for *Saint Joan*

Suite fantastique: see incidental music for *Deburau*

Suite française, op 22 (1910)(20m)

  1) *Les Zouaves* (Alla marcia vivo)

  2) *Le fée Tarapatapoum* (Allegretto moderato)

  3) *Hymne héroique à la France* (Solenne)

  4) *Joie de vivre* (Molto vivace)

Suite picaresque (in the Spanish style)(c.1935)(sketch)

Undine (suite extrait de musique de la Fèerie, par Gustave Froissart), op 3 (c.1899)

  1) *Prélude romantique* (Presto comodo)

  2) *Barcarolle des Undines* (Larghetto mosso)

  3) *Carnaval et menuet de Maïa* (Allegro giovale)

Symphonic Studies for string orchestra, op 101 (1938)(lost)

  1) *L'Allegro*

  2) *Il Pensieroso*

Symphonies

Pasquinades symphoniques, op 98 (1935)

  1) *Classical* (Allegro non troppo)(10m)(arr. & expansion of *Pasquinades* for 2 pianos, op 93.1)

  2) *Romantic* (Lento quieto)(7m)

  3) *Modernist* (1/2 = 100)(unfinished)

Symphony (op 8): see Transcriptions & arrangements (SCHUBERT: *Death and the Maiden*)

A Symphony of East and West for European symphony orchestra & ensemble of Indian instruments, op 100 (c.1937-38)(lost except for sketches)

Tzigeuner (Gipsy Czardas) for solo violin *obbligato* & small orchestra (publ. 1935)(6m)

● **TRANSCRIPTIONS & ARRANGEMENTS:**

BACH (JS)/FOULDS

Bach-Fantasia for orchestra, op 31 (c.1914)(lost; prob. a pot-pourri on well-known themes)

[TRANSCRIPTIONS & ARRANGEMENTS (continued)]

Crucifixus and Resurrexit (from *Mass* in b) arr. for small orchestra (c.1918)(partly lost)

BEETHOVEN/FOULDS

Excerpts from "Mass" in D arr. for small orchestra (c.1918) (lost)

3 Sacred Songs (in Liszt transcription) arr. for piano, strings & timpani (c.1918)

BERLIOZ/FOULDS

Grand Fantasie on Berlioz's "The Damnation of Faust" for orchestra (1922)

Love Scene from "Romeo and Juliet" arr. for small orchestra (1929)(lost)

Symphonie fantastique: movements (.2,.4,.5) arr. for small orchestra (movements (.2,.4) also arr. for military band)

BORODIN/FOULDS

Nocturne and Serenade (from *Petite Suite*) arr. for small orchestra (1927)(*Nocturne* lost)

BRAHMS/FOULDS

Symphony 1: Andante sostenuto arr. for strings (c.1918)(lost)

DVORAK/FOULDS

Dmitrij: Overture arr. for piano, strings & percussion (c.1918)

GLAZUNOV/FOULDS

Meditation (op 32) arr. for small orchestra

Serenade espagnole (op 20) arr. for orchestra

GOTTSCHALK/FOULDS

Pasquinade arr. for small orchestra (c.1918)(partly lost)

HANDEL/FOULDS:

Largo (from *Semele*) arr. for strings (c.1918)(partly lost)

MacCARTHY (MAUD)/FOULDS

England My Country (harmonized & orchestrated)(c.1917)

A Solemn Song of England (harmonized)(c.1917)

A Song of home (harmonized & orchestrated)(c.1917)

MENDELSSOHN/FOULDS

Mendelssohn-Fantasie for orchestra (publ. 1932)(pot-pourri on well-known themes)

RIMSKY-KORSAKOV/FOULDS

Chant Hindou arr. for indian ensemble (1938)

[TRANSCRIPTIONS & ARRANGEMENTS
    (continued)]
ROSENTHAL (A)/FOULDS
    Denia: Tango Sérénade arr. for orchestra
        (1933)
SAINT-SAENS/FOULDS
    Fantasie on Saint-Saëns "Samson et Dalila"
        for small orchestra (c.1918)(partly lost)
    La Jeunesse d'Hercule arr. for piano &
        strings (c.1918)
SCHUBERT/FOULDS
    Death and the Maiden (*Quartet 14* for strings)

[TRANSCRIPTIONS & ARRANGEMENTS
    (continued)]
    re-imagined as a *Symphony* for full or-
        chestra, op 8 (1930)
    Schubert-Fantasie for orchestra (publ.
        1933)(pot-pourri on well-known themes)
TCHAIKOVSKY/FOULDS
    Tchaikovsky-Fantasie for orchestra (publ.
        1934)(pot-pourri)
VERDI/FOULDS
    Marcia trionfale (from *Aida*) arr. for orchestra
        (c.1918)

SUPPLEMENT: WORKS BY OPUS NUMBER

N.B. that many of Foulds's works were not given opus-numbers, while the
numbers 35, 46, 53, 56, 62, 63, and 74 seem to have remained unused.

OP 1   *Music-Poems* (1: *Lyrics*) for piano
OP 2   *2 Songs* for baritone (voice & instrument(s))
OP 3   *Undine* (Suite extrait de musique de la Fè-
            erie, par Gustave Froissart) for orchestra
OP 4   *Variazioni ed improvvisati su una thema
            originale* for piano
OP 5   *3 Marching Songs* (chorus)
OP 5a   *3 Marching Songs* for male voices (chorus)
OP 6   *Sonata* for cello & piano
OP 7   *The Vision of Dante* (dramatic works/
            concert-opera)
OP 8   *Death and the Maiden* (symphonic vers. of
            Schubert quartet)(transcriptions & arran-
            gements)
OP 9   *Impromptus on a Theme of Beethoven* for 4
            cellos
OP 10   *Music-Poems* (2: *Epithalamium*) for orchestra
OP 11   *3 Songs of Beauty* (voice & instrument(s))
OP 12   *Lento e Scherzetto* for cello & orchestra
OP 13   *Music-Pictures* (Group 7: *2 Landscapes*) for
            piano
OP 14   *Music-Poems* (3: *The Wanderer*) for piano
OP 15   *2 Songs* for tenor (voice & instrument(s))
OP 16   *Holiday Sketches* for orchestra
OP 17   *Concerto 1* in G for cello & orchestra
OP 18   *Music-Poems* (4: *Apotheosis (Elegy in
            Memory of Joseph Joachim)*) for violin &
            orchestra
OP 19   *Concerto 2* in d for cello & small orchestra

OP 20   *Music-Poems* (5: *Mirage*) for orchestra
OP 21   *Music-Pictures* (Group 8: *For the Young*) for
            pianoOP 22   *Suite française* for orchestra
OP 23   *Quartet 8* in d for strings
OP 24   *Trio* in F for violin, viola & cello
OP 25   *2 Pieces* for cello & piano
OP 26   *Solomon* (dramatic works/operas)
OP 26a   *An Eastern Lover* (scena)(see *Solomon*,
            Op 26)
OP 27   *Cleopatra* (dramatic works/miniature opera)
OP 28   *Keltic Overture* for orchestra
OP 29   *Keltic Suite* for orchestra
OP 30   *Music-Pictures* (Group 1) for violin, cello &
            piano
OP 31   *Bach-Fantasia* for orchestra (transcriptions
            & arrangements)
OP 32   *Music-Pictures* (Group 2: *Aquarelles*) for
            string quartet
OP 33   *Music-Pictures* (Group 3) for orchestra
OP 34   *Wonderful Grandmama* (orchestral/inciden-
            tal music)
OP 35
OP 36   *The Tell-Tale Heart* (dramatic works/melo-
            dramas)
OP 37   *Sinfonietta* for orchestra (orig. *3
            Pasquinades*)
OP 38   *Miniature Suite* for orchestra (see *Wonderful
            Grandmama* (orchestral/incidental
            music))

OP 39   *Julius Caesar* (orchestral/incidental music)

OP 40   *4 Pieces* for violin & piano

OP 41   *2 Excerpts from "The Vision of Dante"* for string quintet (see *The Vision of Dante*, op 7)

OP 42   *3 Pieces* for violin & piano, for orchestra

OP 43   *6 Songs in Indian Style* for mezzo-soprano (voice & instrument(s))

OP 44   *12 Dedicated Works* (Set 1) for chamber orchestra

OP 45   *5 Recollections of Ancient Greek Music* for piano (rev. as *Hellas (A Suite of Ancient Greece)* for double string orchestra)

OP 46

OP 47   *12 Dedicated Works* (Set 2) for chamber orchestra

OP 48   *Impressions of Time and Place* for piano, for orchestra

OP 49   *Gandharva-Music* for piano

OP 50   *Lyra celtica* (concerto) (voice & instrument(s))

OP 51   *Mood-Pictures* (Set 1) (voice & instrument(s))

OP 52   *Mood-Pictures* (Set 2) (voice & instrument(s))

OP 53

OP 54   *The Song of Honour* (dramatic works/melodramas)

OP 55   *Music-Pictures* (Group 4) for string orchestra

OP 56

OP 57   *12 Pièces d'occasion* for chamber orchestra

OP 58   *The Return of the Legions* (marche militaire) for chamber orchestra

OP 59

OP 60   *A World Requiem* for solo voices, chorus & orchestra

OP 61   *Avatara* (dramatic works/operas)

OP 61b   *3 Mantras* (see *Avatara*, Op 61)

OP 62

OP 63

OP 64   *Sakuntala* (orchestral/incidental music)

OP 65   *The Trojan Women* (orchestral/incidental music)

OP 66   *Sacrifice* (orchestral/incidental music)

OP 67

OP 68   *A Gaelic Dream-Song* for orchestra

OP 69   *3 Songs* (voice & instrument(s))

OP 70   *5 Scottish-Keltic Songs* (chorus)

OP 71   *2 Pieces (Spirituals)* for orchestra

OP 72   *Deburau* (orchestral/incidental music)

OP 72a   *Le Cabaret (Overture to a French Comedy)* (see *Deburau*, Op 72)

OP 72b   *Suite fantastique* for orchestra (see *Debureau*, Op 72)

OP 73   *Music-Pictures* (Group 5) for flute, clarinet, violin & cello

OP 74

OP 75   *The Goddess* (orchestral/incidental music)

OP 76   *The Fires Divine* (orchestral/incidental music)

OP 77   *The Cenci* (orchestral/incidental music)

OP 78   *Essays in the Modes* for piano

OP 79   *Baldur the Beautiful* (orchestral/incidental music)

OP 80   *Cymbeline* (orchestral/incidental music)

OP 81   *Music-Pictures* (Group 6: *Gaelic Melodies*) for orchestra

OP 82   *Saint Joan* (orchestral/incidental music)

OP 82b   *Saint Joan Suite* for orchestra (see *Saint Joan*, Op 82)

OP 83   *Masse-Mensch* (orchestral/incidental music)

OP 84   *Hippolytus* (orchestral/incidental music)

OP 84b   *3 Choruses in the Hippolytus of Euripides* (chorus)

OP 85   *The Dance of Life* (orchestral/incidental music)

OP 86   *Garland of Youth* (voice & instrument(s))

OP 87   *Henry VIII* (orchestral/incidental music)

OP 87b   *Henry VIII Suite* (see *Henry VIII*, Op 87)

OP 88   *Dynamic Triptych* for orchestra

OP 89   *Quartet 9 (Quartetto intimo)* for strings

OP 90   *Music-Pictures* (Group 9: *Indian Scenes*) for orchestra

OP 91   *Sappho* (symphonic ode) for orchestra

OP 92   *Music To-day* (book)

OP 93   *Pasquinades* for 2 pianos

OP 94   *Deva-Music (Symphonic Pieces)* for orchestra

OP 95   *Chinese Suite* for orchestra

OP 96   *Indian Garland* (piano solo)

OP 97   *Quartet 10 (Quartetto geniale)* for strings

OP 98   *Pasquinades symphoniques* for orchestra (orchestral/symphonies)

OP 99   *Poetical Reveries* (lost work for unknown forces)

OP 100   *A Symphony of East and West* for orchestra

OP 101   *Symphonic Studies* for orchestra

OP 102   *Indian Melodies* for piano

Discography

This listing falls into two parts, reflecting the wide gap between the early recordings issued mainly within Foulds's lifetime, and the modern LP discs that have begun to appear with the revival of interest in the composer since the centenary of his birth.

PART 1: BEFORE 1980

This lists all pre-Hi-Fi recordings of music by Foulds which I have been able to discover. These were mainly devoted to his lighter music ("All my poorest stuff," he scribbled on one record catalogue) and, since nearly all belong to the 78 era, the music is often severely cut. (The worst offence is the *Hebrew Rhapsody*: the Paxton record contains only about a fifth of the whole work.)

The listing is alphabetical by first significant word of title. Different recordings of the same piece are alphabetical by name of recording company. All records listed are 78 rpm unless otherwise stated. Where it has not been possible to obtain a copy of a record, it has sometimes not been possible to identify the performing artists involved.

Le Cabaret: Overture, Op.72a, from incidental music to Sacha Guitry's *Deburau*. Paxton PR 406

Canadian Boat Song, Op. 25/1, for cello and piano (1914).
W.H. Squire (vlc), Hamilton Harty (pno) Columbia L 1042

Dream Waltz from *A Puppet Ballet Suite* (1934) Paxton PR 426

La Fée Tarapatapoum from *Suite Française*, Op.22 (1910). This was recorded by Boosey & Hawkes but apparently not issued and the metal scrapped.

Fiddler's Fancy from *Music-Pictures* Group IV, Op.55.
New Concert String Ensemble, cond. Reginald Leopold. Boosey & Hawkes S. 2132

Gaelic Melodies (*Music-Pictures* Group VI, Op.81). Paxton PR 404

Hebrew Rhapsody (c.1936).
London Promenade Orchestra, cond. Walter Collins. Paxton PR 454

Henry VIII Suite, Op.87 (three movements only: Queen Katharine's Vision; Passamezzo for Anne Boleyn; Baptism Procession). Bosworth BC 10-?

Keltic Lament from *Keltic Suite*, Op.29.
The Jacques Orchestra, cond. Reginald Jacques[†] Columbia DX 925 (33 rpm)

Keltic Overture, Op.28. Bosworth BC 10-?

[†] An enigmatic aspect of this particular recording is that the *Keltic Lament* is presented in a version for string orchestra and harp. This must in fact be its original version, now missing, as No. 2 of the three *Keltic Melodies* for strings and harp which preceeded the *Keltic Suite* proper.

Keltic Suite, Op.29.
(1) Regimental Band of HM Grenadier Guards, cond. Captain G. Miller.   Columbia 9249/50 (80 rpm)
(2) New Conservatoire Concert Orchestra.   Edison Bell (Electron) 0299-300

Schubert-Fantasie.
Regent Classical Orchestra   Bosworth BC 1036

The Tell-Tale Heart, Op.36 (1910).   Paxton PR 443

PART 2: FROM 1980 ONWARD

April-England, Op.48/1, for solo piano (1926).
Peter Jacobs (pno).   Altarus AIR-2-9001

Aquarelles (*Music-Pictures* Group II) for string quartet, Op.32 (1914?).
Endellion String Quartet   Pearl SHE 564
(reissued as compact disc SHE CD 9564)

Dynamic Triptych for piano and orchestra, Op.88 (1927-29).
Howard Shelley (pno), Royal Philharmonic Orchestra, cond. Vernon Handley (with Vaughan Williams
Piano Concerto).   Lyrita SRCS 130

Essays in the Modes, Op.72 (1920-27). Complete (including "Egoistic").
Peter Jacobs (pno).   Altarus AIR-2-9001

Gandharva-Music for solo piano, Op.49 (1915-26).
Peter Jacobs (pno).   Altarus AIR-2-9001

Lento Quieto (from *Quartetto Geniale*, Op.97) (1935).
Endellion String Quartet.   Pearl SHE 564
(reissued as compact disc SHE CD 9564)

Mirage, Op.20 (1910).
Luxembourg Radio Symphony Orchestra, cond. Leopold Hager (3-record set with music by Parry,
Brian).   Forlane UM 3529/3531

Pasquinade Symphonique No. 1, Op.98/1 (1935).
Luxembourg Radio Symphony Orchestra, cond. Leopold Hager (3-record set with music by Parry,
Brian).   Forlane UM 3529/3531

Quartetto Intimo, Op.89 (1931-32).
Endellion String Quartet.   Pearl SHE 564
(reissued as compact disc SHE CD 9564)

Saint Joan Suite, Op.82b (1925).
Luxembourg Radio Symphony Orchestra, cond. Leopold Hager (3-record set with music by Parry,
Brian).   Forlane UM 3529/3531

Three Mantras, Op.61b (1919-30).
London Philharmonic Orchestra, cond. Barry Wordsworth.
                                            Lyrita (number not yet assigned; unissued as of April 1988)

Variazioni ed Improvvisati su una Thema Originale for piano, Op.4.
Peter Jacobs (pno).   Altarus AIR-2-9001

As this book goes to press, Lyrita records have announced plans to record Foulds's *April-England, Le Cabaret, Hellas*, and *Peace and War* for release on Compact Disc during 1990.

Index

Other Music Titles Available from Pro/Am Music Resources, Inc.

BIOGRAPHY

ALKAN, REISSUE *by Ronald Smith.* Vol. 1: The Enigma. Vol. 2: The Music.
BÉLA BARTÓK: His Life in Pictures and Documents *ed. by Bonis.*
LIPATTI *by Dragos Tanasescu & Grigore Bargauanu.*
MASCAGNI: An Autobiography Compiled, Edited and Translated from Original Sources *by David Stivender.*
MAX REGER *by Gerhard Wuensch.*
MICHAEL TIPPETT, O.M.: A Celebration *edited by Geraint Lewis. Fwd. by Peter Maxwell Davies.*
MY LIFE WITH BOHUSLAV MARTINU *by Charlotte Martinu.*
PERCY GRAINGER: The Man Behind the Music *by Eileen Dorum.*
PERCY GRAINGER: The Pictorial Biography *by Robert Simon. Fwd. by Frederick Fennell.*
VERDI AND WAGNER *by Ernö Lendvai.*
ZOLTAN KODALY: His Life in Pictures and Documents *by László Eosze.*

GENERAL SUBJECTS

AMERICAN MINIMAL MUSIC, REISSUE *by Wim Mertens. Transl. by J. Hautekiet.*
THE FOLK MUSIC REVIVAL IN SCOTLAND, REISSUE *by Ailie Munro.*
KENTNER: A Symposium *edited by Harold Taylor. Fwd. by Yehudi Menuhin.*
MODERN MUSIC: Selected Essays by Malcolm MacDonald (Volume 2).
THE MUSICAL INSTRUMENT COLLECTOR, REVISED EDITION *by J. Robert Willcutt & Kenneth R. Ball.*
MUSICOLOGY IN PRACTICE: Collected Essays by Denis Stevens *edited by Thomas P. Lewis.* Vol. 1: 1948-1970. Vol. 2: 1971-1988.
THE PIANIST'S TALENT *by Harold Taylor. Fwd. by John Ogdon.*
THE PRO/AM BOOK OF MUSIC AND MYTHOLOGY *compiled, edited & with commentaries by Thomas P. Lewis.*
THE PRO/AM GUIDE TO U.S. BOOKS ABOUT MUSIC: Annotated Guide to Current & Backlist Titles *edited by Thomas P. Lewis.* 1986 Ed. & 1987 Suppl.
RAVEL ACCORDING TO RAVEL *by Vlado Perlemuter & Hélène Jourdan-Morhange.*
TENSIONS IN THE PERFORMANCE OF MUSIC: A Symposium, REVISED & EXTENDED EDITION *edited by Carola Grindea. Fwd. by Yehudi Menuhin.*
THE WORKS OF ALAN HOVHANESS: A Catalog, Opus 1–Opus 360 *by Richard Howard.*

GUITAR

THE AMP BOOK: A Guitarist's Introductory Guide to Tube Amplifiers *by Donald Brosnac.*
ANTONIO DE TORRES: Guitar Maker—His Life and Work *by José L. Romanillos. Fwd. by Julian Bream.*
CLASSIC GUITAR CONSTRUCTION *by Irving Sloane.*
THE FLAMENCO GUITAR, REISSUE *by David George.*
GUITAR HISTORY:Volume 1—Guitars Made by the Fender Company *by Donald Brosnac.*
GUITAR HISTORY:Volume 2—The Gibson SG*by John Bulli.*
GUITAR REPAIR A Manual of Repair for Guitars and Fretted Instruments*by Irving Sloane.*
AN INTRODUCTION TO SCIENTIFIC GUITAR DESIGN *by Donald Brosnac.*
LEFT HANDED GUITAR *by Nicholas Clarke.*
LIVES AND LEGENDS OF FLAMENCO, 2ND EDITION *by D. E. Pohren.*
MANUAL OF GUITAR TECHNOLOGY: The History and Technology of Plucked String Instruments *by Franz Jahnel. English vers. by Dr. J.C. Harvey.*
THE STEEL STRING GUITAR: Construction and Repair, UPDATED EDITION *by David Russell Young.*
STEEL STRING GUITAR CONSTRUCTION *by Irving Sloane.*
A WAY OF LIFE, REISSUE *by D. E. Pohren.*